# *A Most Uncommon Journey*

◆

# A
# *Most Uncommon*
# *Journey*

◆

Jackie Richards

Writers Club Press
San Jose  New York  Lincoln  Shanghai

A Most Uncommon Journey

Writers Club Press
an imprint of iUniverse.com, Inc.

For information address:
iUniverse.com, Inc.
620 North 48th Street, Suite 201
Lincoln, NE 68504-3467
www.iuniverse.com

ISBN: 0-595-13715-6

Printed in the United States of America

Books by *Jackie Richards*


A Most Uncommon Journey

Charlie Dog Two and Mustard
(A Children's Book)

# A MOST UNCOMMON JOURNEY

*A Fictionalized Memoir Set in the Year 1939:
A year long journey on many roads, the most important of which was a
premature journey from childhood to maturity.*

*With the exception of historical figures,
all names have been changed.*

# *Acknowledgements*

◆

My gratitude to Doug Deringer and the late Jane Flower Deringer who were the first to read the story-in-progress. They did not discourage me and offered valuable suggestions. I am grateful to Doug for editing. Any mistakes are my own. My thanks to manuscript readers Julie Crews, and Ron Carter for their encouraging comments. And to manuscript reader, June Stephenson, who says, "Stunning. The angels have watched over you, how did you not get hurt?"

I am continually bolstered by my association with the Chesapeake Bay Writers' Club.

The support and love given me by my husband, children, and grandchildren are my strength. Their advice is always invaluable.

And—to the friends and relatives who shared memories, especially my brother, I am indebted. One cannot pass safely through the stages of life without debts.

# *Dedication*

◆

*To Jim*

*I have this overwhelming feeling that I have been married to the same person through several lives. May we continue to find each other.*

# Prologue

◆

One of my granddaughters was celebrating her twelfth birthday
when a natural question came to her mind.
"What was your twelfth year like Grandmom?"
I replied truthfully.
"It was a most uncommon journey."
And of course, her next question was, "What do you mean?"
That is when I promised to write it all down.
I began to remember and when I remembered, I knew that
I had never learned as much in any one year of my life
as I learned in my own twelfth year.
I shall tell my story in the voice of my youth and in
the voice of the times.

*Folks in My Life*

*Spring of 1939, Washington, D.C.*

*Family*
    *Mother*
    *Larry, stepfather*
    *Buddy, younger brother*

*Friends*
    *Sue Lankford*
    *Jimmy Ray Perkins (as it turned out)*
    *Richard*
    *Cookers, schoolmates at H. D. Cooke Elementary*
    *Raggedy Ann and Andy*

*Teachers*
    *Mrs. Stubel*
    *Mr. Gorge*

*Apartment Folks*
    *Old Mr. Swift, neighbor*
    *Mr. Orman, janitor*

*Relatives passing through*
    *Uncle Walter*
    *Aunt Maime and cousins Doadie, Jean and Ruth*

# Spring

◆

### The Birthday Celebration

From beneath the shrubs that lined the front walk of our apartment house, a few ragged crocuses struggled to make their way into spring. Their trampled condition was brought about by youthful feet more intent on a game of hide-and-seek than preserving the first sign of spring.

I sat on one of the benches that lined the short sidewalk leading to our apartment house door. Clouds were in contest with the morning sun leaving me alternately warmed and chilled. It was not the rising breeze that sent a shudder through me as I stared at the ailing crocuses, it was their timid promise of summer. The first crack of a baseball bat sent most of my friends into a frenzied summer countdown, while I dreaded the whoop and holler of the last day of school. Even though that day was three months away, thoughts of it sent me into a foggy gloom. Except for thoughts of summer, I actually felt happier than I had for years.

The day was Saturday, March 4, 1939. I was eleven years old. The next day, March 5, I would be twelve. Along with my family, I moved to Washington, D.C. in 1937. There were four of us, my mother, stepfather, younger brother Buddy and me.

After being passed around among relatives for several years, I loved the feel of being a whole family. I loved having a real home. From our apartment I could look out on busy 14th Street in Northwest Washington. Built of mustard colored brick in a U shape, our apartment house faced Columbia Road. The second floor apartments in the right hand wing were above stores that faced onto 14th Street. I lived in one of those. I loved having friends. I loved the Tivoli Theater that was just up the block at Park Street. I especially loved the ushers in their bright red uniforms. I loved the cling and clang of the streetcars as they rumbled past my window. And I truly loved Franklin Delano Roosevelt who had been president since I was five.

"You look so far away. What are you thinking about?" Sue asked.

I had not noticed her until she was directly in front of me. Sue was my best friend and I had been waiting for her. As I glanced up, I saw that she was dressed exactly as we had planned. We looked as much alike as possible. She had reddish-blonde hair, brown eyes and lots of freckles. I had dirty blonde hair, pale blue-green eyes and a trace of freckles. I stood a head taller. Otherwise, we matched perfectly. Each wore dark blue skirts and light blue sweaters buttoned up to our white blouse collars. Our coats were identical because I wore her sister's outgrown navy blue. Our saddle shoes were freshly polished. We wore blue socks.

"I wasn't thinking of anything much except summer. Anyway, I'm not going to let it spoil our day. We've planned this too long."

We started walking to the corner where the streetcar stopped.

"Do you think we'll get lost?" Sue asked.

"Get lost, how can we get lost? We're only doing downtown. We've both been downtown a thousand times with our parents. Besides, they have drilled us for a week on what number streetcar to take and where to get off to walk to the Smithsonian."

"I know, but we aren't going to the Smithsonian. It's scary."

"It's only scary because you fibbed to your mother about where we're going."

"Well, how else could I get to go?"

I nodded in agreement. I considered it a miracle that her parents let her go at all. My patience sometimes wore a little thin with Sue. Each summer for the past two years I traveled on the train by myself all the way to Birmingham, Alabama. Well, almost by myself, I corrected my thoughts. Little brothers hardly count. How could she be scared of getting on a streetcar right here at home—she had me, didn't she?

The streetcar clanged to a stop and we climbed aboard. I asked the conductor what time it was. We wanted to make the ten forty-five show at the Capitol Theater so we would be home way before dark as we had promised. Keeping his eye on the coin box, the conductor pulled out his pocket watch and held it out for me to see. We had plenty of time.

"You didn't tell your mother did you?" Sue asked as we settled in our seats.

"Well, yeah, I did."

"You told your mother. What if my mother finds out? I won't be let out of the house ever again." Her voice raised a couple of decibels as she talked. The lady under the felt and feathered hat in the seat in front of us turned around and stared. We withered.

When the lady finally turned back around, I whispered, "Dummy, my mother never sees or talks to your mother. My mother couldn't care less if I go to the Capitol Theater. She'd go too if she didn't have to work on Saturday mornings. I won't get in trouble for going to the movies, but I would for lying. I don't have to lie to go, so it doesn't make any sense to lie and get in trouble. Don't you see?"

"I guess."

"Mother says it's in the Bible. 'Tell the truth and the truth shall set ye free' or something like that."

Sue turned her head and quietly watched out the window for awhile. Then she began to get fidgety. "Are you sure you know where to get off?"

"We're going to get off at F Street and walk a block. I've done that hundreds of times with my mother."

"Smarty. Just because I've never been to the Capitol Theater before, you don't have to rub it in."

Sue had very strict parents. She lived over on 16th Street, a ritzy part of the neighborhood. Meridian Hill Park sort of divided us. Sometimes she was allowed to go with us kids to the Tivoli on Saturdays when her parents approved of the movie that was showing. She couldn't go anywhere on Sundays except to church.

My family didn't go to church on Sunday. I knew all about church, of course. I spent a lot of time in church every summer. Mother read the Bible all the time on account of the book she was writing. She said preachers had a way of talking for God and making God's simple rules almost impossible to live by. That's why our family didn't go to church.

My family went to the movies mostly. I think my mother wished that she were a movie star instead of a secretary. Or maybe she wished I could be a child star like Shirley Temple. Every now and then she reminded me that it was a movie star who gave me my first kiss. I was six weeks old when Wallace Beery came to Birmingham where I was born. He appeared on the stage at the movie theater. Mother stood holding me in the back of the theater as he left. He stopped, peeked into my blanket, leaned down and kissed me on the forehead kind of like a blessing. Maybe Mother thought something rubbed off that would make me a movie star. It might have if the kiss had come from Robert Taylor, my absolute hero. Anyway, I caught the whooping cough right after that and nearly died. It seemed to me that the whooping cough was all that rubbed off from that Mister Wallace Beery.

Sue fidgeted again. "Did you check the movie. Are you sure it's a Mickey Rooney?"

"I took three cents out of my savings and went downstairs to the drugstore and got *The Washington Post* first thing this morning. It was right there, Mickey Rooney starring in *Huckleberry Finn*. I even read Mr. Nelson Bell's column. He says it's a good movie and that Mickey is just right for the part."

"Oh, this is so exciting."

I continued my spiel. "At twelve-forty the stage show starts with Frankie Albertson, a comedian, and the Rockets. They're dancers, you know. It will be much better than that Adolph Menjou and Jack Oakie movie playing at the Tivoli today." I didn't much care for Adolph Menjou.

Sue and I had been saving up for my birthday celebration since Christmas. We began by avoiding the five and dime store where we usually hunted for treasures that we could afford. We often spent at least an hour in the store every Saturday. We browsed from counter to counter savoring all the items we knew by heart. We squealed in delight if something new had been added. But for weeks we had forgone the temptation, giggling that it served old Mr. Crail right for us to keep our money. He kept an eye on all us kids, trailing after us suspiciously, muttering to himself. We teased him unmercifully by picking up a pencil or a small pad. Then we passed it around from one to another while he tried to keep track of his merchandise. It always was something we didn't want and eventually the item was put back in its place.

As we neared our stop, Sue piped up with, "Do you think I should get a chicken salad or tuna salad? Should I get a soda or a cherry Coke?"

"Get whatever you feel like having when we get to the drugstore after the show. It's no big deal."

Even as I said it, I knew that was not true for Sue who rarely ate anything away from home. When her parents went out to all those big parties, she and her sister ate in the kitchen with their cook, Bessy. At times I envied Sue. Mealtime was one of the times I had to admit to being jealous of her. Our family mostly ate out at the cafeteria or the drugstore soda fountain. My mother always came home too tired to cook. She didn't really know how anyway. Sometimes, if we were in a hurry to get to the movies, Mother stopped at High's Ice Cream Store and got us each a "Quart for a Quarter." That was our supper.

It hadn't always been that way. Down in Birmingham, back before things went every which way, Pearl did our cooking. In fact, Pearl did just about everything. She was our colored housekeeper and nursemaid. Her big arms hugged tight when I got hurt. She was also some kind of cook. Once she cooked a rabbit and fooled Mother into thinking it was chicken just so Mother would quit fussing about my father raising rabbits in the backyard for no good reason. Pearl took care of all the grocery shopping too. She claimed that when Mother went to the grocer's, the budget just plain got busted. Pearl haggled over just about everything; Mother never did.

Startled out of my thoughts, I jumped when the conductor yelled, "14th and F Streets."

We had some spare time so we decided to look in the windows of Garfinkle's Department Store. Only the ladies who appeared in the society section of the paper could afford to shop at Garfinkle's. But, like Mother always said, "It doesn't cost to look."

The window backgrounds were blown up pictures of people waving from departing ships. Steamer trunks and suitcases sat piled up beside nattily dressed mannequins.

"The mannequins seem to be dressed for a European voyage on the Queen Elizabeth." I said.

"I heard my mother talking to a friend. They said people aren't traveling to Europe much these days what with the war talk and all," Sue replied.

"Well, I don't have to worry about that for sure. All I really want to do is go to the World's Fair in New York. That doesn't look too promising."

We looked both ways and crossed the street.

Mr. Bell of *The Washington Post* was right. It was a great movie and Mickey Rooney was a great Huck Finn. I ought to know; I must have read the book ten times. Sue couldn't believe her eyes when the Rockets started dancing. She had never seen a stage show before. She didn't seem to understand half of what Mr. Frankie Albertson said, but I supposed that was just as well. Truth was, I didn't understand some of it myself.

It took a couple of minutes for my eyes to adjust to the light after the dark theater. Then I began to search the skies.

"Sue, see if you can find the Yankee Clipper."

"The what?"

"You know, the dirigible. It's supposed to fly over Washington today to help celebrate the 150th anniversary of Congress. I read about it in the *Post*."

We stood for several minutes craning our necks skyward to no avail. We gave up and headed for the drugstore.

I would rather have gone around the corner to the Neptune Room, a restaurant next door to the Earle Theater. There, after you got your lunch from the cafeteria line, a waitress brought desserts around on a big tray. I always chose the Napoleon pastry, my absolute favorite dessert in the whole world. Sue and I just had not had enough time to save up for that much of a birthday treat.

As we walked along, Sue decided she might order a tuna fish sandwich and a chocolate soda. That sounded all right to me.

"I might have the same," I said.

We found two empty stools near the end of the counter. Sue slid the menu out of its holder and began to question her lunch selection.

"I didn't know they had hamburgers, maybe I'll have a hamburger. Look, they have egg salad sandwiches. I've never had an egg salad sandwich. I love fried eggs. I wonder how they make them into a salad?"

By this time the counter lady was standing in front of us. She wore a white triangle shaped cap on her head and a starched white apron over her blue dress. She held a pad in her hand ready for our order.

The counter lady smiled at Sue and said, "Egg salad sandwiches are made about the same as tuna or chicken salad. The egg is hard boiled first and then chopped up. Stir some mayonnaise into anything chopped up, add some onion and pickles and you've got yourself a salad. Would you like to try one?"

Sue thought a minute. "I don't know—there's so much on the menu."

"Tell you what. You take your time deciding. I'll check back in a couple of minutes."

"She's very nice."

"Yeah, but she isn't going to wait all day," I replied.

"Bessy makes chicken salad a lot but she hardly ever makes tuna salad. I'm not sure I would like my eggs in a salad. I guess I'll just have the tuna salad and chocolate soda."

The counter lady reappeared and smiled at us again, her pencil poised above her pad.

"It's her birthday celebration," Sue said as she pointed to me.

"Well now. Let me guess." She patted my arm. "I'd say about thirteen."

Although flattered to be thought of as older, I 'fessed up. "No, just twelve tomorrow."

Sue gave the waitress her order. It sounded all right to me, I said, "Me too."

I had just taken a big sip of my soda when lunch was suddenly spoiled. A colored man bumped my elbow as he climbed onto the seat next to me. The bump didn't spoil my lunch. I had been hugged and squeezed so many times by warm and loving brown skinned Pearl that I knew there was no harm in his touch. It was the counter lady who spoiled my lunch.

Scowling, she said gruffly, "We don't serve coloreds." She didn't even say she was sorry.

Suddenly a bite of my tuna sandwich stuck in my throat.

He was light skinned. Neat. His slicked back hair had a fresh cut look.

"Miss, I'm hungry, been travelin' a long way," he said. "Came down from New York to live here. I've got a government job come Monday. Don't know my way around the city yet."

The counter girl just shook her head. He stared at her for moments then his shoulders slumped as if suddenly weighed down by an invisible yoke. Slowly he reached down and picked up his small suitcase and moved toward the drugstore door. I watched him through the window until he was out of sight.

"Mama says some coloreds just don't seem to know their place these days," Sue remarked.

My sandwich continued to stick in my throat. I felt guilty. I knew that my mother would have thought to give the man half of her sandwich.

After lunch we walked on down F Street and browsed through the first floor of L. Franks Ladies' Shop, then crossed the street to window shop at Lerner's Shop.

"Someday I'm going to work at Lerner's," I proclaimed to Sue. "Or maybe I'll choose L. Franks, it's classy. I'm not sure which right now."

Sue was used to my proclamations. She just sighed and did not respond.

We made our way back to the streetcar stop. Just so Sue wouldn't be fidgety going home, I asked the conductor if we were on the right streetcar even though I knew we were.

We had just gotten seated when Sue asked, "Do you think you'll get it?"

I knew what she meant but I asked anyway, "Get what?"

"You know, a bicycle for your birthday."

"Don't know. Sometimes I think yes and sometimes I think no. Mother keeps mentioning that she is saving up for a duplex house across the river in South Arlington somewhere. They cost over five thousand dollars. Also, maybe not on account of Randolph."

"Who's Randolph?"

"He's a colored man who works in Mother's office at the Department of Agriculture."

"What's he got to do with your bicycle?"

"Well, my mother was supposed to get a raise. Her boss, Mr. Clary, called her in and told her so. Then Mother asked Mr. Clary if Randolph got his raise because he was next in line. She said Mr. Clary seemed real surprised and upset at her question and told her that Randolph hadn't gotten a raise. So, my mother refused her raise until Randolph gets his."

Mother very often told Buddy and me that what's right is right and what's wrong is wrong and that's all there is to that. I figured this was one of those right is right times my mother came on strong about. I tended toward staying on the right side as much as I could. Being on the wrong side around Mother could get very serious what with her having a redhead's temper. My stepfather, Larry, had not quite learned that. He got on the bad side of Mother's temper a lot. I hated the quarrels, the yelling. I often wondered why my mother bothered with a husband at all. She didn't seem to like living with a man. There were many times when I thought she didn't like living with Buddy and me either.

Sue was silent for a few minutes as she looked out of the window. Without even turning toward me, she quietly said, "Your mother is a little weird you know."

I didn't bother to answer or get myself all riled up. It had to do with comparisons and, compared to most of my friend's mothers, what she said was true.

Sue had to get right home when we got off the streetcar. I was relieved that I didn't have to ask her up to our apartment. It was a mess when I left and I had no reason to believe it would be any different now. I was the only one messes seemed to bother.

I called after Sue to remind her, "Don't forget to talk about the museum whale and the mummies when you get home."

She waved and went on.

The whole family was in the apartment when I got upstairs. Mother said that we were just going to get a sandwich at the soda fountain for supper since we would have a big day on Sunday for my birthday. I chose to go to King's Chinese Restaurant across the Potomac River in Alexandria for my special dinner. It meant that we had to take the streetcar and change to a bus on Pennsylvania Avenue at the post office.

We didn't go often and it always took a long time but it was worth it. Mother heard about the restaurant from someone at her work who lived in Alexandria. We all liked the chicken chow mein best. It had piles of slivered chicken all over the top. Besides, it was the cheapest thing on the menu.

"We'll come back here for cake and ice cream. I got a cake from the market on my way home from work today," Mother said. "Then maybe there will be a surprise," she added.

I crossed my fingers and made a wish. Then I began to pick up the strewn papers and coats until Mother said I was making her nervous. Mother and I never saw eye to eye about keeping things straight. We didn't see eye to eye about a lot of things. It was just as well that I was told to stop. I needed to do my homework if I wanted the whole Sunday cleared for my birthday.

Mother seemed anxious for us to get to bed that night. I was tired anyway so I didn't mind. Buddy and I didn't have a set bedtime. It was mostly set by Mother's moods. Sometimes that made it hard to get my homework done so I usually did it right after school.

Buddy and I shared the same bedroom. We had twin beds. It was easy to tell whose bed was whose. Each morning when I got up, I carefully made my bed. I learned to do that while I lived in Alabama with my Aunt Bea. Mother and Buddy just threw the covers up to the top of the bed and left them however they landed. Also, Raggedy Ann and Raggedy Andy rested against my pillow. They were more like friends than rag dolls. I told them everything.

During the night I heard an awful scream. I jolted upright and grabbed Raggedy Ann. Then I realized Buddy was having one of his nightmares again. Every now and then he saw monsters at our second floor bedroom windows. I never saw them but they were very real to Buddy. They terrified him. I ran to get Mother as she had told me to do. She wasn't in her bedroom. She wasn't in the kitchen or the living room either. Larry, my stepfather, was gone too.

Now I was scared. I ran back to Buddy. He kept crying and hollering. I told Buddy that there weren't any monsters, just the streetlight filtering through the sheer curtains. He cried louder. I opened a window and leaned out moving my arms back and forth so that he could see that nothing was there. He pointed to the next window over. I repeated my performance. Finally, he pulled the covers over his head and settled down. I lay in the dark squeezing Raggedy Ann and Andy. I waited and waited until I heard a key in the lock. I held my breath.

I heard familiar voices. I got up and ran to the living room and tearfully asked of my mother, "Where have you and Larry been? Buddy's monsters scared him again. I couldn't find you."

Mother laughed. "Just over to the dance hall. We weren't far away. Besides, you are a big girl now. You just turned twelve years old."

I didn't think there was anything to laugh about. I had been very worried. I guess Mother could tell I was really upset.

"I promise, I'll tell you when we are going out from now on."

"Buddy and I are used to being home alone in daytime, I guess we will get used to it at night," I whispered to Raggedy Ann and Andy as I crawled back in bed. I lay in the dark a long time wondering what being twelve would be like.

The rain pelted the windows as I woke up on my birthday morning. Buddy was still head and all under the covers. I got up and looked out. 14th Street was quieter on Sundays. The streetcars didn't run as often. As I watched, I saw a few people dashing about huddling under umbrellas. Off in the distance I could hear church bells ringing. I tiptoed into the kitchen. Mother and Buddy were late sleepers on Sundays. Larry was always the first one up. As usual, he had already been down to the drugstore and the bakery to get *The Washington Post* and our Sunday morning breakfast treats.

He sipped his coffee as he read. I made myself a cup of Ovaltine and dug a honey bun out of the waxy bag on the counter.

The two of us split the paper every Sunday. My part lay by my place at the table. Larry just read the want ads, the car ads, and the sports section of the paper. Mostly he read detective stories. Sometimes I glanced through his magazines but I thought they were horrid. People sticking knives in people just didn't sit right with me.

Larry became part of my life just three years earlier. Mother met him while she was working in Jacksonville, Florida. Most of the time she was working there, I lived with Aunt Bea in Florence, Alabama. Buddy was further down state with my father in Alexander City. Larry and Mother got married before Buddy and I ever met him. It took awhile to get used to him. For one thing, he had short grayish hair that rolled itself into tight curls. I had never seen hair like that before. One time I heard a neighbor say that he was a milquetoast. I thought maybe this meant that he was tall and thin, but I decided to look it up. Miss Jessup at the library helped me because I didn't know how to spell milquetoast. I found out that it was probably a very good word to describe him. I used it sometimes when I talked with my friends. I just never bothered to tell them what it meant.

"I see Arcade Pontiac has a new car advertised for $758," Larry commented in his whispery Sunday morning voice. Mother would be angry if we woke her up.

I didn't know why he kept looking at car ads. Not only could we not afford one, we didn't need one. He worked at Riggs National Bank as a teller. The streetcar took him right to the front door down on F Street.

"I'll have to go take a look," he continued.

"Hey, Hedy Lamarr married Gene Markey, the director." I read the whole article out loud.

"You sure are taken up with movie stars, just like your mother."

"Well, I guess I have a right. Did Mother ever tell you that she named me after a famous silent movie star that she liked in her younger days?"

"I think I've heard that once or twice." He went back to reading the paper.

I settled down to read Mary Haworth's advice column to myself. It was all about a man who was 31 and a woman who was 25. The woman wanted to know if she should get a divorce because she wasn't happy with the way things were going. Mary told her that divorce should be avoided where at all possible but since there were no children, she guessed it might be all right. I was glad she said the stuff about children. When my mother divorced my father it just about tore me up. I was only six when everything turned topsy-turvey. They fought all the time. That year neither one even took time out to come to school for the big fair where everyone brought embroidered pillowcases, and jellies, and pies; all sorts of things. So I walked the few blocks over to school and just pretended to a couple of smart alecks that my folks were over in another room looking at all the fancy quilts hanging on the walls.

I didn't want to think about that anymore so I piped up with, "I hope we get back from dinner in time for Jack Benny and Edgar Bergen and Don Ameche."

"Don't leave out Rochester," Larry added. "We'll get back in time. We're going early so we can celebrate here later."

I got out my paper and pencil and began copying the dress and suit ads for Hecht's and Lansburgh's Department Stores. Sometimes I dreamed of becoming a dress designer. After I copied a suit with a bolero jacket, I added my own touches here and there and thought it looked much better. It might even sell for as much as ten dollars, I thought. I studied my drawing and decided I had better take art lessons sometime in the future. The new style wedgie shoes were difficult to draw.

By the time I got around to checking on Winnie Winkle and Dixie Dugan in the comics, Mother and Buddy were up. My birthday celebration soon began.

Due to the gully washing rain, our trip over to Virginia was messy. The cold rain chilled us too. But, Mother was in good spirits so we all were. When we passed over the 14th Street Bridge, down below the Potomac River looked choppy and gray matching the sky. When I peered through the clouded windows on the right side of the bus just past the bridge, the airport looked deserted.

Buddy soon spotted some freight trains moving along the tracks on the left. The smoke from the engine rolled down toward the tracks and back under the wheels. He moved over to an empty seat on the other side of the bus so he could see clearly.

I fell to studying the bus driver as the bus stopped and started down Route 1 towards Alexandria. He seemed a nice enough sort. Every time some poor soaked rider got on the bus he apologized for being late.

"The weather, you know," he repeated over and over.

Even when they appeared nice, I didn't much trust bus drivers. I remembered for a while I had trusted them down in Jacksonville, Florida. When I first got there, Mother and Larry were running an old hotel downtown. Mother worked days as a secretary in her government job while Larry stayed at the desk. I guess I was underfoot a lot. I didn't know anybody and Mother didn't much like the men that hung around the lobby. Weekends she gave me a dime to ride the bus. It was just for riding, not going anywhere. I got on and rode to the end of the line and then came back. It got so the drivers let me do it over and over for the same dime.

One day the driver and I were the only ones on the bus at the end of the line. While we sat and waited for a customer, he had me sit on his lap so I could pretend to drive the bus. Pretty soon I got this funny feeling. The bus driver squirmed and made weird noises. I tried to get away—he pulled me back kind of rough. I was scared. Just then, I heard someone pounding on the door wanting in. I got away and ran to the back of the bus where I stayed until my stop came around. Then I dashed down the aisle and got off as quickly as I could. That ended my bus riding. Mother seemed puzzled as to why I didn't want to go anymore and I didn't know exactly how to explain, so I didn't. Anyway, she bought me a bunch of paper dolls and I stayed in our room a lot when I wasn't in school.

That summer, Mother rented a place at Jacksonville Beach. Buddy came and so did a cousin who stayed with us while Mother and Larry worked. It was one of my better summers.

We finally got to the restaurant. Our walk from the bus stop made us wet and cold. We ordered two pots of tea and asked the Chinese waiter to bring it right away. The chow mein we ordered tasted especially good. Buddy told the waiter about my birthday. After we finished eating, he brought out a little candle stuck in a saucer along with the fortune cookies. Everyone in the restaurant sang 'Happy Birthday'. My fortune said, "The sun will always shine on your head." It struck me so funny that I laughed until my side hurt. It was still pouring down rain outside.

We dashed from the streetcar and dripped puddles as we climbed the stairs to our apartment. Buddy started giggling. Mother shushed. Then I saw it. A brand new bicycle leaned against our apartment door. A big piece of cardboard hung from the handlebars. I just about died on the spot from happiness. The cardboard read, 'Happy Birthday to You'. The whole family had signed it.

Mother said that old Mr. Swift who lived in the apartment next to ours had kept it hidden and put it in the hall while we were gone. He kept an eye on it until we got home. When he heard us, he stuck his head out and waved and wished me a happy birthday too.

I wheeled the bicycle inside and sat on it all while listening to Jack Benny.

That night I could hardly sleep. My bicycle and I had a project to carry out and it would take some planning. I had been thinking about it for a long time. That's why I needed a bicycle. First I had to practice up some. I hadn't ridden since last summer down at my grandmother's farm in Alabama. There were a couple of old rusty bikes in the barn that Buddy and I used. I wondered if it would be different on a new bike.

As I drifted off to sleep, I again wondered what my twelfth year might be like. As far as I knew it would be like the last couple of years. I would finish the school year; get on the train and go South; then come back to enter Powell Junior High. That much would be different as I would be finished with Cooke Elementary. I'd go to the Tivoli on Saturdays with friends and on Sundays with Mother, Larry, and Buddy. We would go to the zoo a lot when the weather was good. I kept adding to the list until I drifted off to sleep.

But as fate would have it, that's not the way it would be, not with my mother arranging our lives.

## School Plans

My teachers, Mrs. Stubel, and the gym teacher, Mr. Gorge planned a lot for us sixth graders to do in the spring of 1939. When I returned to H.D. Cooke Elementary on the Monday after my birthday, Mr. Gorge said it was time to get started. There were two big events that were his responsibility. Among the lucky ones, I was to be in both.

One event was the big safety day parade coming up in May. Mr. Gorge got those who were going to be in the parade excused from Mrs. Stubel's verb lesson so he could explain everything. That suited me just fine.

"We will start training soon. I'm going to teach you to march in step and make soldier sharp turns. You'll have several drill maneuvers to learn. Later on we will learn to march with other elementary schools over on the high school field. Then, in May, everyone will be ready for the big parade. We are going to march down Pennsylvania Avenue." Mr. Gorge said all this in his funny accent.

He came from down in South America somewhere. His skin stayed very brown. It didn't even lighten up in winter. He once told us that he had lived in Washington a long time. He didn't sound like it. He had a big toothy smile and seldom got mad at us. When he did, he blew his whistle, talked loudly and waved his arms around. We couldn't under-stand a word he said. Then he would suddenly stop, laugh, and say "again" in English. We all adored him and he managed to get the best out of us.

I reveled at the thought of marching on Pennsylvania Avenue. Besides the Virginia bus stop being on the Avenue, it was the same route that President Roosevelt used to go back and forth between the White House and the Capitol building. I saw him do it once. I never ever dreamed that I might be in a parade on that same Avenue.

Mr. Gorge chose me because of my job. It was my job to stand on the corner further up Columbia Road from our apartment toward the park. I made sure all the little kids got across the street. As a safety patrol, I had a white belt to go over my shoulder and around my waist. This showed the automobile drivers why I was there. Because my corner was so busy, Mr. Johnson helped me. He was the neighborhood policeman who knew all the kids by name.

Mr. Gorge went on to say that the safety patrol parade would be on May 13. We needed uniforms of white duck pants and red jackets topped off with slick black high hats. We would wear our safety belts over our red jackets. As Mr. Gorge talked, I envisioned us looking like my brother's tin soldiers.

I raised my hand. "Where do we get our uniforms?"

"A group of volunteer mothers will make them. Does anyone here think their mother might volunteer?"

I didn't raise my hand. Several others did. I looked around enviously as hands shot up. My mother had never picked up a needle as far as I knew. Most mothers didn't type though, I thought defensively. Maybe Mr. Gorge would need some typing done sometime I hoped.

Jed Thomas asked, "How much will the uniforms cost?"

Mr. Gorge figured no more than three dollars. "You'll need black shoes too," he said.

I had a sinking feeling. I dreaded telling Mother. She said all these school things that popped up were unexpected and that the teachers really knew how to spend a person's money. I'd just have to watch for a time when she was feeling good. I hoped that was soon. It was puzzling to me that we always seemed to have enough money for movies and ice cream and eating out. When I needed a new dress or school stuff, money got really scarce all of a sudden. However, we were not going to start marching practice for a week and that gave me time. Besides, I didn't want to think about it right then.

## The Bicycle

I could hardly wait for school to let out that Monday after my birthday. I threw my books onto my bed as soon as I got home and grabbed the storeroom key off the kitchen cabinet door. Our storage space was small and set off by a chicken wire wall from the others. There was plenty of room for my bicycle since we didn't have anything to store but some old suitcases and a lamp that Mother no longer liked. There were three steps up to the first floor front hallway and I managed that. I struggled to get the bike out of the door because it kept shutting on me before I got the front wheel out. Finally Buddy saw me and left his marble game long enough to hold the door open.

"You are going to break your neck you know."

I just made a face at him and wheeled the bike out to the sidewalk.

My new bike was bigger than the ones down at Grandmother's farm in Alabama. I wobbled a little at first and again each time I hit a big crack in the sidewalk. It got dark before I realized it. I barely got home before Mother did. That mistake might keep the bike locked up. I'd have to be more careful. Mother didn't like to wait for anyone, although we waited for her a lot.

That night we went over to the cafeteria for supper. Mother started in right away fussing at Buddy for taking too many dishes as he went down the line. She said he would have to eat it all. He managed to get a stom-achache and cry. The two of them went through this same thing all the time, sort of like an Amos and Andy routine. I hated it. My stomach always ended up in knots. The wrangling also interrupted my thoughts about how long it would take me to practice up on the bicycle for my secret project. It was definitely not a good night to mention the parade. Anyway, I had homework to do on account of riding the bike all after-noon. When we got home, I jumped in the middle of my bed and read my geography book out loud to Raggedy Ann and Andy.

At the end of the week on Friday, I had good luck. The boys in my class goaded us girls with the news that they were going camping over the weekend with Mr. Gorge. I was delighted. It meant that they would not be around in the park. That night, Mother came home with the news that Mr. Clary had called her in again and told her that he had found some extra money. She and Randolph were both getting a raise. Right then and there I told her about the parade and she said she guessed she could manage three dollars. It was a big load of worry off me.

I stayed in bed on Saturday morning until I heard Mother and Larry leave for work. I dug down in my drawer for an old pair of pants that I wore down on the farm and put them on. I looked over at Buddy to make sure he was sound asleep. The covers were pulled right up to his eyelids. I figured he would stay asleep until about eleven o'clock. Just to be safe, I knocked on Mr. Swift's door before I went downstairs and told him that Buddy was alone for awhile. He said he would keep an ear open. This meant I was free for a good two hours.

Mr. Orman, the janitor, was working in the boiler room and helped me with the bike.

"It's a little raw to be out this morning, misty too. Are you sure you want to take your bike out?"

I was sure.

I rode the few blocks over to Meridian Hill Park. If us kids weren't at the movies or over on the school grounds, we'd be in the park.

Surrounding the park was a tall pebbly concrete wall. I entered from the corner of Euclid and 15th Streets. From this point the park graduated downhill toward W Street by terraces. Steps led from one terrace to another. These steps were involved in my project.

All last fall I watched as the boys rode through the park from Euclid down the terraces toward W Street, out the 15th Street exit, doubling back up to Euclid to start over. Sometimes they skidded on leaves, dumped their bikes, and scraped elbows. Nobody broke a leg or anything. They rode down the steps. It was a challenge I had to try.

I had more luck. The misty dampness and cold wind kept people out of the park. Once in awhile someone hurried across. My headscarf became soaked as I waited for an all clear. My hands turned cold. I didn't know if it was from fear or the weather.

The front wheel of my bike was in position. I spotted the slight grooves worn in the steps from the boy's wheels. Then came the moment when there was nothing to do but shove off.

There were only a few steps in the first set. I did fine. My wheels stayed straight and rolled steadily across the terrace to the next set. Then my speed increased. I couldn't find my brakes. I couldn't find the grooves. I just went with the wind. I thought about veering off into the bushes and crashing but before I could make a decision, I was right up on the next set of steps and down again. I became terrified. It seemed like I would never stop thumping down steps. I thought my head would jerk off. My fingers froze to the handlebars. Finally, I reached the last terrace. My feet felt for the brakes on my runaway bike. As I hit the brakes, my bike slid out from under me. I went one way; the bike went another.

The next thing I knew someone pulled me up by my elbow. That someone laughed for all he was worth. It was Jimmy Ray Perkins. Jimmy Ray was the biggest tease and bully around and the last person I wanted to see. He was already in junior high school but often hung around with some of the sixth grade boys. He was bound to tell.

"You done good, squirt. You got anything broke?"

"Nope." I wouldn't have told him if I had.

"Your pants are torn."

"Don't matter."

He went over and stood my bike up straight. He looked it over. I caught my breath and carefully moved my arms and legs to see if they really worked.

"Wheels are O.K. You've got a long deep scratch along the side here—a shame, looks brand new."

"Don't guess that matters either," I snapped.

"Better get home, squirt. It's too wet to be doing them tricks. Besides, that's boy stuff."

"Humph."

I dabbed at the small cut on my chin. He rolled the bike over to me and said that I ought to think about walking it home. He was acting awful nice for Jimmy Ray.

Luck ran out. Buddy was in the basement talking to Mr. Orman about how the furnace worked when I got back. Buddy liked to know how everything worked. If nobody told him how something worked, he usually ended up taking it apart. Of course, he noticed the gouge on my bike right off. I knew there wasn't any use in asking him not to tell. He got fussed at so much at the cafeteria and for tinkering with everything that you could hardly blame him for wanting me to share Mother's pepper-sauced tongue some of the time.

Buddy followed me upstairs. I went in the bathroom and closed the door right in his blue-eyed freckled face. When I pulled down my pants, I saw a big red and lavender place on my hip and a couple of deep scratches. I rummaged in the medicine cabinet until I found the all-purpose salve. Mother got all her medical advice from Dr. Judd at the drugstore. He mostly dispensed the greenish-black salve to take care of the outsides and a cherry-flavored syrup that took care of the insides. Once in awhile, he sent you over to Mrs. Judd at the soda fountain. The dreaded bottle of castor oil stood ready on the shelf in back of the fountain. When

Mr. Judd said it was needed, Mrs. Judd ceremoniously poured out a teaspoon and mixed it with a choice of orange juice or a Coke. She always made a horrible face right along with you while you held your nose and swallowed. Then you and she shivered.

Sure enough, Mother was hardly through the door when Buddy told her about my falling and getting the bike banged up.

"Hmmm," she muttered absently while looking through the mail. Luck was back. Even though I was relieved, I was also upset. She didn't even ask if I had gotten hurt.

Another week went by and it was Monday again. Mr. Gorge explained more about the spring playground track meet and how we had to start practicing hard.

"We are going to move outside now that the weather is better and really get into practicing. You will probably need to stay after school some. Please bring a note giving you permission before Friday."

That would be easy. Anything that kept me busy and out of the apartment, Mother signed.

Mr. Gorge had a list in his hand and started calling names. All winter he had scratched out and rearranged his list while we tried out in the gym. My name came up on two lists, the hundred-yard dash and the high jump. It was on account of my legs. My stepfather sometimes called me 'Olive Oil', like in the Popeye comics. He said it was because my long and skinny legs sort of got in the way of each other. I guessed I would show Larry. Mr. Gorge said I had a real good chance of bringing in a blue ribbon or two for our team but that I would have to work hard. He said that to everybody on the team.

Mrs. Stubel, our regular teacher, was very different from Mr. Gorge. Short and blonde, she had a way of smiling that crinkled up her eyes some. She never lost her temper no matter how many tricks the boys played or how many notes the girls passed. A few in my class really prided themselves on all A's. I was very content to be a mediocre student.

Mostly I got C's and that was just fine with me. Mrs. Stubel seemed content to let me be mediocre most of the time.

We'd hardly gotten settled into drilling and running and jumping when Mrs. Stubel gave us a new assignment. We were going to study the western pioneer trails and then do a play about them for our outdoor graduation celebration. Our scenery would be a covered wagon and a campfire made of red cellophane. The play was called 'Trails West', she announced. I raised my hand fast when she asked who would like to be in the play. I got chosen.

It wasn't on account of my legs that I got chosen. I figured it was on account of English. Mrs. Stubel had a thing about English. She frequently had us write a composition for homework. First I wrote mine with a pencil on one of the big pads that Mother used for her Bible writing. Then second, I put a piece of paper in Mother's typewriter and pecked away until I got it typed. Sometimes Mother was impatiently waiting to use the typewriter and would type it for me. It was neater then. I was the only one who turned in a typed paper. Besides, Mrs. Stubel liked the way I occasionally didn't write sentences. Every now and then she would question me.

"Did you intend to leave the subject out? It's a good tool in writing." Or, "Did you use only one word to describe your feelings on purpose? That's very good." That day I got an A.

Sometimes she said, "You really ought to think about being a writer."

I didn't have the heart to tell her that I was going to be a famous designer and go to Paris. Besides, it wouldn't have been very smart. As long as she thought I might be a writer, I was sort of a favorite. I liked that. That's how I got chosen for the play.

Richard was chosen too. Richard wasn't my boyfriend exactly. Sometimes we hung around together on the playground. Sometimes he walked me home after I got through with safety patrol in the afternoon. It wasn't on his way. He had to turn around to go back over close to 16th Street somewhere. Sue said that made him my boyfriend. I said, "Does not." Once he bought me a soda. That almost made him my boyfriend. It would be fun being in the play together, but I wasn't ready for that boy and girl stuff.

Despite how late in the year it was, a new girl came to Cooke. Her name was Alice. Sue and I sort of took up with her and tried to help her fit in with our friends. I told her that my favorite song was *Alice Blue Gown.* We invited her to join us at the Tivoli for the Saturday matinee.

One afternoon as we were walking across the playground at recess time, she began to snicker. She pointed at the socks that one of the boys walking in front of us wore. The socks were shiny stiff and a large hole appeared above the shoe line on each foot. The boy had sandy-red hair. The boy was Buddy. My face must have reflected my embarrassment, not only for him, but also for myself. Many days, my socks were in the same condition.

"Tacky, tacky, tacky," her singsong voice repeated as she continued to point.

I felt a real jolt. I wanted to put my hands over my ears. I wanted to shrivel up. I wanted to hide. I raised my chin and hoped the tears in my eyes would not trickle down my cheeks.

This was something new and decidedly unwelcome. The people in our neighborhood were family. Our school was just another home where all sorts of kids came together. Even those from Embassy Row were nice. Sure, we teased and poked fun occasionally, but we weren't mean. Maybe remembrance of hard times from the depression still lingered and the thought that it could creep back again kept us from taunting each other about our haves and have nots.

Sue took my hand. Together we silently returned to class. When one hurt, both of us hurt.

I slammed every door as I entered our apartment that day after school. I found every sock in every drawer and under every bed and dumped them in the furnace room trash. My tears made it impossible to sort the good from the bad. I didn't care what Mother might say or what she might do to me. I raged inwardly. How could she let us go to school that way anyway, I thought as I brushed more tears onto the sleeve of my dress and stomped back upstairs to flop on my bed. Raggedy Ann and Andy were no help. I shoved them off the bed and onto the floor.

Luck came back. It was Friday and payday to boot. When I declared on Saturday afternoon that new socks had to be on the shopping list for Buddy and me, Mother gave me a quizzical look but asked no questions. She bought the socks. From that point on, I rinsed out socks every couple of days for both Buddy and me.

The weather got warmer and warmer. Daffodils and tulips bloomed in people's yards. Soon the cherry trees would bloom. Mother promised that we would go see them. Because of the warm weather our family did more roaming around on 14th Street, wandering up and down and poking around in the stores and the Arcade Market on Saturday afternoons. I particularly liked it when Buddy needed a haircut. Mother and I always went with him and sat reading the magazines. Mother usually read *Life*. Buddy and I grabbed a comic book while we waited his turn. Sometimes I just pretended to read when I was really listening. Mr. Anthony (that was his first name) came from overseas in Italy. Mother said she thought he was a bookie from the things that went on in the barbershop. I knew a bookie didn't have anything to do with books. Now and then someone started an argument with Mr. Anthony about how things were going over in Europe. He got all excited and waved his scissors and comb all around the customer's head. Like Mr. Edward R. Murrow on the radio, he took off on Hitler and Mussolini and just about everybody he knew over there. Mother would say, "Not again." That's because she knew we would have to wait a long time when Mr. Anthony got excited like that.

At school I marched and jumped and ran. The spring track meet was getting closer and closer. Everybody said that I was bound to win. I felt pretty cocky about it myself. I loved being the center of attention when I soared over the high jump bars doing just as good as the boys. I figured I could do just about anything as good as a boy. It was a little weighty though being expected to win like that. I began to get butterflies in my stomach. On the Saturday before the meet on Monday, I persuaded Sue and a couple of other girls to meet me over at Meridian Hill Park. I brought a broom and showed Sue and Carey Smith how to hold it higher and higher until I said stop. They were following my instructions fairly well—and then…

"Stick 'em up!" The yell came from a close by. A bandanna covered face suddenly peered through a bush.

Sue jumped a mile. Up went her end of the broom just as my right leg began to go over the broom handle.

Three young boys about Buddy's age went scampering away, pointing their toy pistols at everyone who passed.

Sue looked back toward me. I lay on the ground. I was used to falling on the ground but I had fallen short of the grassy plot we were on and had landed on the edge of the sidewalk. The end of my spine was sending shock waves through the whole of me. Tears welled up. I didn't know if I could move. I didn't want to try. The girls hovered around, then finally just sat down beside me until we decided what to do. I don't know how long we sat there.

Finally I said, "Help me up. Mr. Gorge says it's always better to move around and walk it off when you fall." It didn't feel better.

"I could just die," Sue said.

"Not your fault."

"We'll walk you home. You'd better go home and lie down."

I wouldn't let them help me up the stairs, but before I got to our apartment door I wished that I had. I gingerly crawled onto my bed and hugged Raggedy Ann. When Mother came in I told her I had a book report to do and had to read all afternoon. The family went to the Tivoli. I cried. They brought me a quart of ice cream for supper.

Sunday came. I lay in bed longer than usual. Finally, I hobbled out to the kitchen. I walked a little better. Before I got out of bed I prayed that I would be better. Mother didn't cotton to people praying all the time for every little thing. She said that every time someone prayed for some self-ish thing it counted against the times when you really needed a prayer.

"If you are going to pray at all you need to make sure you can't take care of the problem yourself. God helps those who help themselves." She said that a lot. I figured this was one of those times I had better pray.

My part of the Sunday paper lay on the kitchen table. Larry wasn't anywhere around and I was glad. For awhile I sat and read. Hedda Hopper didn't have much exciting Hollywood news. The lady on the society page must have been important. She had on a long dress and sat regal-like in a high backed chair. The picture was right in the middle of the page. There was long story about her but I didn't bother to read it.

Buddy straggled in rubbing his eyes. "What are you looking at?"

"This picture."

"It doesn't look interesting to me, just some old lady."

"Well, someday I'm going to have my picture in the middle of the page in *The Washington Post*. You wait and see."

"Look at this." He held up a page with pictures of planes and tanks. "Now that's interesting." There had been a lot of those pictures in the paper lately.

"How's your back?" he continued.

"Don't ask"

"O.K. I won't"

"And don't tell Mother."

He didn't have to tell. Later that afternoon she could see the problem very well for herself no matter how hard I tried to walk straight. She rubbed the green-black salve on my spine and gave me an aspirin. Much to my relief, she reckoned castor oil wouldn't do much good. Towards suppertime I felt well enough to make it downstairs and over to the cafeteria and back again. It was slow going though.

After Jack Benny, I hobbled toward the bedroom.

"You'll be all right in a couple of days," Mother called to me.

"I have a track meet tomorrow Mother," I lamented.

"Well, don't worry about it. I can't see much point in jumping over a pole anyway. It's not that important."

Tears came. It's important to me I thought. I pulled Raggedy Ann and Andy close to me. I worried. I tossed. I sniffled. I prayed again. Maybe I slept some toward morning.

Monday morning dawned bright and clear, just right for a track meet. I discovered that if I moved in a certain way I didn't hurt so much. I moved in that certain way all the way to school. I hardly spoke to anyone. Ten o'clock came and busses from other schools pulled up out in front of Cooke Elementary. Mr. Gorge gathered us Cookers in one corner of the playground to give us a pep talk. I thought I would die just listening. I had this terrible feeling. I couldn't even fake a smile.

"Don't be so tense." Mr. Gorge said as he patted me on the shoulder. "You did great on Friday and you'll do great today." Mr. Gorge moved on patting everyone else on the shoulder.

Friday was Friday, today is today, I thought to myself.

There were several events before my turn. I walked back and forth as straight as I could, limbering up as best I could—wincing at the slightest wrong move. There was quite a crowd. Lots of mothers came. Some of them were putting out lemonade and cookies for an after the meet treat. Neighborhood folks hung over the fence watching. For once, I felt relieved my mother never appeared at these school events.

First came several boys' races. Richard won a red ribbon for second in his race. Us Cookers cheered.

Then the boys chosen to do the setting up began to get the high jump ready.

The boys competed first. A Cooker boy won first place. When he stepped up to get his blue ribbon, Jay Winthrop looked as proud as the peacocks that my Aunt Allison raised down in Alabama. The Cookers were really cheering now. My heart was doing flip-flops.

The time came to take my place. I saw a teacher on the sidelines point toward me. "She's a sure winner," I heard her say. My stomach rolled over and its contents lurched toward my throat.

First I had to run distance enough to get my speed up to send me over the bars. This distance was laid out with chalk. As I stood tensely looking down that line, it seemed much longer than usual. I drew a deep breath. The first two running steps didn't hurt too much, but as my right foot again touched the cinders of the track, the searing pain came back— strong. I kept going anyway. The bar got closer and closer. The Cookers were cheering me on. I felt tears trickling down my cheek. I twisted my left leg to get in position to scissor over the bar by throwing my right leg up. My right leg simply wouldn't go. I crumpled to the ground.

For the first time in my life I really knew what was meant by a deafening silence. After the first chorus of "Oh no's," there was total quiet.

I lay very still and kept my eyes closed, never wanting to open them again.

Then I felt a hand on my forehead. "Are you all right? What happened? Did you twist your ankle? Did you hurt your head when you fell?"

My pain was terrible. My pride hurt the worst. I'd barely turned twelve and already I was a failure.

As I opened my eyes, other teachers closed in around me and kept the Cookers shooed away.

Mrs. Stubel pushed her way into the circle.

"Can you sit up?"

Tired of questions, I whispered, "I'll try."

I managed to sit up and slowly Mr. Gorge and Mrs. Stubel helped me stand. They helped me hobble off the playground. Tears streaked my cinder-dusted cheeks.

I spent the rest of the track meet on the cot in the nurse's office. She called my mother at the Department of Agriculture who told her to call a taxi after I had rested some. The nurse lent me money from the principal's special fund for the taxi. The taxi man helped me to the door and Mr. Avery, the janitor, helped me upstairs.

I did not go to Cooke Elementary the next day, or the next, and then it was right up to Friday when Easter vacation started. I stayed out all week. Mother used up a whole jar of the green-black salve. Sue came to see me once. She said everyone was sorry. Mr. Gorge gave a lecture about how trying to be brave when you're hurt wasn't such a good idea. The Cookers won three blue ribbons and four reds. It wasn't enough to win the track meet. They had counted on me.

The next big shock came with the Sunday *Post*. I couldn't believe my eyes when I saw it. There it was in the youth section—a picture of Buddy riding on the shoulders of some of the Cookers with his hands thrown up in the air like some bigwig. I remembered newspapermen taking pictures during the track meet.

I stared at it for the longest time. I felt pain all the way through to my soul. Buddy's picture was actually in *The Washington Post* before mine. I really wanted to tear it out of the paper and put it in the trash before anyone saw it. Nobody would know the difference I reasoned. But, suppose somebody showed it to Mother or Larry at work on Monday. They would know what I did. For a good five minutes I wrestled with myself before I tore the whole page out and laid it carefully aside for the family to see.

From some unfamiliar place deep inside I conjured up a smile when Buddy appeared to claim his jelly doughnut.

"Look here, there's something very interesting in the paper this morning."

"More society ladies I bet," he said as he picked up the page.

"Wow! That's me. Hey Mother, I'm in *The Washington Post*," he yelled as he opened her bedroom door.

Mother didn't even fuss about being awakened.

## Spring Continues

We dressed up on Easter even if we weren't going to church. Mother said that since I needed a new dress anyway, she bought the one I wanted and a new hat to go with it. The hat was straw with the brim turned up all the way around. My walking had improved enough so that we could go on *The Potomac* cruise boat down the Potomac River to visit Mount Vernon like we planned. Buddy had a new striped shirt and Mother had a new hat too. Larry didn't want anything new. He got out his old straw hat and set it at a jaunty angle on his head.

All of us grabbed a seat on the upper deck so that we could really see everything. Powder puff clouds hung low in the sky edging the blue like a picture frame. The clouds didn't interfere with the sun that seemed to be flinging glitter on the water. A soft breeze appeared to be pushing us gently downstream. Mt. Vernon soon came into view.

I really liked President Washington's home. For awhile, I stood on the wide veranda pretending that I was Nellie Custis, his stepdaughter, welcoming all the people to my home. Play acting ceased as the family headed for the grave where George and Martha were buried. It was one of those days when everything goes right. Mother and Buddy didn't even fuss later at the cafeteria. I began to think maybe luck was back.

I was wrong again.

The bad luck started before the bell rang for classes on Monday morning. Real or imagined, I was greeted with silence that signaled everyone's disappointment about the track meet. I tried hard to ignore the cold shoulders and busied myself telling Sue all about going to

Mount Vernon. She said she knew all about Mount Vernon and didn't want to listen to me a minute.

"I go by Mount Vernon every summer. I go all the way down to Colonial Beach on *The Potomac.* We have a big summer house that sits right across the road from the river and right close to where Alexander Graham Bell lived when he was young." She went on to tell me all about the blue crabs you could buy for a nickel from boys who caught them along the shore.

She said, "I can stand out a little way in the water and spread my legs far apart and be standing in both Virginia and Maryland at the same time."

There were times when I couldn't stand Miss Sue Lankford: my best friend. I didn't even know what a blue crab looked like, not that I would admit it.

Thank goodness the bell rang. Those of us in the safety parade didn't stay inside long. We were excused for a special practice. Our uniforms were going to be handed out. When I got to the place where I usually stood, which was right up on the front row, the row was full. Anne Marie Sloat stood in my place. I was about to protest when I saw Mr. Gorge beckon to me. He explained that I had missed so much that he had put Anne Marie up front because that was the lead line and had to be full for practice. I knew before he finished that I had been moved to the back.

I prayed. By Mother's standards, I knew it was wrong. I did it anyway because I didn't think I could solve the problem by myself.

I was praying that Anne Marie Sloat would get sick or break a leg or something. And I reminded God he had only two weeks to see to it. I knew my mother would never approve of that prayer.

Luck or God came back in my life. A terrible spring flu was going around. Two days before the parade, Anne Marie's mother sent a note to school. Mr. Gorge moved me back up front.

I had awful guilt pains but they did not affect my marching. On Saturday the weather turned cold. The temperature hovered in the low 50's as we boarded our bus early in the morning. The sun finally stole some of the chill as we found our places.

The parade was glorious. There were bands. People rode in open cars. There were hot dog stands and little kids sitting on the curbs. Policemen blew whistles on the corners, keeping cars off Pennsylvania Avenue. I wouldn't have been surprised to see Mr. Roosevelt riding up ahead somewhere. We hutted right and hutted left and fell in and out of formations exactly right. I had difficulty keeping a serious face. I wanted to smile so badly. My chin strap helped me keep a straight face. Mr. Gorge walked beside us close to the curb so as not to seem part of the parade. His grin was so wide that all his teeth showed. We won a trophy.

All during the parade I tried not to think about Anne Marie, but when I did, I prayed for God to make her well for the 'Trails West' play. He had plenty of time.

After the bus dropped us off at school following the parade, we walked through the neighborhood and up and down 14th Street showing off our uniforms.

The *Post* news article headlined the "Schoolboy Patrolmen Parade." The article said there were 15,000 safety patrols from 19 states in the parade. Further down the column the reporter mentioned that there were a few girls among the boys. I nearly puked. I scanned the pictures. I was not in them. I didn't read the *Post* again for a week.

The Saturday after the parade, we girls were walking in the park while the boys whizzed past us biking down the stairs. They taunted us each time they rode by.

"Sissy girls," smart aleck Tom Adams called the loudest.

When they had had enough riding, they gathered around us on their bikes.

"Bet there's not one of you who would even try the short steps," Tom chided.

Jimmy Ray Perkins was with them that morning. He looked over at me, grinned and winked.

He kept quiet. I kept quiet. If I had been a puppy dog, I would have wagged my tail. I did not want to repeat my performance. Once was enough. He understood. After that, I took on an entirely different opinion of Jimmy Ray Perkins.

Uncle Walter came to town again—our rich uncle on Mother's side from Alabama. About twice a year he came to Washington to meet with some congressmen and other important people. It had something to do with a business he owned. He stayed at the Willard, the famous hotel on Pennsylvania Avenue. He never came to our apartment. Uncle Walter always called and asked Mother to come downtown to see him. Sometimes the whole family went with her. This was one of those times.

I always felt out of place when we entered the lobby. We dressed up in our very best outfits. Somehow, we never seemed dressed up enough. The lobby was really classy and had an antique look about it like my Aunt Helen's parlor down in Alabama. Mother said there were always some dignitaries sitting around so people could see them. Sometimes she pointed them out, but they seemed about the same as unimportant people to me.

Soon after we got to his room, Uncle Walter ordered dinner for all of us. He never asked what we wanted; he just ordered steak that came with fancy vegetables. A hotel waiter brought dinner right to the room on a special cart. Uncle Walter never ate his dinner. He was too busy sipping on his drinks. Sure enough, he was soon plastered. Then he begged

Mother to stay with him. That night she couldn't because she had to get up really early and go to work because of a special breakfast meeting where she had to take what she called 'conference dictation'. That was her specialty.

"Then let Buddy stay," he drawled as he took off his tie and rumpled shirt.

Buddy's eyes got as big as moon pies. He looked at Mother hoping she would say no.

"What do you think Buddy? Tomorrow's Saturday. I can pick you up when I get off at noon."

Buddy hemmed and hawed but when Uncle Walter said there was a five-dollar bill in the deal for him, Buddy nodded a yes. That was a lot of money for Buddy. Uncle Walter sometimes gave Mother 100 dollars when she stayed with him. He didn't trust himself by himself. Mother said sometimes he got in trouble when he was out of town because it was then that he let the bottle get hold of him. He needed someone to watch and see to it that he didn't go down to the lobby or out on the street and make a fool of himself. By the time the rest of us got up to leave, he was stumbling about in his undershirt trying to unbutton his pants.

"It was awful. I'm never going to do that again," Buddy said when he got home on Saturday afternoon. "He up-chucked half the night and hollered a lot—nearly scared me to death."

Funny thing. Uncle Walter was like another person when we visited in Alabama—all starch and dignity and didn't seem to have the time of day for us.

When it happened I couldn't figure out whether I was in luck or out of luck. We Cooker girls didn't talk about it much because it had not happened to very many of us. But, when it did, we referred to it as 'the curse'. The moment of announcement gave a person a certain amount of respect. We whispered to one another.

"Did you know you could have a baby now?"

"For heaven's sake, I'm twelve years old. What would I do with a baby? Besides, I think there is more to it than that even if I'm not sure just what all is involved."

"Does it hurt?"

"It's messy."

I attempted to change the subject but before I could, another girl chimed in.

"It makes you almost a woman. Doesn't that make you feel just wonderful?"

"It's messy," I repeated.

I did know that I was luckier than some. Mother told me a little about it just before I was twelve. She figured that I would start early since she had. She told me that she started when she was twelve and that nobody had told her anything about 'the curse'. It nearly frightened her to death. Mother said her sisters were so dumb not to explain it.

"People back in my day shied away from what they called 'delicate subjects' as if they did not exist at all. Ridiculous," she explained.

Mother showed me where she stored the box of pads. There was a brand new belt for me. She also told me just what to do when it happened. I thought I handled the situation splendidly. All the same, a dreadful feeling came over me when I realized I would be handling this situation for a long, long time.

As the weather got warmer, my friends and I spent a lot of time walking through Rock Creek Park. We pretended to be in the deepest jungles as we approached the Washington Zoo at the far end of the park. There were times when we acted as silly as Buddy and his pals. It was great having a zoo practically in your backyard. We got to know the animals by name and their keepers too. Tassy, my favorite monkey, was thin and wiry with a particularly wrinkled forehead as if she worried all the time. She seemed to resent being a monkey. When we threw her a peanut, she always threw it back.

One of the favorite games played by the keepers was to give the orangutans the hoses to clean out their own outside cages. The shaggy red-orange giants put on a great act as they hosed carefully around the walls of their confine. With obvious coyness, they worked along the back corner of their cages ignoring their audience. Suddenly one, then another, would turn the hoses on us. Their upper lips curled in a triumphant smile and we pretended great indignation as we marched back through Rock Creek Park soaking wet.

When the lioness had her twins, keeper Sam tricked the mother into her indoor house using a hunk of raw meat. Then he let us pet the babies through the bars.

Sometimes while in the zoo, we split up, agreeing on a meeting place. Occasionally, when something was troubling me, I wandered off alone to sit on a bench outside the elephant house. There, while I brooded, I observed both people and elephants. Their personalities weren't too far apart. I soon relaxed.

Jumbina was usually in the elephant yard near the moat. Jumbina, the largest of the four elephants, seemed to be the smartest. When she was outside, her favorite pastime was attempting to unscrew the giant metal bars from the posts that surrounded her pen. She worked steadily with her trunk, stopping now and then to make a full body turn, checking to see if a keeper was around. She did not concern herself about spectators. They never scolded her. My blues vanished one day when I saw her actually unscrew the top bar. It hit the ground with a bounce that sent one end clanging into the lower metal bar. The noise scared Jumbina so badly that she let out a bellow like I had never heard before. In a trot, she headed for the safety of her indoor pen. I laughed out loud and clapped my hands. My mood had completely changed as I ambled down the path to the meeting place by the water fountain to join my friends.

Each visit to the zoo left me convinced that I lived in a wonderful place. I wished living on Columbia Road could last forever. Of course, I knew it wouldn't. My mother was bound to become bored. Her moods were like funnel clouds spinning in the distance. Where would they strike? When?

## Kinfolks

Kinfolks were coming. We had never had company at our apartment before. In May, Mother got a letter from her sister Maime. She and three of my older cousins, Aunt Bea's Doadie and Aunt Maime's Jean and Ruth, were stopping by the last Sunday in May on their way to the World's Fair in New York. Right away, I was jealous that they were going to the fair. Then I began to worry about their visit. There wasn't much furniture in our apartment. Whenever we moved, Mother never took the furniture. She just picked up the pieces she bought through the newspaper ads. Then she sold it all when we moved again. I closed my eyes and conjured up a recollection of all my Alabama relatives' homes. They were full of furniture collected over many years, warm and familiar. When I opened my eyes and looked around our apartment again, my heart sank.

The reality was grim. A dusty brown sofa and two mismatched chairs, one blue, one rose, dominated the living room. At one end of the sofa stood a floor lamp with a tasseled cream-colored shade. At the other end under a pile of newspapers stood a watermarked end table. Along the 14th Street wall, our radio stood atop a drop leaf table where Larry also stacked his detective magazines. The floor and walls were bare. Near the kitchen, a chrome table and matching chairs completed our living space.

Food was another thing to worry about. Suppose Mother decided to serve a 'Quart for a Quarter' ice cream supper. I could just see the expressions on their faces—what a shocker that would be. It was times like these that I really wished with all my heart to be a normal family or least-ways to appear normal. Another thought—Mother might decide to do her tomato supper. I don't know where she got the recipe but all she did was open a can of tomatoes, dump them in a bowl and chop them up. Then she chopped some onions and threw them in too. The third thing she threw in was crackers after she crushed them on the counter with the bottom of a glass. Then she stirred it all, shook on some salt and pepper and called us to eat. Sometimes she opened two cans of Vienna sausages to go with it. Actually, the recipe wasn't all that bad but somehow I didn't think it would go over with my fried chicken and pork chop cousins from Alabama.

Another situation I had to worry about was religion. Mother claimed that Aunt Maime was afflicted with religion. According to Mother, she gave no quarter to anybody's views but her own, which she totally believed were God's too. Since Mother spent most of her spare time reading the Bible and then doing her Bible writing, it was hard for me to figure out just what was what between the two of them. Anyway, best as I could decipher, Mother and Aunt Maime just didn't agree on what they were reading in the same book.

It all turned out pretty well. The Sunday they were to arrive, I managed to pick up all the papers without Mother fussing. I found a pair of old underpants to use for a dust rag. Buddy stuffed all his soldiers, marbles, and toy guns into a big box and hid it in our closet. Larry put all his detective magazines in a paper bag and put them in his bureau drawer. While shopping at the Arcade Market on Saturday, I persuaded Mother to buy some flowers for the kitchen table. She bought a couple of extra plates and glasses at the five and dime store too.

All in all, things didn't look so bad. I guess Mother reached back in her memory because she bought two fat chickens that she put in the oven that Sunday afternoon. Our place smelled scrumptious by the time we heard a lot of noise on the steps.

There was a lot of hugging and "look how you have grown." Our apartment quickly settled back to its accustomed clutter as our four guests crowded in with their baggage, quart jars of pickled watermelon rind and Mother's favorite pepper sauce. By nightfall quilt pallets were arranged in every bare space.

At first I was content to sit on the floor and listen while Aunt Maime and the cousins told us about their adventure thus far. They stopped in Savannah to look at mansions and the Suwannee River. They ate at some fancy tearoom in the downtown hotel.

"Why they've got more Spanish moss on their trees than they do in Mobile," exclaimed Aunt Maime. "It's just a hangin' ever'where. Makes it kinda musty-like though."

Aunt Maime's accent was somewhere between downright-country and sticky bun southern. She and Mother didn't favor each other in looks. When she was all dolled up, Mother came close to being beautiful with her auburn hair, green eyes and pale white skin. Her sister was a weatherworn, brown-haired plain Maime. They didn't favor each other in accents either. In fact, Mother never had a southern accent. She spoke plain English splattered with lots of big words. Come to think of it, I didn't speak southern either, even though I spent a good deal of my life "deep into Alabama's innards," as my father would say. Mother told me once that she was born into the wrong family. "It was not the family I chose." I never figured out how you could pick the family you wanted to be born into. She never explained. If she was right, then she must have been born with the accent of some other family.

Aunt Maime continued. "Along about church time, down Virginia way, we came on the purtiest white clapboard church you'd ever want to see. We went right in and ever'one made us as welcome as a coconut creme pie at a revival meetin'."

She didn't come right out and ask Mother if we had been to church that morning. She looked sideways down her straight nose and rolled her eyes. The unasked question kind of hung up in the air near the ceiling ready to pounce.

Larry changed the subject. He was catching on about how to live with Mother.

I was at my obnoxious best when the talk turned to the World's Fair.

"Well, I don't really think it will be as great as the King and Queen of England. They are coming here early in June, you know." I announced this bit of news when I couldn't stand the fair talk another minute.

Aunt Maime and the cousins all smiled and went right on telling about what they were going to see in New York.

"Mercy sakes, I read as how we are going to see pictures of Jack Benny right in a box—same as the radio program only we can look right at him. Do tell!" Aunt Maime exclaimed.

I interrupted again. "I wouldn't want to miss royalty for the World's Fair. The whole town of Washington will be there to see them come down Pennsylvania and Constitution Avenues from Union Station all the way to the White House. It's a big holiday." Nobody even turned their head my way. Everybody kept right on talking about the wonders coming up in the future.

The next time I started to open my mouth, Mother gave me one of her redheaded, storm brewing looks that said a very solid but silent, "That's enough." I thought daggers and slunk off to the pallet that lay between the twin beds, grabbed Raggedy Ann and sulked.

By eight in the evening, Edgar Bergen time, I had recuperated some and the rest of the evening went smoothly as the subject changed to home folks gossip. It was good to catch up because soon I would be back among them for my summer stay. God and the Bible didn't come up again. Aunt Maime did say she would pray for Mother as they went out the door early the next morning to journey on to New York. Mother clinched her teeth. She refrained from her usual retort that would have been, "Save it for yourself Maime."

## Their Majesties

The news in *The Washington Post* was so exciting I could hardly stand it. Their British Majesties were in Canada and soon would be in Washington.

June 8th finally came. It was royalty day. Pomp and circumstance were words that came to my mind. King Arthur and the Knights of the Roundtable popped in too, but I didn't think they fit somehow. Palaces and crowns; Princesses and Princes; Kings and Queens; royal guards and royal horses strolled through my mind. It was a vision oh so much more romantic than our country's pompous politicians shaking their fists from the back of cross-country trains. Larry called them, "Snake oil peddlers."

I loved Washington in spring. The city gussied up like the finest lady wearing an Easter bonnet brimming with flowers. As fine a place as it was in spring, Washington was no place to be in the summertime. In summer, the heat wraps itself around the city and squeezes. Even though we were only into the fading days of spring, the royalty morning arrived steeped in summer's hot sultry haze.

Mother and Buddy got up really early like everybody else in Washington. Every city streetcar was on the tracks, clanging downtown full and returning uptown empty. Already overflowing with passengers, three streetcars went right past our stop as we waited. The fourth stopped. It was a good thing we were at the head of the line. Only our family and the couple behind us got on. We were squashed. We decided to get off at Garfinkel's and walk over to 15th Street to get a place near the end of the procession. President and Mrs. Roosevelt were scheduled to escort King George VI and Queen Elizabeth from Union Station down Pennsylvania and Constitution Avenues, then up to the southeast gate of the White House. If on time, the blue and silver train would pull into Union Station at eleven in the morning. We had a long wait ahead of us on a downtown curb.

I'd never seen so many people. The sun bombarded us. Buddy managed to squiggle up front to the curb leading me with him. Mother and Larry stayed two rows behind. The snowball man ran out of ice before he'd hardly started selling his delicious flavors. Buddy and I were really put out about that. I'd had my heart set on grape. I felt almost melted when we finally saw the cars coming. The crowd roared. I spotted Mr. Roosevelt in his top hat. His smile spread all over his rugged face. Beside him sat King George. The King seemed much smaller than I thought he would be. Instead of a crown and robe, he wore a splendid uniform. Occasionally he bowed his head down and then up to the crowd and now and then he gave the crowd a regal gesture that was less than a wave.

Then came the queen. The crowd's roar seemed louder.

"She's so dainty," I said over my shoulder to Mother.

Her white satin gown had long sleeves trimmed in white fur. She wore a white hat that fanned up off her face. It was trimmed with wispy feathery stuff. Her smile made her seem like the kindest person you'd ever want to meet. Her right hand lifted and dipped as though she was offering the crowd an invisible bouquet. In her left hand she carried a beautiful frothy white parasol. She held it high, valiantly trying to share a fragment of shade with Mrs. Roosevelt who sat wilted in the ninety-degree heat.

I just plain loved Franklin Delano Roosevelt. I liked Eleanor Roosevelt, a great first lady. She impressed me as being spunky. I got that impression from reading about her in *The Post*. But, that minute I was a little ashamed of her too. She looked especially dowdy sitting there next to the queen. Her clothes were drab; her hat drooped. She did have a nice smile even if her mouth was too big and toothy. Seeing the two together was like comparing a plain gold locket with a rare jeweled necklace. For the moment I envied the British their royalty. Such pomp! Such circumstance!

By the time we saw the procession, the people further down Pennsylvania and Constitution Avenues had already peeled away from the curbs. Some were picnicking on the mall. Others were jamming streetcars.

Mother thought about the situation and then announced. "As long as we are downtown, let's walk over to the Neptune Room to eat and then take in a movie at the Earle or Capitol."

Immediately, I pushed aside thoughts of the morning events and concentrated on a Napoleon pastry at the Neptune Room.

## Spring Wanes—Summer Approaches

A few days later a letter arrived addressed to Mother. It was from my Aunt Pauley in Birmingham. I knew what was inside. She confirmed the date and time that she or Uncle Rob would meet Buddy and me at the train station. My summer fate was sealed again.

It wasn't that I didn't like the folks in Alabama. I loved most of them a whole lot. It was just that every summer I had to try to fit in where I didn't quite fit. It was like when you are the last one to be squeezed into a double bed that's already full. The quilt never quite covers your backside. Part of you always sticks out in the cold.

Anyway, for now I had to think about the graduation play, 'Trails West'.

When Mrs. Stubel started us studying about going west, she told us all about Route 66, the new way to travel west. She said it followed some of the same trails that the pioneers used.

"The whole way to California is now paved for automobile travel," she said. "Route 66 was completed just two years ago in 1937. The road was the dream of a Mr. Cyrus Avery. I expect that almost every one of you will travel it someday. In a way, it's a modern trail."

It didn't seem likely to me that I would ever travel on Route 66. We didn't own a car. I feared I was doomed to travel up and down the Southern Railroad route for the rest of my life.

All of us kids felt sure that we knew all about the old West. The Tivoli regularly scheduled cowboy movies. Our history books told the stories differently. There didn't seem to be any Lone Ranger types in our books. But, by patching the movies and the books together, we got a pretty good idea of what moving west in the old days was all about.

For the play our Conestoga wagon was made of cardboard. All our audience could see of it was the front end because that's all there was. Two girls in our class stood on milk boxes and poked their heads through the hole in the covered part pretending to be in the wagon. The painted cardboard cottonwood trees wobbled in the breeze. The rest of us sat around a make-believe fire made of red cellophane. The girls wore long skirts, long aprons, and sunbonnets. The boys got off easy. Most of them already owned flannel shirts, cowboy hats, and BB guns. Tim Flanagan was our fiddler. We held the play in a back corner of the playground. When the play started, some housewives were busy hanging out wash on their upstairs porches above our heads. When they finished their wash, they hung over the banisters and watched the play.

We told stories and sang songs. Our favorites were *Git Along Little Dogies, Home on the Range,* and *Old Chisholm Trail.* "Come a ti yi yippi yappi yay, yappi yay." We really got into that one.

The ending was sad. The story wasn't sad, I was sad. It meant that in just a few days I would leave my home, my friends, and once again be parceled out to relatives. Insecurity ruled my life. Why didn't Mother see that? I knew in my heart it wasn't something she worried about. Like a loaf of bread, for her life sometimes got stale. She looked for a chance to move on—get a new loaf of bread somewhere else. Until I grew up, I was stuck with Mother's whims.

## All Aboard

We were up early that Thursday morning—bags packed and waiting. Buddy and I had a few new summer outfits. Mother said that we would get a breakfast treat at the station. She took a few hours off from work to take us to the train station.

For all the sadness, there was a part of leaving that I liked—Union Station. The huge hollow sounding main room was filled with polished benches. Voices and clattering noises bounced off the walls and mingled about in a jumble. I especially liked going to the bathroom. Two wide archways opened wide for the men and ladies' rooms on either side of the main room doorway. Inside, the ladies' high heels made a static sound against the tile floors. There was a long row of sinks where the arrivals spent a good deal of time washing up and repairing their powder and rouge. Rocking chairs seemed to beckon to the weary traveler. When I stepped up to the sink, I wondered if maybe Queen Elizabeth had used the very same sink when she arrived.

By 1939, Buddy and I thought we were expert train travelers. We learned to get on early so that we could turn one of the green velour seats back. That way we had seats facing each other and both of us had a window. If we were lucky, the train would not be crowded and we would have the double space to ourselves. It was a great arrangement for naps and sleeping overnight.

Nonetheless, when we heard the final "All aboard," we felt a little shaky. No matter how many times Mother told the conductor that we were traveling alone; no matter how many times I touched the note in my pocket that explained where we were going and who was meeting us, we were frightened but determined not to show it.

The train took us through a ramshackle section of Washington, then across the Potomac River through Alexandria, Virginia and on into the country. I liked the small towns with stations right next to the tracks. I liked watching people welcoming or saying good-byes. Most of all, I liked it when the porter stopped by to tell Buddy and me that we could go to the dining car. I felt very elegant in the dining car. The tablecloths were starched white linen. Each place had a huge linen napkin. It covered my whole lap and hung over. The silverware was heavy and ornate like my Aunt Helen's in Alabama. A small vase of flowers decorated every table.

The dining car stewards were grand. They were colored men who dressed in black pants and spotless white jackets with a black bow tie. They served with a white towel over one arm and with a special kind of flair. One had saved my pride two years before when I was ten and making my first trip with Buddy.

After dinner, the steward brought two little bowls with a piece of lemon floating in each.

"What's that for?" Buddy asked me after the steward turned to the next table.

"I'm not sure. Don't touch it," I replied. That was my standard solution. If I didn't know about something, I ignored it.

When the steward turned around, Buddy pointed to his bowl and said loudly, "Hey, what's this for?"

I nearly died. Buddy was showing off our ignorance to all the fancy people in the dining car. I could feel my blood rising to a full-blown blush.

The steward didn't laugh at us. He was most dignified.

He leaned over the table and quietly explained, "Little master, missy, that's a finger bowl. Just touch your fingers ever so lightly in the water to clean them and wipe them on your napkin."

I looked around. He had been so quiet about his explanation that nobody had noticed. Even though my fingers weren't sticky, I did as he said. Buddy held up his fingers and examined them. He had already licked off all the chocolate pie but he dutifully plunged as much of his hands in the bowl as he could manage then wiped them on his napkin.

This trip we were at ease with the fanciness.

Down North Carolina way I stayed alert. I didn't want to miss the sign. Near the tracks, outside a small town, there was a lumberyard. On top of its largest building there was a sign that told who owned the company. The owner's last name was the same as mine. It was not too common a last name and I really wanted to get off the train long enough to see if he was a relative. Since I couldn't, I daydreamed about my rich relations in North Carolina as I stared out the window.

The train then followed the tracks through swamps in South Carolina, through the red clay banks of Georgia and rolled into the station.

"Atlanta. All out for Atlanta."

Atlanta? I became alarmed. I beckoned to the conductor.

"This is where you change miss," he said.

"Change what?" I asked, trying not to sound petrified with fear.

"Trains," he replied. "I'll show you." He pointed out the window. "You just walk along the concourse over to gate Number 5 and get on the train to Birmingham. We're a mite late so she's about ready to leave."

Never before in my whole life had I needed to change trains. No one told me anything about this. I felt sure nobody told Mother either. I immediately became certain that we were lost forever. The conductor pulled our suitcases off the overhead rack. We thanked him and each of us took a suitcase. Buddy didn't seem disturbed, but he did slip his hand into mine as we reluctantly stepped onto the wooden stool at the bottom of the train steps. We trudged along the strange and unknown station platform toward where the conductor had pointed. My heart pounded louder than the puffing steam engines and the clanging iron gates. We reached gate Number 5 safely.

Close to tears, I asked the uniformed gatekeeper, "Is this the train to Birmingham?"

"It certainly is," he jovially replied as he checked our tickets.

Buddy cocked his head and furrowed his brow. "Are you sure?" he queried.

"Positive." He pulled out his pocket watch. "Now get aboard you two, we've got just fifteen minutes before we pull out."

We boarded. The train pulled out right on time. I was sure we were on the tracks to nowhere…lost forever. I began to twist the hem of my dress. I had a habit of doing this when I became really nervous.

I did less daydreaming and paid more attention to the towns we passed. Their names became more familiar as we got closer to Birmingham. I straightened my twisted skirt as best I could.

Both Buddy and I breathed a sigh of relief when the conductor opened the door between the train cars and yelled out, "We're coming into Birmingham. All out for Birmingham."

Summer began.

Folks in My Life

Summer of 1939, Alexander City, Alabama


Family
>Dad
>Ilene, Stepmother
>Buddy
>Grandmother

Aunts and Uncles
>Uncle Rob (Dad's brother) and Aunt Pauley
>Aunt Maggie (Dad's sister) and Uncle Brady
>Aunt Nan (Dad's sister) and Uncle Lawrence
>Aunt Allison (Dad's sister) and Uncle Tom
>Uncle John (Dad's brother) and Aunt Beth
>Uncle Ed (Dad's brother) courting Laney
>Aunt Lillian (Dad's sister) and Uncle Peter

Cousins
>Melvin and Jamey
>Danny and Joanie, the young towheads
>Tommy

Friends
>Raggedy Ann and Andy

Others
>Tommy Lee Jones, a neighbor's son
>Mr. Juleson Morley (Mr. Jule), a so-called friend of my Dad
>Bailey, Mr. Jule's meaner than a rattlesnake son

# Summer

◆

## In the Country

For the first six of my twelve years, Birmingham had been home as well as my birthplace. While the train slowly approached the station through the train yards, my mind conjured up scraps of my past life there. Thoughts came in bits and pieces. I remembered our brick house in East Lake. It was a busy home with relatives and friends coming and going. It sat on the slope of a hill with many steps leading up to the front porch.

There were rabbits and chickens in the backyard. An elderly neighbor down the street taught me how to appliqué butterflies onto squares of soft white cotton. I remembered a place that we used to visit on Sunday drives. Except for a roof, it was an open building that covered a huge pond of gold fish. I thought about the time I swallowed a pin and had to eat mashed potatoes for three days.

Even though she didn't work in it, Mother owned part interest in a beauty parlor. There I got my first permanent when I was five. The hair-dresser hooked me up to a machine with long wires that pulled at my hair and singed my scalp. After that I decided I definitely did not want any more curls. And, I remembered my colored nursemaid, the gentle Pearl.

About the time my eyes became misty and my throat lumpy, the engineer blew his whistle to signal that we were pulling into the station.

Presently, Birmingham was just a city to hurry through on the way south or north depending on the summer schedule. This year I would be traveling south to my dad's home for the first part of summer. In August, I would go north to Mother's folks. Buddy asked to spend the entire summer with Dad in Alexander City.

Aunt Pauley and Uncle Rob acted as go-betweens for the north and south folks. Uncle Rob was my father's brother. I loved Uncle Rob. Somehow he seemed to sense the turmoil that all this shifting about caused Buddy and me. Because he could rearrange his schedule easier than Aunt Pauley it was Uncle Rob who usually met us. Then whoever picked us up for our summer stay stopped by their house later in the day or the next day and loaded Buddy and me along with our two suit-cases into their car.

Uncle Rob waved from down the tracks as we stepped off the train. I knew what his first words would be. I could count on them like a needle stuck in the same spot on a cracked record.

"Well, there you are," he said as he stooped to hug. "My, how you two have grown."

He put one suitcase under his arm and grabbed up the other using the same arm. With his free hand, he took hold of Buddy while I scur-ried along to keep up with his long stride.

I didn't mind that we hurried through the station. It was smaller and dirtier than Union Station. I couldn't imagine that a queen would stop there.

Uncle Rob's house was on the side of a hill just like our old home. Lots of houses in Birmingham clung to hills. We were soon sitting at his kitchen table eating sandwiches.

"Your dad will be along pretty quick. He had to get the milking done and feed the chickens before starting out. He took the day off from the mill."

I wondered if my stepmother, Ilene, would be with him. Uncle Rob didn't say. I didn't ask. I hoped not. If Ilene came along, we would not stop off at my grandmother's on the way home. It might be several days before I saw Grandmother. Ilene didn't understand that she belonged in the new part of my life and that Grandmother belonged to the old, the more secure part of my life—the part that I clung to.

Dad arrived a couple of hours later. Luck was with me. Ilene was not with him.

"Well now, look who's here," he said as he came through the back door. Dad was a big man, both tall and broad. He rubbed his hand through Buddy's sandy-red hair, a gesture that silently relayed his fondness.

I rose to greet him. Then he said, "Sis, you sure did go and get tall on me."

Dad always called me 'Sis'. There were times when I didn't think he even knew my name. One summer I paid close attention to what other girls were called. I decided that their fathers called at least half the girls in Alabama 'Sis'. When there were several girls in the family it saved a lot of time trying to remember who was who.

Dad lost no time packing us into his brand new Chevrolet. Buddy took the front seat beside Dad which really puffed him up. No matter how young, being a male put you in the front seat.

"When did you get the new car Dad?" Buddy asked.

"No more'n a week ago. She's a beaut'. Runs like a dream. We'll open her up when we get away from the traffic some."

"I guess things are going good at the mill."

I groaned to myself. I knew what Buddy was thinking. Dad had been promising him a pony for years. "When I get a little ahead," he would say each summer. Even though ponies only cost about ten dollars, I knew Dad would never get ahead enough. Never in our whole lives had Dad bought us a present.

"The mill's coming along. Growing all the time," he answered Buddy.

Because of traffic and people stopping and starting for mail and turns along the narrow two lane road, we were more than an hour getting as far as Sylacauga. There wasn't much of anything between

Sylacauga and Alexander City. The next 25 miles whizzed by as Dad opened up.

We didn't ever stop in Alexander City on our way to the farm. I never really got familiar with the town. When anyone asked where my father lived, I always answered Alexander City. I couldn't say down in the country in Alabama because that would sound ignorant. But the truth was that I rarely saw anything but the farm; or someone else's farm where we visited; or the family church; or somebody else's family church when we went to revivals. I had never been to Froshins' Department Store, Meig's Cafe, or the Strand Theater. For me, Alexander City was a place to pass through on the way to my dad's farm.

The road curved into Alexander City. The first thing I saw was the water tower at Russell Manufacturing Company. Everybody around called it 'Russell Mills'. Dad often referred to it as the "lifesaver" plant. He meant that it had saved the life of 'Ellick City' as most folks called the town. Until the mill came, most everyone had been struggling on small farms. Old man Benjamin Russell started the plant in 1902 with eight knitting machines and twelve sewing machines. There were six mills now. Dad worked in mill number two.

Dad gestured toward the mill. "Orders are coming in right and left since we went vertical. Got to hand it to Ben, he sure knows his business."

Buddy perked up. "I'm sure glad to hear business is so good."

I made a mental note to talk to my Cooker friends about my dad working at Russell Manufacturing where they were so modern they went vertical. I knew that I would have to explain that going vertical meant the mill went from raw off the vine stuff to finished stuff like underwear and long johns. I liked to have something to talk about that the other kids were ignorant about. It made me feel important.

"Yes sir, he sure saved our hides. Keeps right on doing all kinds of nice things for the town. We'll let Ben know we're grateful too. Ain't none of them union bosses ever going to get their hooks into Russell Mills."

I'd heard all this before. Buddy and I had been on a tour with Dad where he explained every detail.

We crossed the railroad tracks. One spur went into the mill, the main track went straight through town and the road went into town right beside it. The trains stopped in Alexander City right smack in front of Carlisle's drug store. I suddenly thought, now that I knew how to change trains maybe Buddy and I could come all the way by train. Maybe we could even wait at Carlisle's and have a soda if Dad arrived late to meet the train. I'd never been in the drugstore, but I had heard it was a nice place.

I looked to the left over toward the hardware as we passed through town. My Uncle Brady worked there. If there were no customers inside, sometimes he sat out front in one of the cane chairs that lined the side-walk. I didn't see him.

"What's all the flags for?" Buddy asked as we got into the heart of town.

"Big celebration. Not only for the 4th of July but we got us a new courthouse to dedicate too. Big doings." Dad drove on past the bank with the big clock. We hadn't gone far when the pavement dropped off to a bumpy dirt road that led into the countryside.

"One of these days we'll get the politicians to pave this here road. It'll wait a mite though on account of this year we've got electricity coming. The wires are already down some roads. I thought I'd never live to see the day," Dad said as he stepped on the gas leaving a thick trail of dust behind us.

We'd heard it before, but he told us again. "The second thing I'm going to get when I get electricity is a washing machine. The first thing being light bulbs of course."

Growing up, all the children in my grandmother's family had to help wash clothes on washday. His chore had been to stir the big iron pot that boiled the clothes clean. Then he had to lift them out into a rinse tub and wring them as dry as he could under grandmother's eagle eye.

The girls were assigned the task of filling up the clotheslines. When the lines were full, the girls spread overalls, shirts, and aprons on every available bush. Dad always hated washday.

We drove right past Aunt Maggie's house. Besides being my dad's sister, she was Uncle Brady's wife. Everybody around called her an angel because she did so much for folks. I considered all four of my father's sisters angels because of the way they tried to help Buddy and me fit in every summer. I nominated Aunt Maggie as the head angel. The next landmark was the white church that was less than a mile from Grandmother's house. I knew I would be spending a goodly amount of time there.

I asked the question that I would not have dared if Ilene had been along.

"Well, we don't have much time before supper, but I reckon it won't hurt to stop in at your grandmother's for a few minutes," Dad replied to my question as he turned into her horseshoe shaped driveway.

The white clapboard house, adorned by a flowerpot-laden porch, sat at the wide bend in the driveway. Each year it saddened me to see the family homestead slowly eroding away like all the other memorized fragments that I cherished. The house no longer teemed with young people scattering about the farm to complete the daily assigned chores. The ring of metal-to-metal no longer called me to the blacksmith shop. There were no hams or bacon slabs hanging in the smokehouse. The barn stood empty. There was no Collie dog to bound out and greet me. Here and there, white paint peeled back to reveal the gray of aged boards.

All this change had slowly come about after my grandfather died. Could it have been eight years ago I thought to myself in half denial. That scorched, sun bleached day in July was one of the blackest days of my life. I think it was then that I began to associate summer with trouble. This old house mourned on, as did I.

Dad stopped the car beside the well that stood just left of the house. He rarely went into the home place without first drawing a bucket of water and then dipping himself a cool drink. As it always had, the dipper hung ready on the well roof post.

"Best water in Tallapoosa County," he reminded Buddy and me as he drew a bucket.

While he went through his ritual, I went through mine. I stopped under the giant oak that stood close to the well and checked the century plant growing in a big washtub. There was no bloom. There never was. I figured I'd have to live the whole hundred years it took to bloom if I was ever going to see its elusive flower. Then I looked over at the oak on the other side of the house. They were still there, the giant oak and its partner, the swing. The rope swing that hung some forty feet high from a muscular limb had always been a source of wonderment and pleasure for us grandchildren. We could never figure out how the swing ropes got that far up in the tree. Uncle Ed told us the swing started off low to the ground and just grew up with the tree. We all knew we couldn't believe a cottonpickin' thing that he told us, but he never told us different—no one else did either. When we persuaded someone to swing us, we went almost to the sky.

I inspected what was left of my grandfather's prize flower garden. Roses still struggled up through the weeds. Purple hydrangeas persisted. The blacksmith shop in back of the garden leaned. I hope it would last a little while longer.

Buddy had already lapsed into his summer melding. He became glued to Dad's leg from the moment of contact. He waited patiently for his turn with the dipper before we went in the house to find my grandmother.

"Yep, best water in Tallapoosa County," he mimicked Dad.

We found Grandmother on the back porch. She was rocking and stringing beans. The half dozen hens that had been keeping her company on the porch scattered, cackling in protest.

"Well now, how you two have grown."

As much as we had grown, Grandmother had shriveled. I knew she was only sixty because I had asked about her age the summer before.

This year she seemed even more worn down with time. Her soft gray hair was pulled straight back in a bun accentuating every line in her pale powdered face. Even her blue eyes seemed to have faded to gray. I supposed that raising eight children out here in the country with no electricity and no plumbing probably made her grow old so fast. The way I figured, she wasn't much more than one step away from being a pioneer woman. She had moved from Virginia with her mother and father when she was a youngster.

Grandmother set her stringing pan down and got up to hug us. "Well now, aren't we going to be good company for each other this summer."

"Now Mama, don't start." Dad spoke loudly even though Grandmother denied being hard of hearing. She hadn't heard us arrive.

"Well son, it doesn't make any sense. I'm rambling around all day in this old house by myself and these young'uns don't need to be staying up the road all by themselves. It just isn't right."

My grandmother, Buddy and I were in perfect agreement about that. I could have told her there wasn't any use standing her ground. My dad and the rest of the family were good at spouting quotations from the Bible to suit most any occasion. I fully expected Dad to come out with the "cleaving to your wife" part. For some reason known only to her, my stepmother had decided we were old enough to stay by ourselves all day that summer. Dad informed us of this fact just outside Birmingham as if he wanted to get it off his chest right away. And that was that.

In reply to Grandmother, all Dad said was, "Come on young'uns, time to go. See you Sunday Mama."

"Well, I should hope so. I surely am not stringing all these beans purely for my health," she said as she gave Buddy and me her squeeze on the arm sign of affection.

"I forgot to tell you young'uns that Sunday is reunion day," Dad said as he settled into his seat behind the wheel.

There was no need to explain further. When Buddy and I were at Dad's, the entire family gathered at least once. This was because we were the only ones that lived outside Alabama, too far away to come just any old time. Two families would come from Montgomery, Uncle Rob and Aunt Pauley from Birmingham and the rest would amble in from other dusty roads surrounding Alexander City. All the cars would be laden with food. Dad would pluck a few watermelons and go to town for blocks of ice and soda pop.

As we approached my dad's house, I wished that I had gotten Raggedy Ann or Andy out of my suitcase. I would feel better with one of them at my side. Instead, my hand reached for the hem of my skirt. I wadded it into a ball. I was overcome by dread.

Dad's house stood on a rise of land in plain view from the road. Its unpainted, weathered siding supported a rusting tin roof. I truly believed that my dad loved this old house and the 200 acres that surrounded it more than anything or anyone else in his life. This section of land had once been part of my grandfather's farm and his father's before him. I had long ago reckoned that his love of this land had a lot to do with why Mother left him. The country bored her, as did small towns.

At least once each summer, Dad reminded Buddy and me that he was born "right over there in the northwest corner." He was referring to one corner of the big room that served as the sitting room and bedroom. A huge stone-faced, walk-in fireplace dominated the north wall. Several wooden rocking chairs faced the fireplace all winter. All but two were dragged to the front porch in summer. Quilt covered double beds flanked the front door. An assortment of tables holding kerosene lamps and two clothes chests completed the furnishings. On the west and east walls there were doorways. One led to the narrow kitchen that hugged the depth of the house. The other led to an enclosed side porch where Buddy and I slept on day beds. I knew nothing would be changed.

Dad drove the Chevrolet up the inclined dirt driveway and parked at the back door.

Out from under the house came a brawny-chested, stomach-hanging, mean-mugged bull dog named Pug. He swaggered his whole rear end in greeting and bared his teeth slightly as if mustering an unaccustomed smile. The only person who got this greeting was my dad and whoever was with Dad. Pug growled furiously and bared his teeth into kill position when any other car came up the drive. Those who knew him would slowly talk their way out of the car. Those who didn't sat there until someone rescued them.

"Nobody is gonna' get by Pug, are they boy? Pug will keep you young'uns safe this summer," Dad said as he stooped to pat the broad brown head.

I was never sure which scared me more, strangers or Pug.

Buddy dashed toward the barn right away. I knew what he hoped to see but I also knew there would be no pony. Dad was unconcerned by his sudden dash. "I reckon he misses Matilda. He'll get a surprise. There's a calf along side her."

Ilene did not come outside. When we went inside, she wasn't in the big room so we went to the kitchen. Her floured hands were deep inside a wooden biscuit bowl.

"Supper will be ready 'terectly. I just got home from the mill. Lem dropped me off. There won't be much. Too tired to fix much. There's plenty of tomatoes. I've got some taters frying."

She went right on rolling the ball of biscuit dough around in the flour. That was about as good a greeting as I could expect. Ilene made it plain that she would just as soon Buddy and I disappeared off the face of the earth. I was sure when we weren't around she pretended to herself that Dad had never had another wife.

Dad married Ilene about the same time that Mother married Larry. Buddy and I didn't know anything about either one of them until letters arrived in Florence where we were staying with Aunt Bea. The letters weren't even written to Buddy and me. I figured a person should tell a person in person when a person had important news like that to tell. I figured wrong a lot of the time.

Buddy came in from the barn and stayed quiet for a long time. By evening, we were as settled in as we'd get. Our suitcases were under our beds. We used them as drawers. I reckoned dresser drawer space would make us look too permanent. I settled Raggedy Ann and Andy up against my pillow. They looked as out of place as I felt.

There would be some good times ahead. I knew that. Most things weren't all bad. I dwelled on and grasped at that thought as I drifted off to sleep that night.

The next day was Saturday. Dad shook us awake at dawn.

My dad's life habits were formed way back when he was a boy. In my grandfather's house nobody was allowed to sleep past the first gray light of dawn. Until his dying day, my grandfather believed that the workday was from dawn to dark. If he could think of something to stretch it out a little further by lantern light, he'd see it was done. This applied to six days of the week. On the seventh, the rest part of the Lord's Day began only after the cows were milked, chickens fed, and eggs gathered. Also after the womenfolk had prepared breakfast and the big Sunday dinner to be eaten following church.

To get all this done, he roused everyone at dawn on the seventh day of the week. My grandfather applied these rules to every person under his roof. My dad did too. Being a person who slept late at every opportunity, my mother surely hated this routine. I knew it must be one more reason that my mother left my dad.

Getting up at dawn didn't bother me much but Buddy took after Mother and liked his morning sleep. It was a struggle for him, but on the second shake he rolled out of bed and pulled on a pair of his overalls that had hung on the hook on the wall since last summer. They were too long the year before and had to be rolled up. This year they fit him just fine.

Buddy made his way to the barn with Dad while I crossed the big room and went into the kitchen. Ilene had just pulled a pan of biscuits from the oven and was busy frying the morning sausage.

"You can set the table then run on down to the barn with your daddy 'til he's finished milking," she said without looking away from the wood stove. Her tousled auburn hair framed a face I saw as set in a permanent frown.

A red clay path, packed stone hard from use, led to the barn. When wet the path became as slippery as ice. Along the path I passed by the chicken pen. I did not pass by the outhouse since I was beginning to hurt from holding it so long. I hated to use the slop jar. I opened the creaky door and peered in. Inspecting for rats and snakes was a must before I dared step inside. While I positively hated this necessary building, Dad seemed very proud of his 'two-holer'. I guess he liked company but I couldn't imagine anybody wanting company for the necessaries. When I was much younger I felt certain that one day I would fall in one of the holes and die a ghastly death. I still wasn't sure it wouldn't happen. I thumbed through the Sears catalog as I sat.

As I came out, I heard peels of laughter. I hurried on down the path.

Just as I entered the barn, Buddy said, "Do it again."

A gray striped mama cat and three half-grown kittens sat beside Dad's milking stool. Their eyes were glued to the cow's udder and their tails flicked back and forth in anticipation. Dad obligingly angled the cow's tit and squirted milk down the line into each open mouth.

As I reached to pick up one of the kittens the whole group quickly vanished. I had forgotten how wild the farm cats were. The daily milking was a weak point in their skittish nature.

Dad's buckets were almost full.

"You chill'un run on up to the chicken house and get the eggs. I'm almost done here. Don't forget, don't be making a lot of noise and upsetting the hens."

I reached for the egg basket hanging on the chicken coop wall. Buddy found a box to stand on so that he could reach the nests. I had permanently assigned Buddy the egg hunting part of our chores since the time I felt around in a nest for eggs and grabbed hold of a black snake eating his breakfast.

Buddy began peeking in boxes checking for eggs while hens began their chorus of clucking protests.

"Someone ought to tell the hens to be quiet so as not to disturb me," he said as one Rhode Island Red pecked in protest when he shooed her from the nest.

When the eggs and milk were stashed in the icebox, we washed up in the big bowl on the kitchen shelf and sat down to breakfast. Dad bowed his head for the blessing. I noticed that his light brown hair was getting scarce on top of his head.

Then came the problem. I didn't know about the problem until Miss Stubel taught us a health section. Ilene put a whole glass of milk by my plate of sausages and biscuits. I knew it was yesterday's milk cooled in the icebox. It didn't look any different from the milk that I had always had at the farm. I stared at the glass and studied the unpasteurized milk. I conjured up bugs and bacteria and stuff that caused all kinds of sickness and even death. Miss Stubel told us about it. They were in there. I just knew it. Besides, I thought, the milk would most likely taste like bitterweed. It usually did.

"I don't drink milk anymore," I said as I pushed the glass away.

"You do too," piped up Buddy. "You did just yesterday at Uncle Rob's."

I glared at Buddy, then looked straight into Dad's eyes. He looked straight back into mine and studied for a minute as if he was reading my mind.

"I reckon you've become a city girl straight through. I 'spect you mean you only drink milk that comes from a dairy bottle."

"I guess."

"Sis, your daddy and my daddy and his daddy before him drank this good old cow's milk that the Lord gave us. Didn't no harm come to any of us. I don't reckon none will come to you either."

I could either throw a tantrum, which I wasn't good at anyway, or drink the milk. My dad was known as a very even-tempered man except if you got him real riled up about something. I saw by the way he was looking at me that he could get real riled up about his milk. I drank it. And it did taste like bitterweed.

Right after breakfast, Dad said to Buddy, "Come on son, we got to get into 'Ellick City' and get some ice and sodas for the reunion tomorrow.

I felt a pang of jealousy toward Buddy. I was left with Ilene.

She dipped hot water from the wood stove reservoir into the dish-pan. "I reckon you can dry the dishes. The Sunday school lesson is out on the table by the fireplace. You best study it. Later on you can icing the cake and put on the coconut. I reckon you can peel the eggs too when I get them boiled. The front yard needs sweeping, the porch too. Water the flowers while you're out there. When we're finished with the dishes, throw these here leftover biscuits out to Pug." Her litany finally stopped. My day was set.

I threw the biscuits out the back door to Pug. He gulped them down quicker than I could shut the screen door. I knew he would plop down under the back steps to snooze off his breakfast and leave me alone. I made a beeline across the big room to the front porch and grabbed the willow branch broom. I actually liked sweeping the yard. While I was at it I rearranged some of the stones lining the front path. Then I shuffled some of the flowerpots around on the porch to show off the colors better. After awhile I stood back to survey my handiwork. I began to feel more at ease. The Sunday school lesson loomed as the hardest task. I decided to put that off as long as I could. It wasn't easy being plunked down in the middle of the Bible after a long dry spell. I figured I'd be on shaky ground come Sunday morning.

Luck was with me. I moved up to a new Sunday school class. Aunt Maggie sat in the teacher's chair. She knew Mother pretty well because she had lived with us in Birmingham for awhile. She knew that Buddy and I didn't go to church regularly. Aunt Maggie led a discussion of the lesson and asked a few questions, none of them directed at me. It was just as well because I was distracted.

Tommy Lee Jones stared at me. All the girls sat on one side of the room and the boys on the other. Aunt Maggie sat at one end of the small room in the middle of the rows of benches. From across the room, I first felt his gaze. Then our eyes met. We locked in for a few seconds. Slowly, his dark brown eyes wandered down my body and back up. He winked and his lips moved into a tight smile—or a smirk. I couldn't tell which. I tugged at my skirt to make sure my knees were covered. Tommy Lee was three years older than me, a neighbor's son.

It's that curse thing again. I just know it I thought to myself. I must have a different scent, maybe like the farm animals when at certain times they sniff at each other. I knew they made babies after all this sniffing.

"Oh Lord!" I heard a quiet voice say and then was startled to find it was my own.

As we filed out of the Sunday school room and into the sanctuary, Tommy Lee managed to brush up against me.

"Hey there. You growed up a heap," he whispered.

His family sat behind mine during the preaching. All during the service I felt his stare. It penetrated my back like a hot sunbeam streaming through a windowpane. I kept my Abram's Funeral Parlor fan going back and forth in an effort to cool my flushed face. I contemplated turning around and telling Tommy Lee that the Lord surely would not approve of what he was doing to me right here in church. Instead, I concentrated on listening to the preacher. That didn't work out so well because he was in a hell and damnation mood. I quickly tuned him out and let my eyes wander around the familiar room.

Wooden sconces holding oil lamps lined the walls ready for night meetings. There were seven down each side, two in the back and one on each side of the pulpit. The walls and ceiling were made of a narrow wood paneling painted a restful pale blue. To the right of the pulpit stood a wood stove that gave off enough heat to make the building tolerable in winter. Oil polished, the wide pine floors shone with care. My eyes came to rest on the empty space below the pulpit. It was here that

my grandfather's casket sat back in the summer of 1931. His funeral was
my first and only. I shuddered as I remembered leaving my seat and
stepping forward to ask my grandfather to please get up. "It's after dawn
Grandpa, it's after dawn."

Buddy brought me out of my reverie by shoving an open songbook
toward me to share.

I glanced down at the page where his finger pointed and joined in the
singing. "Jesus loves me this I know."

Ordinarily Dad and Ilene hung around after church to visit with
folks. Today was different.

"Go on young'uns. Get in the car. We got to get home; pack up and
go to your grandmama's."

I looked out the window as we waited for Dad to say a quick good-
bye to the preacher. As if willed, my glance went directly to the old oak
on the north side of the church. Tommy Lee leaned against it. His eyes
met mine. He pushed his cap back on his head releasing a shock of coal
black hair. He slowly raised his right knee and rested his foot against the
tree. A rakish half-smile crept to the corners of his mouth.

I quickly turned away. I did not like what I was feeling. I thought
about it all the way up the road. It must be what the actresses feel when
they melt into Clark Gable's arms I reasoned.

By the time we got to Grandmother's, some of the folks were already
gathering. Every chair Grandmother owned and a long table from the
kitchen sat in the front yard. They were placed to catch the shade from
the canopy of oak limbs. Dad, Uncle John and Uncle Ed brought extra
chairs the day before. Each of them had a beat up old truck for hauling.

Grandmother often said, "Turn a rock over anywhere between
Birmingham and Montgomery and you will find a relative under it."

We certainly had our share just like most farming families in Alabama. Every few years somebody arranged a big reunion—bigger than most revival meetings. Buddy and I never seemed to be around for those. The reunions at Grandmother's house were for gathering her own four daughters and four sons, their husbands and wives, and the seven grandchildren.

From slivers of conversation that I sometimes overheard at these reunions, I knew that my relatives were not surprised when Mother and Dad divorced.

"The two of them are like a pair of mules in a pullin' contest—both backin' up in the wrong direction. Never was a chance of them getting' to the finish line, none a'tall," I heard Uncle Rob say right after things went topsy-turvy.

I knew they did not take kindly to Ilene either.

"Seems like he goes pickin' for a wife in the briar-patch."

"She treats those children like flies on a blackberry puddin'. Always shooing them away."

Careful not to cross a line that would irritate my stepmother, my aunts and uncles managed ways to soften the smoldering hostility Ilene had for Buddy and me. The reunion was one way of making sure we felt a part of the family.

"Mama won't stand for having the reunion until they come," one of them explained to Ilene each year.

Aunt Nan and Uncle Lawrence came out of the house to greet us. They came all the way from Montgomery so they must have gotten up really early. Uncle Lawrence worked in a famous men's clothing store in Montgomery. He was very tall and dignified. His hair had been snow white ever since I could remember.

"Well now, you're just a sight for sore old eyes," Aunt Nan said as she reached the bottom porch step. "Come on over here and give me a hug."

I dutifully obeyed. Aunt Nan managed to refer to herself as old in almost every conversation. She was the spitting image of my grandmother and only a shade younger looking. It was impossible to think of her as ever having been young.

"Now let's have a big hug for your old aunt. I brought you a jar of your favorite scuppernong grape jelly. And Buddy," she said as she pulled him toward her, "I have a bag of my special tea cakes just for you."

Aunt Nan and Uncle Lawrence did not have any children. I heard her say one time, "Not everyone is meant to have children. The Lord has other assignments for some of us."

Every now and then I thought about that. I figured the Lord must mess up on his assignments sometimes. It seemed to me that there were some folks that had children that clearly never should. Sometimes I felt that way about my own mother and father. But then, I did realize that I wouldn't be born except for them. Maybe the Lord knows what he's doing I reasoned. It was just hard to figure sometimes.

By the time we had our greeting out of the way with Aunt Nan and Uncle Lawrence, more cars were swinging into the driveway.

From Aunt Allison and Uncle Tom's car poured the Stevens family. I was really glad to see my cousins Melvin and Jamey. They had been our cousins longer than the rest since they were older than Buddy and me by a couple of years. Melvin was the oldest and Jamey was one year older than me. They were children of Aunt Allison's first marriage. The four of us were the only cousins who had known my grandfather. We were pals. Toddling out of their car were two younger cousins that I hardly knew. Danny was four and Joanie was two. The towheads clung to Aunt Allison's skirt. It took them awhile to warm up to folks.

"Look at you chill'un. Buddy, you are going to catch up with Melvin and Jamey in no time. We've got a little surprise for you that we'll tell you about later," said Aunt Allison.

Aunt Maggie and Uncle Brady arrived empty handed. Their picnic fixings were put in Grandmother's kitchen not long after daybreak. When it came to early rising, Uncle Brady was champion of them all. He and Aunt Maggie didn't have children either. I figured God meant for

Aunt Maggie to spread herself around helping other folks with their children. That's why I considered her the 'head angel'. We knew that she would slip treats to us whenever she got a chance. I loved visiting her house too. I really loved her photograph album. I made sure I saw it each time we came south. The picture of Dad holding me in his right hand just after I was born was the one I loved most. I fit just fine since I weighed slightly less than four pounds.

Uncle John drove in, riding Uncle Ed's bumper in a cloud of dust as the two cars rolled past our gathering place and came to a stop down the far side of the driveway.

"I declare," I heard Grandmother say. "It just don't seem like those two ever plan to grow up."

Redheaded and freckled, Uncle Ed still lived at Grandmother's. He occupied the small room off the back porch where he came and went as he pleased. He worked at the mill and in his free time courted Laney. That didn't leave much time for chores around the home place. My dad and Uncle John took up his slack when Grandmother complained. On our reunion day Uncle Ed, spruced up in his Sunday best and polished up on his manners, stepped around the car to open the door for Laney.

Uncle John pulled his small son, Tommy, off Aunt Beth's lap and threw him up onto his shoulders. "Look out, here we come," he announced with a laugh.

He had a smile that hardly ever quit, making it impossible to know when he was serious and when he wasn't. He belonged to that part of the family who weren't redheads, inheriting instead the same light brown hair that topped my head. Since Uncle John had finished with his courting days, he left Aunt Beth, who was obviously expecting a baby any day, to struggle alone with the picnic hamper. Dad and Uncle Lawrence quickly went to the rescue.

Uncle John was the youngest of Grandmother's children. She could get aggravated with him but she couldn't stay mad more than five minutes. I'd seen her come close to staying mad two summers past. He bedeviled an old red rooster to the point that nobody could go out the back door without that rooster attacking. Grandmother declared she just knew he was training that rooster for cock fighting, but he just grinned and patted Grandmother on the head. That made her even madder. Uncle Ed finally threw an old quilt over the rooster and carried him to the chopping block. Grandmother baked him but declared later she busted her false teeth trying to eat the tough old bird.

I wouldn't see much of Uncle John and Uncle Ed. They would come around now and then to pick up Buddy and take him off on some adventure. Uncle John was a great one for rattlesnake hunting. Buddy really enjoyed that sport. They presented him with a BB gun the summer before.

Uncle Rob and Aunt Pauley drove in shadowed by Aunt Lillian and Uncle Peter's dust. The four of them greeted each other. Laden down with food baskets, they walked up the driveway to round out the family gathering.

Aunt Lillian and Uncle Peter were teachers. They too were childless. It was easy to see what plans the Lord had for them since between them they had more children to worry over than most folks ever thought about. They married "late in life," as my grandmother put it. Aunt Lillian fussed something awful over Uncle Peter as if he was somebody extra special. He never seemed to want all the attention. It seemed more like he just put up with it. Aunt Lillian was the only member of the family to go to teacher's normal and become educated beyond local schooling.

"I do declare, you have grown like a weed. I dropped off a bag of good reading books in your dad's new car. I know you'll enjoy them," Aunt Lillian said to me as she put her arm around my shoulders.

All during the arriving process, Grandmother sat on the porch fanning and observing. When all had arrived, she made her yearly pronouncement. She rose and stood on the top step of the porch where she could see everybody. "Well now, isn't this a fine group. And not an idiot in the whole bunch."

Uncles swung grandchildren skyward, except for Uncle Peter. He cranked the ice cream freezer. Everybody gorged on fried chicken, ham and all the fixings. Dad cut open several sweet and juicy watermelons. Flies swarmed over cheesecloth-covered pies. Uncle John teased, tickled, and tormented us cousins. All the family gossip was wrung out.

Eventually, the men wandered off to inspect the cars and talk men talk.

Dishes washed, the womenfolk sat on the porch and reminisced.

"Do you remember that last Collie of Papa's? Flapper he called her. She was the best we ever had at bringing in the cows from the back pasture. More than one cow came home without its tail." Aunt Lillian chuckled as she spoke.

"I remember the time when Rob and I were real late riding home from school during an icy winter rainstorm. We were on Buster and Maudlin, those two dumb mules we used to have. Papa came tearing down the road in the buggy looking for us. Tore into those mules as if the weather was entirely their fault. He acted as if those dumb mules had run away with us," said Aunt Allison.

At times the women sat quiet. The rocking chairs squeaked as they conjured up memories.

Aunt Maggie turned to me. "Do you remember the time your grandpa insisted that we make a small cotton picking bag for you. I don't think you could have been more than three or four. You fairly howled to go out in the field with the coloreds and the rest of us. As I recall, it was no more than 15 minutes before you were howling again about your fingers being worn out. You might have had 20 cotton balls in the bag. You sure could twist Papa around."

I smiled and nodded. I loved remembering Grandpa.

For a short while on a July Sunday afternoon, I belonged.

## Settling In

Dawn came draped in a shroud of clouds on Monday morning. After Ilene's first call I sat up in bed struggling to unglue my eyes. A bolt of lightning struck close by. The old house shook. I grabbed Raggedy Ann and Andy and ducked under the bedspread. The rain began with a rat-a-tat on the tin roof and rapidly settled down to a steady drumbeat. On Ilene's second call, I climbed out of bed and shook Buddy. I didn't have any luck rousing him so I went off to the kitchen alone.

When he came up from the barn, Dad pointed to Buddy's empty chair. "Just leave him be this morning. There's not much can be done in weather like this. Looks to me like this storm has set in for a spell."

His rain gear made a puddle on the floor beneath the kitchen coat rack.

"Even old Matilda didn't take much to her milking this morning. I just left her and the calf in the barnyard. You can let her out later if the storm lets up."

I ate my sausage biscuit in silence. I dreaded the long gloomy day ahead.

"There's two sausage biscuits on the sideboard and a couple of early peaches for dinner time," said Ilene as she finished packing two similar paper bags to take to work. "If the rain lets up, go down to the garden and get a few ears of corn and a cabbage for supper."

They were soon out the door. I felt utterly deserted and terribly alone. I began to imagine all the things that could happen, like rats coming up from the barn and invading. Or the bull might get out of the pasture and butt the door down. Pug might go on a rampage and froth at the mouth.

I looked out the back door. Muddy water ran in the gullies along each side of the barn path. I went back to bed nestled between Raggedy Ann and Andy.

After that first blue Monday the rest of the week proved tolerable. Ilene soon got the drift that I did more around the house if it was left up to me. Even though I made beds, dusted and swept each day, my time was not filled. Each morning I hurried through the chores I assigned myself so that I had guiltless afternoons.

Right after Buddy and I ate at mid-day, I headed for the porch swing with book in hand. Aunt Lillian's bag of 'good reading' kept me content. I wasn't as selective as Aunt Lillian. As long as I could understand most of the words, I read any book that I got my hands on.

Not a great deal of traffic came along our road, but each passing car worried me some. I felt uneasy. I actually quivered the afternoon the big black car came up the driveway. There were three men in the car. The man at the wheel didn't try to get past Pug. He just leaned out the window and shouted toward the porch where Buddy and I were sitting on the steps.

"Tell your pa when he gets home that he'd better take a look around the back pasture. He'll know what I mean. Tell him to make it pretty quick. We'll be looking it over ourselves in a day or two. Be sure you tell him now."

I relaxed. "We'll be sure," I answered.

Buddy and I realized they were revenuers when they started talking. Dad had a real problem with bootleggers setting up in the back pasture. The revenuers knew for sure it wasn't Dad's still. They always gave him a chance to take care of the problem himself. Everyone knew Dad hated spirits and what they did to folks. Most of the time Dad knew who set up the still. Whenever he found it, he broke it to pieces and high-tailed it down to Uncle John's house madder than a soaking wet barn cat.

Buddy was out of the house and about the farm much of the time. He discovered that a big black snake lived in a pile of rocks near the chicken pen. As part of his daily rounds, Buddy waited patiently for awhile each day with hoe in hand ready to pounce. Occasionally the snake did appear and slithered away quickly as Buddy dashed after it, chopping chunks out of the red clay soil. Buddy also liked to take Pug down to the barn to bang out the rats that lived in the log walls. He banged with a rusty iron frying pan and Pug snarled and growled. Now and then a rat scurried out and almost always met its fate between Pug's teeth. Target practicing with his BB on old tin cans lined up on the pasture fence kept him busy too.

Although I felt much braver, I was relieved to hear that we were going to spend a week with Aunt Allison and Uncle Tom. That was the surprise Aunt Allison mentioned at the reunion. I suspected our aunts had a conspiracy to see that Buddy and I didn't spend too much of the summer visit alone.

We went on Saturday afternoon. That meant I didn't have to see Tommy Lee at Sunday school and that suited me just fine. Dad took us through 'Ellick City' and then south down another country road ten miles or more to Uncle Tom's farm. Uncle Tom had many more acres than Dad. He also had lots more pigs and cows. He was a full-time dawn to dark farmer like my grandfather had been. Aunt Allison raised turkeys, chickens and peacocks. When she wasn't canning something, she was cooking something. Her kitchen smelled scrumptious all the time.

Uncle Tom didn't like laziness in anyone. He had several colored helpers and saw to it that he got every bit of time out of them that he paid for. Melvin and Jamey usually worked all day too. But as a special treat, because Buddy and I shared their chores, we got some time off in the afternoons.

Now and then the three boys sneaked off by themselves. I began to get suspicious they had decided to do away with me. When I went looking for them I usually fell into a trap. Sometimes their tricks backfired. One day as I was going to the smokehouse for a ham for Aunt Allison I heard the pop-pop-pop of BB guns from the bushes across from the smokehouse door. Then I heard a buzzing that got louder and louder. I looked up to see hornets swarming from a nest in the peak of the smokehouse roof. I froze. I didn't move a muscle. The hornets zoomed over my head and toward the bushes.

"Dang bust it. One got me," yelled Jamey.

"I'm out'a here. Run for your lives," yelled Melvin.

All three started slapping and running for the back door of the house.

I turned and walked slowly around to the front door and through the hall to the kitchen. Aunt Allison was making a soda paste for their bites.

"Don't you dare laugh. Ain't funny," said Buddy

"I suppose you wouldn't have laughed if I'd gotten bitten," I retorted.

"I reckon they would have," said Aunt Allison. "Serves them right. And I reckon that ham will just have to stay in the smokehouse until dark. Then they can go get it."

I snickered.

The next day the boys said I could go with them as they went exploring in the woods. Suspicious, I declined. I spread a quilt under a shade tree and divided my time between reading and watching the strutting peacocks. After their naps the towheads, Danny and Joanie, toddled out and crawled all over me.

Aunt Allison invited Dad and Ilene to come to the revival at their church on the following Sunday, the day Buddy and I would go back to Dad's. Folks had a regular revival circuit during the summer going from church to church spending all day. Aunt Maggie came over on Saturday to help with the cooking. Early Saturday morning, Melvin rounded up a big fat turkey and chopped its head off just above the neck. He tacked the head up on a wall inside the barn where he had collected rows of shriveled chicken and turkey heads—truly weird.

Aunt Allison filled a big tub with boiling hot water and dunked the turkey. We took turns pulling out the stinking wet feathers. We tried to hold our breath as we plucked. The smell gagged us. It was a chore nobody liked. Finally the turkey was carried to the kitchen table ready for Aunt Allison's final touches.

There was a loud whack when Aunt Allison chopped off the turkey neck in one blow with her butcher knife. She shoved it aside with the knife blade.

Looking at it, Aunt Allison said, "Kinda' reminds you of a man's privates don't it."

She spoke to Aunt Maggie whom she thought was the only one in the kitchen. I had just stepped in from the front room and decided it best if I slipped back out so as not to embarrass her. I slammed the screen door as I came in from the back porch. I sidled up to the kitchen table to take a look at the turkey neck. It was purplish-red and sort of rigid. Reminded me a little of the stuffed sausages that hung in the Arcade Market back home. It certainly didn't look anything like Buddy's private parts, not that I had seen much of them. I shrugged my shoulders in puzzlement and asked if I could be of any help.

Most of the family who lived around 'Ellick City' showed up on Sunday for the revival meeting. There was much more hell and damnation at a revival meeting Sunday than on an ordinary Sunday. The visiting preacher pointed out that the road to heaven was a rough one even for the righteous and we were mostly sinners, he said. Sinners had no chance to travel the golden road. We must repent, we were sinners, sinners, sinners. Over and over he repeated his theme. The regular preacher nodded his head in an Amen each time us sinners were mentioned. I felt bad. I sat twisting the hem of my dress. For some strange reason my mind kept repeating, "Step on a crack, break your mother's back."

After the first service, ladies spread the food out on tables under the shade trees surrounding the church. Folks ate and chatted and ate some more for over two hours before the next service began. It was pitch dark before Buddy and I said our farewells and piled into Dad's car.

## The Devil Came Visiting.

I missed the daily newspapers. I felt starved for newsprint. A weekly paper, the *Alexander City Outlook,* came in the mail on Thursdays. Dad made a habit of taking the paper out to the porch after supper on Thursdays where he read the interesting parts out loud. The parts that interested him did not interest me at all. There was little in the paper that interested me. It mostly told about town happenings and the ladies' socials.

"Says here there is going to be a Kudzu Jamboree over at Camp Hill."

Just as he started to read the article to us, his best friend Mr. Juleson Morely turned his truck into the driveway. Pug ambled out and did a half way growling performance then backed off and waddled under the porch. He was used to Mr. Jule, as Buddy and I called him.

"Evening there," he said as he strode up the rock-lined path.

"Come on up. I was just about to read this here article on the Kudzu Jamboree over at Camp Hill next week."

"Yeah, I heard about it." He nodded to Ilene, reached a hand out to tousle Buddy's hair and winked at me as he sat down on the swing beside me.

"It's going on four years since the Alabama Adjustment Administration and the Soil Conservation Service started that kudzu program. I didn't realize it had been that long," Dad commented. "I've been debating about planting some myself. Says here they are paying six dollars an acre for each acre you plant now. They are going to demonstrate all the ways we can use it at the Jamboree."

Mr. Jule farmed full time. He and Dad spent a good deal of time mulling over new farm methods. Most of the time Dad couldn't get a word in edgewise. Mr. Jule was the sort of person that took over a room when he came in as if everything was meant to revolve around him. At church he greeted everyone at the door as if he was the preacher. He especially liked greeting the ladies. Some said he had an Errol Flynn way about him. A stranger probably would never take him for a plain old farmer when he was in his Sunday best.

"Well, if it will stop that water runoff on the terraces the government folks talked us into, it might be worthwhile. Tell you what. Since you can't hardly take a day off from the mill, supposin' I just go on this tour they're settin' up and I'll get back to you with my opinion. Kudzu just might be the answer to a lot of our problems plus being a cheap feed at that."

"Sounds like a right fair proposition. I'd be obliged," Dad replied.

To get my attention, Mr. Jule put his hand on my knee right below where my dress stopped. "Say, how about a nice cool drink Sis?"

I got everyone some sweetened tea from the pitcher in the icebox. To show his appreciation, Mr. Jule patted my knee again when I sat down.

Ilene inquired about the health of the Morley family. Mr. Jule said he would bring his son Bailey over to play with Buddy on his next visit. At this, Buddy grimaced right out in the open. Buddy claimed Bailey was meaner than a two-headed rattlesnake.

For a reason I couldn't quite put my finger on, I was relieved when Mr. Jule finally said, "Well, I'd better call it a night. I've a mind to go to the auction early in the morning, maybe pick up a calf or two." He gave my knee another pat as he rose from the swing.

It was not long after noon the middle of the following week when Mr. Jule's truck pulled into the driveway again. Pug dutifully waddled out to the driver's side of the truck to do his act. He was about to back off when he heard the other truck door open. He wound up his waddle and his growl reaching the door before Bailey could get out. Buddy and Pug shared the same feelings toward Bailey Morely. Bailey slid over and got out the driver's side of the truck.

I sat on the porch reading. Mr. Jule saw me as he came into the driveway. He and Bailey came up the front path. Pug gave in and went back under the house to keep cool.

"Dad and Ilene aren't at home Mr. Jule."

"I know that Sis. Just thought I'd stop by and keep you company for a bit. Where's Buddy?"

"Off in the pasture or down by the barn. I don't know for sure."

"Bailey, why don't you run on and see if you can find Buddy."

"Naw Pa, I'll just wait here and see if he shows up."

I knew Buddy couldn't be too far away because Pug was still close to the house. I also knew he would not come out wherever he was if he had seen our company come in. Just the same, I couldn't help hoping he would. I suddenly had a queasy feeling in the pit of my stomach.

Mr. Jule did have that big-toothed grin like Errol Flynn and dark hair and brown eyes. His smile was different though. Instead of the kind that made leading ladies want to swoon, it was the kind that demanded they swoon. He kept grinning and looking at me. His dark eyes lost their twinkle and narrowed.

"Been noticing how growed up you are. You got right good buds sprouting up top there." His eyes bored into my chest.

I sat stone still, not knowing what to say or do.

Bailey stood beside his pa, a nine-year old grinning replica.

"I just thought if I stopped by you might want to show me how pretty they are."

My breathing got faster and faster. I couldn't seem to slow it down. I decided to get up and run to find Buddy and Pug.

"That's a girl, it's a little public out here. Let's go inside." He grabbed my arm as I rose and pulled me along after him. Bailey trailed behind us.

Once inside, he pushed me down on the bed that was just inside the door. His left arm crossed my chest just below my neck. His left knee and lower leg dug into my legs. While he held me in this lock he unbuttoned the top of my dress. I squirmed under his roughness. He touched one breast and then the other. I screamed. He laughed. Bailey laughed. Pushing me harder into the bed, he unbuckled his belt with his right hand and clawed at buttons. I squirmed enough to free my left knee but he clamped right down again. My fingers dug into the quilt. He pulled at my panties. I screamed full force.

Then he pulled it out. The turkey neck—raw, purplish-red and attached to his hairy body. I screamed again. And again.

As suddenly as the attack started, it quit. He scrambled off me and began adjusting his clothes as if something was after him. He talked quietly through clinched teeth while tucking in his shirt.

"Now Sis, you best keep your saucy play acting to yourself. I just might have to tell your pa how you pestered a grown man into almost doing something against his true nature. The Lord has ways of punishing harlots that make a man stray. And so does your pa. I got Bailey here to prove what you did."

He grabbed Bailey by the back of his collar and the two of them headed for the back door. It was then that I heard Pug's happy bark.

Buddy ran from somewhere yelling, "Hi Dad, whatcha doin' home?"

"Number two mill shut down. Well, hey there Jule, what are you doing here this time of day? Good to see you Bailey."

At that moment, the sound of Dad's voice was sweeter than sugar corn.

"I saw Larson come up the road. I figured the mill shut down. I thought I'd come on by and give you a report on the Kudzu Jamboree."

I lay still, listening. I fought the urge to run screaming to Dad. "Liar." "Demon." I slowly raised myself to a sitting position and buttoned my dress. I was shivering and exhausted.

"Hop in the back of the truck boys, we'll ride out to the field where I'm thinking about planting that kudzu. We might as well talk there."

Ilene's sewing mill must still be operating I thought. She would come home with a neighbor. I had time to collect myself. I buttoned my dress and smoothed the bed. Then I went to get Raggedy Ann. At the moment I did not want to have anything to do with males, not even Raggedy Andy.

I needed air. I sat on the front porch steps. The swing was ruined for me. That's where it began. Why didn't Dad see his hands patting my knees? I tried not to cry but tears rolled down my cheeks. I dried them with the hem of my dress. Unconsciously I began plucking the petals from the can of geraniums sitting next to me. When I noticed the leaves were gone too, I swept the can with its naked stalks off the porch. It landed with a thud. I felt as limp as the doll that lay beside me.

"Raggedy Ann, we got us a mess this time," I whispered. I reasoned that if I told Dad he would either not believe me or he would get out a gun and shoot Mr. Jule. In either case, Bailey would lie. There would be big trouble.

When I heard the truck coming back, I scampered to the kitchen and peeked from the window. Mr. Jule talked to Dad for a few minutes then he and Bailey got in his truck and left.

Slowly my heartbeat settled. By the time we all sat down to supper, I had made a decision.

I said nothing.

The next morning I told Buddy we had to hurry through chores. No more than an hour after Dad and Ilene left for work, we were on the road ourselves—walking to Grandmother's house. I told Buddy to bring his BB gun. We left Pug sitting at the end of the driveway, his head cocked to one side as if studying this new development. I knew that he would not follow us. Pug never left the farm.

"We're not staying up at that house one more day by ourselves," I announced when I found Grandmother sitting on the back porch fanning the flies away.

"She's gonna get us an awful whipping," piped up Buddy. "And she won't tell me why we have to come down here. She just says we hafta."

Grandmother's small eyes squinted until they got even smaller. She looked at me for a long time. Then she said, "Well, I reckon she has her reasons Buddy."

"Grandmother, my plan will work if Buddy and I leave just in time to get home before Dad and Ilene. The only thing is, we might get caught if the mill shuts down."

"That doesn't happen too often. Sounds like a good plan to me. Never did see any sense in you young'uns staying up the road by yourselves.

Besides, if they do find out I'll tell them that I put you up to it. Buddy will be spending some time with me anyway after you leave next week."

She pulled Buddy by the arm until he stood right up against her chair.

"Buddy, there's just one thing. You have to promise me that you won't go foolin' with that old Model T."

We all laughed just thinking about it. Two summers past, eight-year old Buddy bragged to Melvin and Jamey that he knew how to drive the Model T because Uncle Ed had let him crank it up and step on the gas when he used its motor to run the blacksmith wheel. They all piled in and Buddy got it started. Grandmother and I were sitting on the front porch when they came around the side of the house and onto the driveway going lickity split. She started hollering and waving her apron up and down for Buddy to stop. He didn't know how. All he had ever done was press the gas pedal for Uncle Ed.

While Grandmother jumped up and down, I started chasing the car round and round the driveway. Buddy managed to dodge the trees. Fortunately, Uncle Ed didn't keep much gas in it and the car soon came to a halt not two feet away from Grandmother's century plant. All three boys piled out and fell to the ground where they sat and stared at the Model T. Grandmother covered her head with her apron and praised the Lord.

"I kept telling him to step on the brakes, Grandma. He wouldn't listen," Melvin explained.

When Grandmother asked Buddy to promise, she knew she was on safe ground. After Uncle Ed gave up trying to farm the homestead and went to work at the mill, the Model T sat abandoned. There was no gas in it and the grass grew around it as tall as the wheels.

Buddy promised anyway and our plan was settled.

I still had to face Sunday.

He was there in church with his whole family. They sat in front of us. Every now and then he Amen'd the Lord's word. I felt like puking right on the shiny church floor. I hadn't thought about his daughters, but there they sat, the two of them. They were younger than Bailey, pretty, with blonde curly hair and small turned up noses. I sat wondering if their daddy would use their bodies for his pleasuring. He was mean enough. I wanted to get up and shout to the preacher that the devil was right here sitting among us and that he wasn't doing a thing to save us from him.

Instead, I sat dead still and seethed. I felt Tommy Lee Jones' eyes boring into me. I longed to get up, turn around and slap his face.

Finally, I turned my head to the window and sought the sky. Calmness began to seep in. God was out there, not confined to four walls where preachers pretended to talk for Him. I prayed to a clear blue sky that no man would use my body until I said so. Just then a tiny cloud puff scurried into view and just as quickly went on its way.

*Folks in My Life*

*Summer of 1939, Florence, Alabama*


*Family*
    *Aunt Bea*
        *Cousins Charles, Doadie, and Marge*
    *Uncle Tup and Aunt Alice*
        *Cousins Ellie and Johnny*
    *Aunt Maime and Uncle Thad*
    *Aunt Helen and Uncle Frank*

*Friends*
    *Mr. Bill Nolan*
    *Raggedy Ann and Andy*

# *Florence*

◆

My cousin Charles picked me up at Uncle Rob's house in Birmingham. He worked as a traveling salesman so it was easy for him to fit me into his schedule. He was also Aunt Bea's son and it was to Aunt Bea's house in Florence that I was being delivered.

We drove through Sheffield, crossed the Tennessee River and into Florence right on Court Street, the main street. There was also a Main Street but it was one street over where the post office and The Princess Theater were located. This confused out-of-towners. Strangers to town were also quick to ask how the high school came to be called Coffee High. Sometimes they joked and asked, "What brand of coffee and is it perked or boiled?" Indignant natives drew in their stomachs, stood tall, and set the strangers straight.

"Sir, our high school is named for General John Coffee who distinguished himself in the War of 1812. Furthermore, General Coffee, having recognized the beauty of this site on the Tennessee, planned our town. At the time, even General Andrew Jackson and President James Madison agreed with its possibilities for each bought a lot in Florence."

In a few blocks, Charles made a right turn and we headed to Aunt Bea's about a mile out of town. Her house stood on the brink of a hill across from the armory. Steep concrete steps seemed to go straight up from the street. Pink summer blooming rose bushes spread over the banks on either side of the steps. Two sprawling chinaberry trees dominated the small front yard. A sidewalk separated the trees. Aunt Bea stood at the top of the porch steps. I ran to her.

"I declare, I declare—just look at you."

She quickly enfolded me into her large fleshy arms, my head pressed to her buxom chest. She smelled of baby powder splashed with cinnamon. I guessed that my favorite apple pie had not been long out of the oven.

Aunt Bea looked nothing like my mother. Framing her high cheekbones, she wore her long black hair pulled back and twisted into a bun. Her black eyes seemed set in a permanent twinkle that matched the genuineness of her smile. Not much rattled her and there wasn't much she couldn't make better.

Buddy and I went to live with Aunt Bea just after I started second grade. That's when Mother and Dad divorced. Because the school year was well along, the public school principal said there wasn't room for me. Much to Aunt Bea's and my chagrin, she enrolled me in Catholic school. Her protective and suspicious nature included Catholics as well as foreigners and gypsies. Buddy sat on the wall sadly waving good-bye each morning as I made my lonely four block walk.

Two black-robed nuns kept a disciplining ruler close at hand. They taught all grades. Mornings and afternoons, we formed a line and were led into the dimly lighted sanctuary. Shadows bounced off statues of Jesus on the cross and the Virgin Mary. I watched carefully as the other children made strange hand motions across their chests and rose and kneeled on signals I did not hear or see. The unfamiliar rituals seemed perfectly normal to the other children. I tried to fit in by following the motions of the girl next to me. The end of my Catholic education came after a few weeks when the nun who never smiled took a belt to one of the older boys. I walked home sobbing in fright, convinced that I would be the next one belted.

Aunt Bea went to work on the problem by enlisting the help of her minister. Horrified that one of his flock might be contaminated in any way with ideas other than his and 'the true Church', he agreed to help. He scolded Aunt Bea for not bringing this problem to him sooner. Between them they convinced the public school principal, who was also one of the minister's flock, to slip one more child onto his rolls in order to save her soul.

I was happy that Aunt Bea once again had made things better. I didn't tell her that I was just as frightened of her church's Reverend Jones as I was of the nuns. With shouting and pulpit-pounding fists, he demanded that God save his flock from becoming sinners.

In the spring of that same year, the principal pulled my name from a hat. This lucky draw made me the bride in the annual Tom Thumb wedding. This was the big event of the school year.

People came from as far as Rogersville to see it. I felt like Cinderella. Nothing so wonderful had happened to me before.

"Where will we get a wedding dress for me Aunt Bea?"

"Now don't you worry your little head. I expect your mother can spare a dollar or two for material. We'll write her a letter then we'll go down to the piece goods store and get some white satin and make you that wedding dress."

For a whole day, I acted as I thought a bride would, dressed in the most beautiful wedding dress ever made. I wanted to save it for when I grew up and became a real bride. Aunt Bea did not think that was very practical.

She laughed. "I expect we can manage another one when that time comes."

I pushed myself out of Aunt Bea's cuddling arms so that I could return her broad smile. I was safe again.

Charles came up the front porch steps behind me carrying my suitcase.

"I gotta' go Mama, I'm late. See you on Sunday."

He dropped my suitcase, gave us a peck on the cheek and bounded back down the steps.

My cousins, Charles, Doadie, and Marge shared Aunt Bea with Buddy and me. They were all older, only Marge remained at home. I thought of them as my older brothers and sisters rather than cousins. I suspected that Aunt Bea thought of Buddy and me more as grandchildren since she had helped raise my mother. My true relationship never became quite clear in my mind but there was no need to dwell on it as long as her love was spread around.

Marge came through the screen door.

"Hey punk." She gave me a hug as we stood eyeball to eyeball. "Look at you—no fair. Before long you'll be taller than me."

In no time I was unpacked. When I placed Raggedy Ann and Andy on the bed next to Marge's, they looked much happier than they had in weeks.

The next morning I wasted no time in running two blocks down the street toward town. Uncle Tup and Aunt Alice owned the corner grocery and lived in the house next door to it. I counted on Uncle Tup's promise to let me work in the store after I turned twelve.

To be polite, I stopped at the house first to give Aunt Alice a big hug. I heard her in the kitchen where I found her with my cousin Johnny. He and I came close to sharing birthdays. We were born a few days apart. Mother told me that Uncle Tup brought Johnny to Birmingham where I was born and laid us on the bed together. Then he turned to Mother. "I sure did get a lot more for my money than you did, Sis." That was because Johnny weighed almost ten pounds and cost fifteen dollars in trade at the store while I, born early and by cesarean, weighed just under four pounds and cost over a hundred and fifty dollars.

"You want a pineapple sandwich for breakfast?" asked Johnny, busy spreading a glob of mayonnaise on bread.

"No thanks, I've had breakfast already." Much as I liked Johnny, I could not go along with his goofy eating habits. I considered him a great pal when it came to smoking grape vines and climbing the chinaberry trees at Aunt Bea's.

I found my cousin Ellie in the bedroom that she shared with Johnny. I plopped on her chenille bedspread and looked at her reflection in the mirror above her flowered skirted dressing table.

"Well hey there, heard you were back. Want to try some lipstick?"

"When did you start wearing lipstick? What's that stuff you're putting on your cheeks?" I rose from the bed and leaned my elbows on the dressing table. Like several of my Florence cousins, Ellie was close to Hollywood beautiful. Her hair shone silky black; her skin was a soft cream color; she had long black eyelashes.

"It's a blush, makes my cheeks rosy. Here let me try some on you."

"Nah. I gotta' go see Uncle Tup. I've got an idea for him." I bounded out of the room and headed next door to the store.

"Well, I swan. Look who just came strolling in the door like she had all day to get to work."

Uncle Tup was not talking to me. He pointed to me but he was talking to Dr. Jedidiah Carter, the colored doctor. Although an empty field separated them, Dr. Jed lived next door. He and his wife and son were the only coloreds that lived on the whole street. Uncle Tup counted Dr. Jed as one of his best friends.

"Well, I better get out of here and let you set her straight," laughed Dr. Jed.

I went back of the counter to get my hug.

"Up in Washington frozen Milky Ways are selling faster than snowballs Uncle Tup. How about we put some in the butcher cabinet. I betcha' we can sell heaps."

From that point on, my days were divided between Aunt Bea's and Uncle Tup's. I reminded everyone that came in the store that a cool Milky Way tasted mighty good on a hot day. I frequently reminded Uncle Tup that we were selling quite a few.

He laughed and said, "Folks are buying them just to shut you up."

When we weren't busy in the store, I spread the *Florence Times* on the counter. It was so good to have a daily newspaper to read again and one with something besides kudzu and society teas in it.

"Wow Johnny! There's a double feature at the Princess on Saturday. 'Charlie Chan in Honolulu' and Gene Krupa playing in 'Some Like it Hot'. We'll get twice as much for our money." All the cousins got 15 cents to go to the movies on Saturdays, my favorite day. After the movies, Marge, Ellie and I roamed all three floors of Rogers Department Store. Rogers had the only elevator in town. It came close to being as swanky as Garfinkel's back home. The salesladies dressed elegantly and smelled nice. I hoped that someday I would have enough money to buy something. Sometimes Ellie saved up and bought a pair of white cotton gloves or a lace handkerchief. I envied her those days. When Uncle Tup was generous with doling out change, we ended our trip to town with a soda at Southall's Drug Store. That first Saturday I also insisted on a long stroll down Court Street to the Tennessee River before we returned home.

A pattern soon was set. I helped Aunt Bea in the early morning by sweeping and dusting. By nine o'clock, I arrived at the store. Mornings stayed busy from then until around two in the afternoon when folks tended to stay inside out of the heat. Sometimes I walked the older ladies back to their houses and carried the groceries. Johnny didn't much like exertion so he was happy to have me take over that job.

Most afternoons Uncle Tup flipped Johnny and me for a Coca-Cola. "Heads," he'd say as he flipped. Uncle Tup had the worst luck; he always lost.

Aunt Alice usually fussed about the Coke breaks. "Bound to be bad for you. Look how it fizzles."

Uncle Tup always laughed and replied, "Alice, I keep reminding you, if Coke did harm to a person, the South would have died off years back and the North would be rejoicing."

While taking a break, I read the news out loud to everyone whether they wanted to hear it or not.

On August 8th I exclaimed. "Look here! The cartoonist plastered bandages all over President Roosevelt's chin."

Each bandage was labeled with a problem: war, economy, elections and others. On August 10th I read to Johnny about the Swift Jewel Cowboys coming to the Vaudeville Show at Coffee High. We talked Uncle Tup into giving us each of us a two-pound can of Jewel shortening so that we could get a free ticket. By August 12, Mayor Kelly of Pittsburgh was demanding a third term for President Roosevelt in a speech to the Young Democratic Clubs of America. I didn't mention it to Johnny, but I secretly wished I could belong to that club so I could join in on the demanding. I couldn't imagine any other president.

One day something different happened. Old Mr. Bill Nolan called Uncle Tup. He was feeling poorly and wanted some shelf items. Could Johnny or I bring them to him? Uncle Tup handed me the list.

"You've been pestering me with questions about your mother and the old days up in Rogersville. Why don't you go pester Bill awhile? He probably knows your mother better than her kin do."

Rogersville was where the family had lived before they moved to Florence.

"Mind you now, keep his bill under a dollar. He gets right riled if it comes to more than that."

I took the list and began to gather the items. Two cans of Alaska pink salmon at two for 25 cents, Then four cans of Libby's potted meat made 50 cents. After I weighed up three pounds of potatoes and took a can of corned beef hash off the shelf, I was up to 75 cents. When I added a quart of milk and three bananas, I totaled three cents over the dollar. I asked Uncle Tup if I should put one can of potted meat back on the shelf. He told me to forget it. I wrote a dollar on Mr. Nolan's charge slip and clipped it in Uncle Tup's accounts cabinet. I noticed there were several dollar slips.

## Mr. Bill Nolan

"Two blocks up and two blocks over, white house with the only blue shutters in town."

These were Uncle Tup's sparse directions to Mr. Nolan's house. It was tongue hanging hot. When I reached two blocks up the hill the sack full of groceries began to take on significantly more weight. I turned left towards town and started counting the sidewalk blocks. Having been belched up by tree roots, they were uneven and slanted. I got so interested in counting blocks I almost missed the house with the blue shutters.

I knocked on the screen door. For a minute or more all I heard from inside was the whirring of a fan. All I saw of the inside was a dim hallway that ran through the center of the house. Then Mr. Nolan appeared from the rear of the hall beckoning.

"Come on in, child. You must be plumb tuckered. I've got lemonade made."

By this time he was pushing the screen door open for me to enter. His smile seemed genuine and non-threatening. Nevertheless, I hesitated and became a little panicky.

"Your porch swing looks really inviting. If it's O.K. I'll rest a spell out here before I start back to the store."

His smile stayed genuine but a slight wrinkle appeared on his forehead and his dark eyes looked deep into mine.

"Now that sounds like a right smart idea. Here, I'll take the grocery bag and be right out with the lemonade. Do you like it real sweet?"

I nodded and moved to the far end of the porch. The swing was apparently set high to accommodate Mr. Nolan's height. My toes barely reached the floor as I began to push the swing back and forth. The chains squeaked in monotonous, but reassuring discord as I waited. The wait was short.

When he returned, he approached a small table near the swing and shoved a potted plant aside with his elbow to make room for the tray.

"We're in luck. A widow lady down the street brought me some sugar cookies just yesterday. Seems like the widow ladies want to keep me on the sweet side," he chuckled as he spoke.

I jumped up to help myself and settled back to the swing. Then instead of taking the rocking chair, Mr. Nolan sat down beside me. I wiggled over close to the end of the swing. My action did not go unnoticed.

"If I were to guess, I would say you've had a bit of trouble with some men folks. It appears you are learning to take care of yourself though. Mighty handy thing to learn."

I didn't respond. I nearly choked though as I gulped my lemonade. I knew by now that some grown-ups had an uncomfortable way of knowing things that were never said. He must be one I thought to myself.

"Well, just like most everybody, there's good and bad among us men. It takes a bit of sortin' sometimes."

Looking straight ahead, I nodded.

"Did your Uncle Tup tell you I knew your mama from the time she was born 'til she up and left Florence?"

"Yes sir."

"Miss Spitfire. That's what I used to call her. She and my daughter Josie were good friends. Pretty much alike they were, hard to handle. It got so nobody much tried. Since she didn't have no Ma or Pa alive, your aunts and uncles took on the job. Your mama moved from one house to another when she got riled—which was pretty often. They got used to her comings and goings. I expect at times they were glad to see the goings. Come summer, she'd spend a good deal of time in Rogersville and a lot of it at my farm. Now she and Josie never got into any real trouble mind you. They just seemed to stay on the verge of it. And smart? They were always reading and thinking on things, the both of them."

A thought suddenly came to my mind. Nobody ever talked to me about when my mother was a girl, not even Aunt Bea. I turned to look at Mr. Nolan with renewed interest. He reminded me of Jimmy Stewart, drawl and all, except that his hair was goose down white.

Suddenly he reached across my chest with his left arm. Startled, I jumped so high my toes left the porch floor and the swing started going zigzag.

"Well now, Miss Skittish, suppose you and I change places here. I'd like to get to my pipe that sits in the bowl at your elbow there."

My face flushed pink and kept right on going until it reached purple.

"No call for embarrassment. My fault really. I just forgot my manners," he said

I got up and helped myself to another glass of lemonade then resettled into the opposite swing seat.

He stopped talking long enough to light up his pipe and take a few puffs.

"Miss Spitfire and Josie got themselves sort of a reputation. Some old biddies even called them hussies. That was on account of they were fond of wearing pants, especially when they rode my old nag horses all over the place. When they weren't wearing pants, they dressed up mighty splashy in their older cousins hand-me-downs and sashayed around town. They sure could confound a person—tomboy one minute, sashaying the next. I got right smart pleasure out of watching their antics."

"Do you know my Aunt Maime? Is that why she and my mother don't get along, because people thought Mother was a hussy?" I couldn't imagine Aunt Maime being very forgiving of anybody even suspected of being a hussy.

"Well now, I expect it had to do mostly with conflicting personalities. I don't rightly know who your Aunt Maime took after, but I've had my suspicions that your mama took after her papa and her grandpa too. Both men were right smart, like your mama. They liked to question and figure out things for themselves. When they got it figured to the point where they thought they were right, well, no amount of arguing would change their minds."

He puffed a bit more then turned to look at me. "Your grandpa and I were good friends. Grew up on neighboring farms up in Rogersville. Your grandpa became a teacher and moved to Florence, you know."

That much I did know. Mother sometimes spoke of her vague memories of her father. She recalled sitting on his knee for long periods while he read to her. She also said that he wouldn't let any of her sisters and brothers scold her or make her eat anything she didn't want. "You're going to spoil that child 'til she won't answer to anybody Papa."

"Leave her be," he would answer. "Leave her be."

Mr. Nolan went on. "And your great-grandpa…now there was a man for you. A regular one man town he was."

For the first time I turned, lifted my head, and looked straight into Mr. Nolan's eyes. And he looked back. I had this eerie feeling that he could see deep inside me, right down to the lump of hurt in the pit of my stomach that sat there like a piece of Aunt Bea's fireplace coal. I fought hard to keep it from firing up. I felt ashamed that maybe someone might see it.

"Nobody ever told me anything about my great-grandfather." It sounded more like a question than a statement. I was wide-eyed.

"Sometimes folks forget to tell the most important things. Most times it's your grandpa or grandma that fill you in on people and events past. But since you skipped knowing them both, they being dead, I suppose the tellin' got shoved aside. The young ones had a good deal to do just getting themselves together after their ma and pa died. Let's see now. I believe your mama was about three when her mama died and about five when her pa died."

"Mother told me that much. I can't remember anyone ever telling me about my great-grandfather. In fact, I never even thought much about having had one."

Suddenly I was thirsty, and not for lemonade.

"Your mama would have been about a year old when her grandpa died. She wouldn't remember him on her own, so she didn't have any impressions to store away. Yesiree, he was a smart man. When he got back from the Civil War after serving in the 16th Calvary, he staked out a piece of farmland. It might have been part of his father's land before him, I don't rightly recall.

"My great-grandfather fought in the Civil War?"

"Deed he did. Like General Robert E. Lee, he was reluctant to go agin' the Union. Folks in this northwest part of Alabama voted against secession. I reckon they thought things could be worked out peaceable like. Tempers everywhere just got too riled up and the situation got out of hand mighty fast. Once the decision was made, your great-grandpa was duty bound to the South."

Mr. Nolan took a few more puffs on his pipe, and then continued.

"Anyway, it wasn't too long before he built a store on the wagon road that went by the farm and then he became a store-keeper and a farmer. Before long the store became the post office for about a hundred or more folks and he became the postmaster too. It just naturally came about that he fell into being the justice of the peace. Then folks started saying they were going to town when they meant to the store since it was the only convenient place to go. Soon they named the crossroads after him and it became a legitimate town. He was quite a philosopher too. More than one time I heard folks that had some problem or other say, 'I think I'll just mosey into town and see what Solomon has to say.' That was his name you know."

I didn't know. Here I was, 12 years old, and I didn't even know my great-grandfather's name.

"Did I have a Great-Grandmother too?" The words were out of my mouth before I thought. I blushed at the stupidity of the question.

"Of course you did. A right fine woman, half Cherokee Indian I believe she was. She was tall and right pretty with high cheekbones and long shining black hair. She had gentle doe-like eyes. Her name was Sarah. I expect it was on account of her that Solomon wouldn't tolerate anyone speaking poorly of another person no matter who. He nearly tanned me one day for making a disparaging remark about a colored man."

"Billy boy," he said. "You don't know nary a thing about that man, but I do. I'm telling you, if you grow up to be half as good a man I'll be right pleased to see it. And I'll be right surprised too."

I was astounded. My great-grandfather had been somebody important and my great-grandmother was half Indian. I was about to ask a question about my grandmother when Mr. Nolan pulled out his pocket watch and rose from the swing.

"I clean lost track of the time. Suppose we continue this conversation another day. Your Uncle Tup will skin me alive if I keep his new clerk from her duties. I'm sure I'll need something else in a few days."

I didn't have time to ask what had happened to his daughter, Josie. What did my grandparents look like? Funny, I had never thought much about my mother ever being young, much less a hussy. By the time I got back to the store, I had a whole list of questions for my next delivery to the blue shuttered house.

My next trek up the hill and two blocks over came four days later. This time when I knocked on the screen door, Mr. Nolan yelled, "I'm back here in the kitchen." Without hesitating, I went in and down the hall to the kitchen.

"The rheumatism got me today girl. No use fighting it."

I unpacked the bag and put the groceries away while he sat at the table giving me instructions as to where everything went. Then, as if it was perfectly natural, I took a seat opposite him at the table and sipped from the waiting glass of lemonade.

This became our routine for the next couple of weeks that I would be in Florence. I learned that Josie married a salesman and they moved out west. She never did have children.

"She comes back now and then. She's right stylish and doing all right I'd guess. I judge that by the automobile she drives. Josie and her husband wheel and deal in real estate now. She keeps wanting me to come on out west and live with her, but I don't see the use in that."

On the third visit, he took me on a tour of his small bungalow. In the living room he pointed out the grandfather clock; the cabinet with his wife's collection of china vases; the small spinet piano.

"These are Tilly's things. I don't come in here much anymore. You should have heard her play. She could have been a concert pianist. I plain miss her. She's been dead nigh on to ten years now."

The dining room table was pushed against the outside wall, the chairs crowded together surrounding it. An easy chair, table and lamp occupied the extra space. A full size radio stood against the wall near the chair.

"I spend most of my time right here by the radio and in the kitchen."

As instructed, I poked my head into the two sparsely furnished bedrooms. The quilt bed coverings were handmade. I guessed which was Mr. Nolan's bedroom by the well-worn bathrobe hanging over a straight-backed chair. A small bathroom separated the bedrooms.

I became very comfortable with Mr. Nolan. He suggested that I call him Uncle Bill. He felt we didn't need to be so formal since he was practically a member of the family. It seemed as if Uncle Bill forgot something he needed about every other day and that suited me just fine. I always had a question for him.

"Uncle Bill, do you know why my mother quit the church?"

"Well now, she never did just come out and say why. But I do know this. One Sunday she and Josie came home from church just a fumin'.

The preacher spent the entire sermon referring to women who wore pants and painted their faces as sinners—tempting the devil to move in. Your mama claimed he was looking right at her and Josie the whole time. Your mama pointed out that God brought her into the world stark naked. She went on to say that if God cared so much about clothes he would have seen to it that she was born in a flowery dress and with a proper hat too."

Uncle Bill chuckled. "I kept holding my breath all that summer expecting to see those girls riding stark naked down the middle of town. I'm sure they mulled it over but they never did it. Your mama was 16 that summer and just finishing up schooling. Near the fall of the year, she took off for Birmingham. I didn't see a whole lot of her after that."

Through our visits, I gradually came to know my ancestors. I came to see bits and scraps of them scattered here and there among my uncles and aunts. In the secret places of my mind, Aunt Bea, with her black hair pulled back into a bun, her high cheekbones and crinkly smile became my great-grandmother. Uncle Tup, the storekeeper whom everybody consulted, became Solomon. Aunt Maime surely sprung from that austere and ever correct lady, my grandmother. What was it that Uncle Bill said about her?

"Your grandmother was the kind of woman you sorta' skirted when you could on account of she did enjoy lecturing. When you couldn't keep out of her way, well, you'd best pretend you were wearing your Sunday suit and had all your manners straight."

As for my mother, I saw puzzle pieces whirling around like leaves in a windstorm, never quite settling.

And I began to wonder. Which of my ancestors would I be most like?

## Summer Days Winding Down

On Thursdays I liked to dawdle some before going to the store. That day Lilly Mae came to do the ironing at Aunt Bea's. Most southern ladies, even if they had little money themselves, hired a colored lady to do the ironing. Aunt Bea always had the starched clothes sprinkled and rolled up tight. They were just right for ironing when Lilly Mae arrived.

Aunt Bea also chose Thursdays as her baking day. Some ladies chose their ironing day to go shopping, do their family visiting or to participate in afternoon teas. I figured that Aunt Bea chose baking because she enjoyed Lilly Mae's company. When I lived with Aunt Bea, I loved sitting quietly and listening to the two of them. I learned a great deal about the family gossip on those days. I also got to know Lilly Mae's family even though I had never laid eyes on a single one. The two women usually discussed some of the things going on in the world. They always compared notes on the past Sunday preaching at their respective churches. After discussing the preaching, they got into sharing their thoughts.

The day usually went from, "How's your mama this week Lilly Mae?"

To something like: "That man of mine says I have to give him ever' dollar I make ironing. He says the preacher done told that it's in the bible. Says he heard it just last Sunday. I never heard the preacher say that, no way in this world. If the preacher had his way, he'd be the one to get my money. Besides, if I did give Buck my ironing money, he'd go spending ever' penny—forgettin' we need to eat. You know he ain't a bad man Miss Bea. He jes likes to strut around and pretend to be some-body he ain't. Likes to throw money around he ain't got. Do you reckon white men act a fool like that too?"

Aunt Bea nodded. "I know more than one that acts that way. We never would have come out of the depression if the women hadn't held tight to the money jar."

Aunt Bea referred to her jar on the top shelf of the preserves cabinet. From that jar she reluctantly doled out just what she absolutely had to—to the penny.

"Well it jes gripes my soul that most menfolk act so uppity jes cause they was born with a different set of plumin' tools. I say us womenfolk got jes as many brains. The Lord didn't give them to us for nothin'. He meant us to use them no matter what the preacher says."

On the Thursday, two weeks before I was to leave Florence, I went to the kitchen after I dressed.

"Aunt Bea, where's Lilly Mae this morning?"

"Got word that her mama has taken a turn."

Aunt Bea answered while she continued to pack a basket of food. To leftover fried chicken and the pie she'd baked for the church social, she added several canning jars full of string beans and preserves.

"Doadie's coming to get me. We're going over to Lilly Mae's mama's house to see if there is anything we can do."

"Can I come too?"

"If you want to, but you have to stay out of the way and mind your manners."

Doadie turned into a road that I had never known existed. It was not paved. Mud, leftover from a rain three days previously, splashed the wheels of Doadie's shiny car. She pulled up to a small paintless shack. Doadie knew where to go because once in awhile she dropped off her own ironing for Lilly Mae to do. On one trip, Lilly Mae had pointed out her mama's house.

"Watch your step, Mama. The mud is a little slippery and the porch steps look rickety."

Some colored folks stood on the porch. They nodded and moved aside so that we could enter.

Inside, the front room was dark. The two small windows did little to take away the gloom. Lilly Mae pushed her way through an assortment of relatives, young and old.

"Lawd Miss Bea, you didn't need to be haulin' yourself down here, but you shore is welcome."

"We came to see if we could do anything Lilly Mae. Looks like you have plenty of help though. We'll just leave these things for you."

Lilly Mae whispered. "Lawd Miss Bea, seems like folks can smell death before the good Lord is anywhere near ready for the poor soul."

I looked around after my eyes adjusted. The walls were covered with newspaper and cardboard held in place with strips of wood. A small wood stove stood against the back wall. A single cabinet stood beside the stove. I realized the stove served for cooking as well as heating. A time worn table took up most of the space in the room. Mismatched wooden chairs surrounded it.

One rocking chair and a lamp that sat on a small table were the only other furniture. An open bible lay beside the lamp.

Lilly Mae said to Aunt Bea, "She'd feel some proud if you graced her bedside. She's heard about you all these years. I know she mus' feel like she already know you."

Aunt Bea followed Lilly Mae into the small lean-to room at the back of the house. Doadie and I returned to the car to wait.

Aunt Bea sat quietly when she returned. Doadie slowly dodged mud holes as we made our way onto more familiar roads.

The only thing Aunt Bea said all the way home was, "I just said my first hello and a final goodbye in the same breath to a woman I feel like I've known for years. Held her hand for a few minutes even. Somehow it doesn't seem right that I haven't been with her before this. I think I'll be going to the funeral Doadie if you will take me."

The remaining days slipped by. Each day as I spread the *Florence Times* on the counter there seemed to be more war news. There were pictures of soldiers training in tanks at Plattsburg, New York. On August 24th the headline read, 'Hitler Demands Free Hand in Eastern Europe.' The article that caught my eye that day was an announcement that Alabama congressman William B. Bankhead was willing to accept a 1940 presidential bid.

"How dare he," I said to Uncle Tup. "Doesn't he know we want President Roosevelt for a third term?"

"Well now, step back a minute. Not everyone agrees that your idol is the answer to everyone's prayers."

"Then they just don't know him as well as I do. If they ever saw him up close, like in a parade, they would know he is somebody very special."

Uncle Tup just laughed.

It was a week left before I was to return to Washington. I wanted to cram in all I could. Aunt Bea promised a trip to Rogersville to visit Aunt Maime and Uncle Thad. I begged to stop by the cemetery too. I wanted to see where my great-grandparents were buried.

I always wanted to check on the dam while in Florence. When the water first spilled over Wilson Dam, I was only five. I still remembered the big celebration.

Aunt Bea said I wouldn't see Uncle Walter this trip. "He's been out of town a spell. I believe your Aunt Marilyn went with him this time."

A good thing I thought to myself.

On Saturday cousin Doadie came and drove Aunt Bea, Marge and I around on our visiting trip.

We were invited to have supper with Aunt Helen and Uncle Frank that evening on our return to Florence. Aunt Bea was having a real vacation from cooking.

Aunt Helen and Uncle Frank lived in a huge Victorian house on one of Florence's streets for prominent folks. They owned a loan business and did well. We always drove up the long driveway to the back of the house. We then went in the back door and sat on the big enclosed sun porch. It was the only room a person felt comfortable in for visiting. We even ate supper on the porch. The rest of the house was furnished like a full-blown museum complete with people's busts sitting on pedestals. Aunt Helen seemed much less pompous than her house.

"I'd love to see your dolls that I've heard about before we go Aunt Helen," I said after dinner.

"Why sure, sweet thing. Let's carry in a few dishes on our way through the kitchen."

Aunt Helen led me through the dining room into the front parlor. She went to her special-built cabinet and opened the doors to display her beautiful 'Gone With The Wind' dolls. Scarlett was the most beautiful doll that I had ever seen—prettier than a Shirley Temple.

"In *Life* magazine, I've seen some of the costumes that they are making for the stars of the movie. I think I copied them pretty well."

"The dolls are wonderful Aunt Helen."

I'm sorry Janey and Keith aren't here," Aunt Helen said as we left. "They always seem to be on the go."

I rarely saw Aunt Helen's children.

On the way back to Aunt Bea's I pondered. Maybe Mother was born to the wrong family. She could never make dolls like Aunt Helen; bake Aunt Bea's pies and cakes; grow a garden and can string beans like Aunt Maime. Or, most likely I thought, she just didn't want to. I figured she could run a store like Uncle Tup.

Doadie dropped us off in the alley that ran behind Aunt Bea's house so that Aunt Bea did not have to climb the steps. All in all, it had been a fine day.

## Uncle Tup and Me

The day dawned cleansed and freshened by the gully-washing storm of the night before. I awoke early, yawned and stretched. I started to get out of bed when I remembered. It was Sunday, the last Sunday I was spending in Florence. Near the door stood two cane-backed chairs, each draped with a flowered dress, pressed and ready for church. I glanced over at Marge. She was sound asleep. As I pulled the covers over my head, I tucked Raggedy Ann under one arm, Andy under the other. Together we thought.

In our silent language, I asked Raggedy Ann if she had any ideas. Right away the answer came. I remembered the time two years before when I had come down with a terrible stomachache. Aunt Bea got worried about the possibility of appendicitis and asked the family doctor to stop by. After looking me over, he asked Aunt Bea what I had eaten the day before. It came out that she had insisted that I eat some of her fresh string beans just out of the garden. I hated string beans. I kept telling her that I was allergic to them. I'd read about allergies in a magazine article only days before.

"Oh come on now, you're spoofing me," she had said with her hearty laugh.

I was.

But that wonderful old doctor just looked at her and said, "Well now, we have the reason for this stomachache don't we. She's allergic to string beans. Give her a little Coke syrup to settle her stomach."

I liked this southern remedy much better than castor oil. He went on to say that I should stay in bed a day or two. I missed Sunday school and church that day.

The door opened. Aunt Bea stuck her head in and called, "Time to get up girls, breakfast is almost ready."

Before she could duck back out, I undraped my head. "I just can't get up Aunt Bea. I've got this terrible stomachache."

Her forehead creased. She crossed the room and put her hand on my head.

"No fever."

"I think I know what the problem is. I forgot. When we had dinner at Aunt Maime's in Rogersville yesterday, to be polite I ate some of her fresh out of the garden string beans." "Oh Lordy. Well, I'll get you a little Coke syrup to settle your stomach. Stay where you are. Marge, up with you."

It was worth missing breakfast. I insisted that since I was now twelve, I could stay by myself for a few hours while everyone else went to Sunday school and church. Aunt Bea decided that Uncle Tup could look in on me.

"He mentioned that he was going to backslide today," Aunt Bea said. "I'll call him."

Backsliding was something Uncle Tup did often. Besides not approving of his skipping church, the family worried when he backslid. Most anything could happen. One Sunday he went over to Aunt Helen's house while she was in church and snatched her whole dinner out of the warming oven and took it to his house. About the time he thought she would be home from church he called her up and invited her to dinner. Aunt Helen was so mad she made the whole family eat peanut butter and jelly. She didn't speak to Uncle Tup for a week. Not everybody appreciated Uncle Tup's tricks.

Another time Uncle Tup was late paying a bill to Uncle Walter's company. Uncle Walter dunned him for more than a month and finally told him it had to be paid by a Monday or his service would be cut off. That Sunday Uncle Walter came home from church to find two heavy bags by his front door. Uncle Tup paid him in pennies.

The house clatter faded. I was alone—for maybe 10 whole minutes.

I heard the front door open and shut.

"Well, what do we have here? I'll bet it's a full blown attack of 'I don't wanta'—betcha me a whole dime."

"I have felt better Uncle Tup, really I have."

"Tell you what. It's such a fine morning I purely would hate to miss out on my fishing. I can't think of anything that cures what ails a person better than fishing on the river. Just suppose you hike yourself up out of that bed and you and I will try us a fishing cure."

"Aunt Bea won't like it."

"You just leave your Aunt Bea to me. Besides, she tends to forgive most things when I bring her a mess of good old Tennessee River catfish. It's just a short run to the river."

It was especially calm out on the river. I had a hard time watching my bobber because I kept soaking in the surroundings. The boat nestled in the top bough of a huge tree that had fallen from the bank and stretched out into the river. Sitting in the shade of the riverbank trees, we felt cool and content. The water sparkled under the morning sun. Somewhere deeper in the woods, a crow squawked. Another answered. I could not spot either in the trees. A snake moved smoothly through the water along the bank's edge looking for its next meal. A spider that had adventured onto the tree trunk busily spun a web between two bare branches. I wondered if spiders swam.

"Watch out what you're doing Missy. That's not your worm that's signaling you."

I pulled up on my bamboo pole. It felt heavy. There was a sudden tug on my line.

"I think I've got a big one Uncle Tup."

"Get him in here now. We've got to get a mess to satisfy Bea when we get home."

We got us a mess. Uncle Tup didn't seem to be in any hurry to go home so we sat awhile longer after the fish quit biting.

"Uncle Tup, how come you and my mother aren't too strict on religion? Aunt Maime says that people who don't go to church just don't believe in God and are sinners doomed to hell for all eternity."

I knew that I had unnerved him when sudden creases appeared across his broad forehead.

He bit down on his pipe, inhaled and then removed the pipe from his mouth. He leaned over the side of the boat and slapped the pipe against his free hand until all the ashes floated on the water. He put it, stem down, into his shirt pocket. Only then did he look at me.

"Is that what you think? That your mama and I don't believe in God?"

"Well, I know you go to church when it suits you, but Mother doesn't go at all. The rest of the family goes every time the preacher thinks up a reason. Aunt Maime says she prays for Buddy and me. She says so far we're innocents but we have to get baptized soon. I don't think Mother will go for that. Aunt Bea goes regularly but she doesn't seem so serious about it like Aunt Maime. Living right just seems to come naturally to Aunt Bea, sort of like breathing."

Uncle Tup looked at me then looked off across the river. Minutes passed. I began to think I had said something terrible and that he might never speak to me again.

Finally, "Missy, I'm not one to talk about religion. I'm sure not one to tell another man how he should feel about it either. But, I reckon you're carrying a burlap bag full of mixed up crop on your back. Before you're grown, it's going to take some sorting. I guess you deserve some kind of answer. First, let me say this, your Aunt Maime gets a mite carried away sometimes."

I nodded. The crows squawked. The snake made its way back up the river. Minutes passed.

"Do you really think I can sit out here on this river seeing how all this comes together—the earth, the water, the sky and not feel the miracle of it around me. Not believe in God! There's no way that all of this is some accident of nature." He looked around as he spoke, taking in the cloudless sky; the woods behind us; the silver waters of the Tennessee. "It's just that sometimes Him and me can converse a lot better out here than in church."

Again it became quiet except for an occasional slap of water against the tree trunk.

"Now don't get me wrong. There's a heap of good in churching too—more for some folks than others you see."

"Well, I just don't get it Uncle Tup. Mother reads the Bible more than anybody I know. She's even writing a book about it. She's strict about telling the truth and doing what's right. And I know you don't have a mean bone in your body, despite your joshing sometimes. You were both raised right along with your sisters and brothers. You're not much different from them except when it comes to steady church going."

He chuckled, more to himself than to me. "Can't speak for your mama, Missy. She and I never talked much about religion. I'm a mite older than her, you know. Went off on my own pretty early in life what with both our parents dying when we were so young. I don't know exactly why it is that we both came to be family mavericks. Maybe we both got a speck of some ancestor's blood that the rest didn't. I just don't rightly know. As to how I got to where I am about church going, well, I just up and graduated myself."

"That's a funny thing to say Uncle Tup. How do you graduate yourself?"

"Well, you study a subject just so long, then you graduate and set about practicing what you learned. Practicing what you learn is the object of religion it seems to me. Now, graduating is not for everybody. Lots of folks need church all their lives. It's like a walking cane—good support. Some need support more than others."

I must have looked as puzzled as I felt.

"Maybe I can explain it this way. I know you like history. You know about President Thomas Jefferson and the Declaration of Independence—his fighting for religious freedom and all that. Do you know that he studied all kinds of religions? He even studied them in Greek and Latin and Hebrew. After awhile, he sat down with the Bible and whittled it down to where it made sense to him. It appears he found out after all that studying that there are really just a few simple rules to live by in all those religions."

"That's what Mother says. She says a whole lot of old men in long black robes tacked on a whole bunch of stuff to God's rules and made a mess."

Uncle Tup burst out laughing.

"Sounds just like her. Well anyway, Jefferson eventually cut up a Bible and left out what he thought some of those old men had made up. Then he got down to the meat of it. In a sense, I guess he graduated himself just like I have. But, he was a most religious person in his own way. Like me, he respected other folks religious ways and went to church when it suited him—anybody's church."

"Did you do the same thing, cut up a Bible I mean?"

"Nope."

Uncle Tup was quiet again as if he wasn't sure he should go on. Then he spoke, almost in a whisper.

"One day I was sitting under a shade tree just resting. For some reason, I fell to studying my hands. All of a sudden, it was like a bolt of lightning struck."

He held both hands towards me, palms up. "Do you see anything about my hands that's different from anybody else's?"

"They sure are big Uncle Tup, but not as big as your feet." I giggled and pointed.

His hearty laugh came right back at me. Uncle Tup had the biggest feet I had ever seen. They were so big that he had to send away for his shoes. Nobody in town sold his size.

He continued. "I did some serious thinking about these hands that day." He rubbed his right thumb across his left hand fingers. "It wasn't a new notion that struck me. I'm sure others have thought about it before. I remember reading a mystery story some time back where two detectives discussed fingerprints. I guess it didn't make much of an impression at the time."

Uncle Tup took his pipe out of his shirt pocket and held it in his hand.

"That day under the tree, it struck like a direct bolt from the sky. There is not another pair of prints like mine in the whole world. Imagine that—in the whole world! See these fingertips. The FBI has my fingerprints in their files on account of my military records. If I do anything wrong that brings my prints to their attention, they will know right away that your old Uncle Tup was up to no good. They'd have a mark against me in their files quick as you can blink an eye."

I looked at my fingertips and studied the tiny lines as he spoke. A picture came into my mind of the rows and rows of cabinets in the file room at the Department of Agriculture where Mother worked. I reckoned God's file room must be stupendous. I was still trying to visualize it when Uncle Tup continued.

"Of course I realize that I don't have my own particular fingerprints just so the FBI and J. Edgar Hoover can keep track of me."

He was quiet for a few minutes while he stuffed tobacco in his pipe. I felt he expected me to sop up his words like gravy on a biscuit.

"Can you picture it, Missy? Millions and millions of people, all identified by fingerprints. New prints come along every day, every time a baby is born. All these people come in different sizes, shapes, and colors. And they all have fingerprints that are different from one another. Everybody has their own mark. It's downright mind boggling.'

He fell silent again while fumbling in his pocket for a match.

"To my way of thinking, the proof that we are all God's work is right here in my fingertips. Every living soul is in God's file box. We all have our very own mark. There has to be a powerful reason for that."

I shuddered. A big lump began to grow inside my throat. Finally I spoke.

"Uncle Tup, does the FBI ever let you erase things you did wrong or do they keep your record forever and ever?"

He smiled and lit his pipe.

"The FBI doesn't put things on your record unless it's really bad. If they did I'd think it would take an army just to keep up with the recording. I expect it's about the same with God about the bad stuff. But I do suspect that God is more likely looking for the good to put in a person's file."

Uncle Tup lit his pipe and took a few more puffs.

"Did you ever read that preacher fella's books? Lloyd C. Douglas is his name. Some of the things in his stories make a heap of sense. I read *Magnificent Obsession* maybe three or four times. It made quite an impression on me. You might want to get hold of the book. It's about the power in doing good. Gives a person right smart to think about."

More silence. Uncle Tup took a few puffs on his pipe.

"Anyway, between reading and thinking, I decided I'd studied enough to graduate and go about doing. You see, I really believe it's the doing that counts. I'd wager a guess that your mama thinks along those lines too."

"Mother never mentioned fingerprints or record keeping, Uncle Tup. Sometimes she seems right mad at God. She told me once that she died. That was when I was born. She said she left her body on the bed and went up to the ceiling and watched the doctors talking about her dying. Then she started down a long tunnel with a bright light. She wanted to keep right on going but somebody told her she had to come back and take care of me. It was important they told her. I don't think she liked that either. Sometimes I think she is mad at God and me for keeping her here. She really is strong on doing what's right though. Maybe she does think God keeps some kind of record."

"Never heard about her dying experience before."

He smiled slightly and dumped his pipe ashes again.

"It's about time we haul in our string and get back to your Aunt Bea's. Before we go, let me say this. Each of us has to figure the best way to get through life without getting black marks while at the same time adding good ones. For some it's one way and for some it's another. Some never seem to figure a way. None of us have any call to judge the next fellow. That's for the record keeper. Seems to me if every single person worried about his own fingerprint file instead of someone else's, it would be a pretty peaceable world."

As he pulled in our catfish, I sighed a deep sigh. The motor whirred to life and my mind whirred to thinking. That bag of mixed grain that Uncle Tup said I was carrying seemed to be getting heavy. I could see that it would take a lot to lighten the load. Maybe it would be easiest just to go to church and pray to God about not putting me in his bad file. But which church? If Uncle Tup was right, I had to find a way to get some good points too. It didn't take much thought to know I was lacking in that department.

We got back to Aunt Bea's minutes after she and Marge returned from church.

"Land sakes. A body can't ever tell what you'll be up to next, Tup. I never thought to tell you not to take this child out of the house. Supposin' she'd started running a fever," Aunt Bea said as she pulled me close and felt my head.

"Calm down, Bea. No harm's done. Besides, we got us a string of catfish just waiting for some hush puppies to go with them. They're out in the back porch sink. I'll clean them. You call Alice and tell her to come on up with the kids. We'll have a Sunday afternoon fish fry."

Aunt Bea threw up her hands in defeat and grabbed her apron off the hook. Marge went to the hall phone to call Aunt Alice.

That night as I lay in bed, I thought about my fingerprints. It truly was mind boggling like Uncle Tup said.

## The Last Days of Summer

Cousin Charles scheduled a sales trip to Birmingham the middle of the next week. He planned to take me back to Uncle Rob's in Birmingham where I would meet Buddy. Uncle Rob would then put us on the train for home.

The first of the week, Mr. Nolan called the store and talked to Uncle Tup. It was late in the afternoon.

He turned to me after he put the phone back in its cradle.

"Bill says for you to bring him a few bananas if there are any good ones in the bin. He needs a box of soda crackers too. Oh, and he'll try one of your frozen Milky Ways if you can get it up the hill before it melts. If you'll stay for a bite of supper with him today, bring two he said."

"Is it all right? Please can I—please?"

"Don't know why not. Johnny is around somewhere if I need a hand. It will be closing time soon anyway. I'll call your Aunt Bea so she won't worry."

I made record time to Uncle Bill's house. This time I didn't even bother to knock. I found him waiting at the kitchen table.

He waved a hand as I entered the kitchen. "A'fore you settle in reach up in that cabinet to the right of the sink there and get us a couple of cans of that potted meat. Put the crackers right on the table, the bananas too."

"I brought two Milky Ways. I'll put them in the fridge for now."

Without being told, I went to the corner china cabinet and got two fancy gold-rimmed plates.

When I set them down, I noticed the red roses arranged very nicely in his wife's favorite green vase.

"I took a stroll out to the back fence. I thought it wouldn't hurt to pick a few of them ramblers. Darned if they don't go pretty good with Tilly's fancy plates. I made us a pot of turnip greens too. They're restin' on the back of the stove."

I glanced over my shoulder toward the stove so he wouldn't see me wrinkle up my nose. Turnip greens did set a little better with me than string beans.

"From what Tup tells me, this is likely to be our last get-together for a spell."

"Yes sir."

He had the can opener handy on the table. While he went about open-ing a can of potted meat he asked, "Reckon we've talked out by now?"

"Well there is one thing I am confused about but I don't suppose anybody can untangle me on that."

"I'm reckoning that would be on the topic of religion. Tup told me you wrestle with that subject now and agin'. Seems like it crops up t'winxt us too."

"Sometimes religion doesn't make much sense. Most all my folks on both sides go to church except my mother and sometimes Uncle Tup. He backslides now and then."

Uncle Bill chuckled. He laid the can opener down and shook his hand to loosen the rheumatism.

"There's hardly any better man around these parts than your Uncle Tup. I suspect half this town is beholdin' to him one way or another. He makes no bugle calls about helping folks. He just gives the Lord a hand now and then, quiet like."

"The thing is, Mother is so sure about her beliefs. Aunt Maime is pos-itive about her religion and thinks everybody else should think like she does. Those in-between like Uncle Tup and maybe even Aunt Bea don't talk about religion much. They don't kick up much fuss about what other people believe."

"Well, let's see. How can we unravel this dilemma a bit?"

He studied a minute. I worried my index finger into a scraped place in the blue oilcloth table cover and made a small black hole a little bigger.

"Now take a look here at this supper. Some folks right around this block would think us plumb crazy to be munching away on bananas and potted meat spread on crackers for our supper. They'd think the turnip greens right fittin' provided there is a good size piece of salt pork simmering with them. Then, there's folks on the other side of the world that would think we were sinning due to the fact that there is cow parts in our potted meat. There's even folks that never heard of potted meat in their entire life. There's some would say we're sinning if we eat meat on a Friday. I heard tell those folks down in Mexico live mostly on beans rolled up in some kind of flat dough. When Tilly and I visited her kinfolks in Germany, they ate mostly sausages and sauerkraut. That dang stuff nearly tore up my insides. It was good eating to them though."

While he talked, I peeled two bananas and arranged slices around one side of each plate.

"I can't see what difference it makes as long as a person has enough to eat. And too, some folks get along on mighty little food. Others gorge and make gluttons out of themselves. They expect everyone around them to do the same. Pretty soon everyone is so stuffed they can't do much but sit at the table and discuss the next meal. See what I'm gettin' at. A little common sense is called for."

The bananas began to turn a tinge brown.

"Well now, folks are pretty much the same about their religion. They're used to what they're used to. That doesn't make the fella half way around the world wrong. It just makes him as puzzling to us as we are to him. But seems to me, as long as we all have enough to eat, there's no use in worrying about what we eat. I 'spect it would cause a heap of problems if we did all go to eatin' the exact same thing. There's no use in calling other folks names just because of a different way of fixing supper. It's all nourishment to our bodies like the preacher prays."

I shooed a fly off the bananas.

"So you see, religion is much like eatin'. Some get along fine with just a little on their plate while others want a heap. Some like it one way, some another. Then there's those that study it so hard that just about all they do is study on it. Good folks mind you, but they think that the word is the important thing and forget the word is supposed to lead to a way of living. One word might be just as good as another as long as it spurs us on to do the right thing by one another."

I began to see the connection.

"Do you talk to Uncle Tup about religion? Do you know about his fingerprint studying?"

"Tup and I do some religious talking now and then. I've thought about his fingerprint idea. There is bound to be a reason for marking us that way."

Simultaneously, we looked at our hands. I wiggled my fingers.

"I can tell you one thing," Uncle Bill went on. "When we go, we end up a pile of bones. It won't matter if they're in some fancy satin lined coffin or just covered over in the dirt. When that time comes, I don't believe it matters one hoot whether we are tall or short—colored, yellow or white. It won't matter if we're Gentiles, Jews, Hindus, Muslims, or whatever. No sir. What will matter is how we lived our days and how we treated each other. That's the whole of it. God surely is not going to favor folks who can't get along in His heaven. The account keeping idea makes sense like Tup says."

The grandfather clock in the sitting room bonged six times.

"Good Lord a livin' child. Dish up the greens and I'll open this other can."

I didn't tell Uncle Bill that a potted meat and banana supper would fit right in with the way my mother cooked.

After we ate, I washed the two plates and silverware, put the leftover turnip greens back in the pot and wiped the tablecloth clean.

"I'd best be going. Aunt Bea might get to worrying."

"I expect you're right. I'm going to miss you young lady. Come back to see me next year, the good Lord willing I be here. Oh, by the way, the next time your Uncle Tup flips you for a Coke, you yell out 'heads' real quick. See if he don't bust a gusset."

He walked me to the porch and settled in the rocking chair as I went down the steps. I turned and waved from the sidewalk. Through misty eyes, I counted lopsided blocks all the way to Aunt Bea's. There were 89.

The next afternoon when it was time for Coke flipping, Uncle Tup reached in his pocket to get out his coin. I yelled "heads" right off the bat.

His jaw dropped. "Doggone that Bill Nolan. He's gone and spoiled everything."

Then he showed me his two-sided nickel, both sides tails. That's why he always called heads.

He lost on purpose.

Aunt Bea gathered up all my clothes and washed and ironed them. She sent me to air my suitcase in the backyard.

"That way you'll carry some Alabama sunshine back with you," she said.

For supper that last night she made two of my favorites, fried chicken and banana pudding. In the evening Aunt Bea, Marge and I sat on the porch and soaked up the sounds and the smells of the waning summer night. I tucked Raggedy Ann and Andy beside me in the big wicker settee that I shared with Aunt Bea. I was not willing to stuff them into the suitcase until the last minute.

Now and then Aunt Bea patted my hand as if to say, 'you have a special place in my heart.' I knew I did.

Now and then I squeezed her arm in reply.

# *Fall*

◆

## Home Again

Buddy did not seem as excited as I became when the train moved through Alexandria on the approach to Union Station. He truly loved the country and would have preferred living there.

Mother appeared happy to see us. She took off early from work that Friday afternoon to meet us and had the whole weekend off.

After we settled on the streetcar, Buddy began to chatter away about his summer. He never did catch up with the black snake but he did help Uncle Ed kill a rattler. I sat alternately listening to Buddy and wrestling with myself as to what I would tell Mother about my own stay in Alexander City. Very little I decided.

Before changing streetcars, Mother wondered aloud if we shouldn't stay downtown and shop for school clothes but she decided the suitcases were a bother.

"We'll shop on Saturday and take in a movie—maybe *The Wizard of Oz*."

"Can we have lunch at the Neptune Room?" I queried.

She nodded.

It was so good to be home again.

As usual, on Sunday Larry and I began our day with the newspapers. The *Post* headlines screamed of war across Europe. War raged far away.

I gave it little thought. I looked for the latest dress styles. Larry zeroed in on car ads.

After Buddy and Mother finished breakfast, Mother said she and Larry wanted to talk to us.

"We've been thinking things over this summer and we want you and Buddy to make a choice," Mother said when we settled down for our talk.

"What kind of a choice?" Buddy piped up.

I was sure he was thinking like me. Did we want to go to the cafeteria for dinner or have High's ice cream? Those were choices we were used to making.

"Well, we were thinking that we could use our savings to buy that duplex in Arlington." There was a long pause. "Or, we could take a trip to California," Mother said.

In a state of complete surprise, I asked Mother, "Do you mean keep on living in our apartment instead of a house and take a trip next summer for vacation instead of going to Alabama?"

"Not exactly. We're thinking of moving to California. It will take a week to cross the country and when we reach California, we'll go to Hollywood to live."

"To Hollywood!" I hoped that I had not heard correctly. Fear that I had set in immediately.

"Would we have to change trains?" Buddy asked.

Larry answered. "No, we'll buy a car. I've had my eye on a good second hand Pontiac at Arcade Motors. It's just two years old and been garage kept. One of the embassy folks owned it—used it for weekend trips out of the city. They got called back home because of the war."

"But I'm going to enter Powell Junior High on Monday. What about that?" I asked plaintively. "I have been so looking forward to moving up from Cooke Elementary."

"The plan is that you will go to Powell for about a month and then we'll start our trip. It will take a little while to complete our plans; buy a car; get rid of the furniture—all those things," Mother replied.

"What about your jobs?" I asked Mother.

"We'll find new ones. In fact I've been reading the Los Angeles papers at the library and there are rooming houses that can be leased to operate. I might try that for awhile. It would give us a home too. It wouldn't be like running the hotel in Jacksonville. Just a few people live in a rooming house."

I knew the reply that I wanted to make to that idea was better left unsaid.

Instead I asked, "What will Larry do?"

"Oh I won't have a problem. Banks always seem to need help," Larry said.

Thoughts of living in Hollywood were exciting. Thoughts of living in a rooming house were not. I so loved having a real home. How could Mother keep doing this to Buddy and me? Still, my friends were sure to be really jealous. My thoughts turned somersaults.

"Do some of the movie people like cameramen or makeup girls live in rooming houses?" I asked Mother as I explored my thoughts.

"I think some of the extras do."

"Extras, what's that?" Buddy asked Mother.

"That's the cowboys and Indians that fall off the horses, dummy," I answered.

He punched me on the arm and went on questioning. He turned to Larry. "Can I drive? Uncle Ed taught me how this summer. All I have to do is sit far up on the seat so I can reach the pedals."

Larry just laughed and shook his head at that idea.

"Suppose Buddy and I decide we want to buy the duplex?" I ventured. By this time I knew full well the decision had already been made. The decision never was ours to make.

"You'd miss a lot of adventures. Think how terrific it will be to live right in Hollywood," Mother replied.

By the end of the weekend, the decision became final. We were moving to Hollywood.

My feelings were certainly mixed that first Monday of September. Powell Junior High was several blocks away. As I walked up 14th Street to Upshur on the first day of school, friends joined me from Cooke Elementary days. We chatted, hoping we would not get lost changing classes; hoping we had the right notebooks; hoping we would get Miss Davidson for English and not Mrs. Nelson whom we had heard was a terror.

Before the day was over, Sue and I hugged and shared our summer news at lunchtime. I didn't mention my horrible experience with Mr. Jule. We both lucked out and got Miss Davidson for English and Mrs. Morgan for homeroom. Richard winked at me during math class. I turned away. That evening the whole world seemed to shudder at the news that Winston Churchill was sending British troops to war against Adolph Hitler.

By the end of the week I had settled back into a happy routine. I wished that something would cause Mother to change her mind about moving. I even prayed. By Saturday afternoon, I knew that was no turning the decision around.

"Come downstairs," Larry called to all of us. "I've got a big surprise."

We walked up Columbia Road toward the park for about a block where he stopped beside a green Pontiac.

"Pile in everybody, let's go for a ride." He had bought the car. He drove on past Meridian Hill Park, through the Rock Creek ford and over to the zoo and back. After we parked, he got a rag out of the trunk and dusted the whole car.

On Sunday we headed to the country town of Centreville, Virginia. There wasn't much there so we decided to go all the way to Warrenton. We celebrated owning a car by having our Sunday dinner in the town's big fancy hotel, the Warren Green. The colored waiters reminded me of the dining car stewards. I had to admit to myself that owning a car had some good points.

The second week in September, both Larry and Mother gave two weeks notice to their bosses. Mother sold most of the furniture by posting notices on neighborhood bulletin boards at the Arcade market and the drugstore. Someone in her office wanted our beds and agreed to pick them up on our last Saturday in Washington. Mr. Orman, the janitor, said he would let them in so we could leave early in the morning. My bicycle was sold to a girl in our building.

Sue, Richard, and some of my other friends walked home with me that last Friday. On the way they chatted about their plans for the matinee at the Tivoli on Saturday; about studying together in the park for the first history test; about who would be chosen for the chorus. When we reached my corner and the goodbyes began, I fought tears by gloating.

In parting I said, "I'll think of you guys sitting in the Tiviloi on Saturdays when I'm out in Hollywood hobnobbing with movie stars."

They were kinder than I. Sue hugged me and handed me a new book to read while traveling. Richard gave me a peck of a kiss on my cheek. I turned and ran up the walk to the apartment before the tears spilled.

Although Mother believed that all a person needed when moving was a suitcase full of clothes, Buddy and I were allowed to bring a few things for the back seat. He selected a shoebox full of toy soldiers and comic books. Besides Raggedy Ann and Andy, I took my school notebooks, pencils and a few books to read.

When we were settled in the car, Larry turned to Buddy and me. "We have to drive nearly 3000 miles and we hope to do it in six days if we don't run into bad weather. We won't stop to see the sights along the way and I'd appreciate it if you two keep the fidgeting down as much as possible."

With that he started the engine and pulled away from the curb and away from a life I was reluctant to leave, even for the glamour of Hollywood.

I was fairly content with absorbing the scenery that first day. The mountains and the villages below them flowed together, joined by the gaudy colors of fall. Traffic on the two-lane road was light so we rolled along at a rate that pleased Larry. He planned to cover at least 450 miles a day. That meant driving from sun-up until dark. We were not sure where we were that first night when long after dark we spied a dimly lit tourist house sign. The proprietor had no visitors and seemed glad to see us at her door. On hearing that we had not eaten supper, she fixed a platter of sandwiches and milk 'for a small extra fee'.

"If we have as good a second day, we'll make it down the road past St. Louis," Larry announced the next morning.

The scenery changed as we got closer to St. Louis. Buddy and I were interested in some of the road signs that promised high adventure while westward bound. One that particularly interested us began appearing on barns. 'Camping at Meramec Caverns; Greatest Show Under The Earth.' We'd never seen a show under the earth. Whenever we saw a sign we punched each other. I passed him a note, "Do we dare ask?" His head bobbed up and down in response. I asked Mother to pass the map so I could check where we were. I quickly located Stanton on the other side of St. Louis. The cavern signs promised this underground wonder was just three minutes off Route 66 at Stanton. Surely Buddy and I were up to wrangling three minutes.

'The world passes through St. Louis, gateway to the West,' another sign proclaimed. I twisted the hem of my dress in excitement.

So far, all our stops had been quick and necessary. Larry pushed the miles through the speedometer. It neared dusk as we caught sight of the steel lacework bridge that would carry us across the Mississippi.

"Man, I hope I see some rafts and steamboats. That'll be the cats pajamas," said Buddy as we began our crossing into St. Louis.

Beneath the bridge we saw muddy swirling water transporting all manner of debris for deposit downstream. Across the river, from behind its cobble-stoned levees, the city sprawled.

"Do you think it's as big as Washington?" I questioned.

"There are sure more boats pulled up along side it," Buddy observed. "I don't see any rafts though."

"Let's take a little spin through. I don't expect we'll get back this way. We'll just roam around a few streets until we connect up with Route 66 and head out," Mother said.

The buildings reminded me of Florence's Court Street in Alabama. They were fancy fronted brick. The traffic interested me most. Streetcars clanged. I spotted everything from Ford Model T's to shiny brand new models looking fresh off the assembly line. Some older cars parked along the streets were piled high with luggage and furniture. From the license tags, I gathered they were passing through just like us. Unlike us, they were trying to take everything with them. People scurried here and there—some in fancy clothes, others in work clothes, even overalls. Saint Louis had the look of a city flavored with dashes of country with everyone on the move. It was too big, too settled. It did not look like the doorway to the west that I had envisioned. I was disappointed.

As we turned onto Scott Street, Mother spotted a large A & P Warehouse Super Market. "Let's stop for a few minutes, we can get some snacks to have on hand," she said.

The market proved to be a modern marvel. Everything was painted white giving it an especially clean look. All through the center of the store, there were rows and rows of shelves about my height. There seemed to be a hundred of everything with clearly marked price signs. On the side walls, higher shelves reached way over my head. That's where I found the candy bargains—Hershey's, Milky Ways—everything 5 for 15 cents. Cracker Jacks were 3 for 10 cents—a gold mine. Buddy and I filled a bag. Mother found drinks, crackers and Vienna Sausages. We quickly got through one of the five checkout stations. I had not expected to find St. Louis so up-to-date. At the checkout counter I began to doubt my movie-digested slant on the west.

As we got back in the car with our treasures, Larry said, "We'd better find Route 66 and get going. The sun is getting mighty low."

We made one more stop at Ted Drewes' frozen custard stand as we wound around looking for the Route 66 sign.

As we licked, Mother studied the map. "I think maybe we can make it to either Pacific or St. Clair now that we've had a bite."

Buddy and I nudged each other and crossed our fingers. The caverns were near St. Clair. Maybe we wouldn't be in too big a hurry in the morning since we had made good time so far.

After a couple of wrong turns, we found Route 66 and left St. Louis behind.

## Route 66

We pushed on past Pacific to St. Clair. All of us were exhausted by the time we saw the sign for Benson's Tourist City. Luckily they had a vacancy with two double beds.

We ate a delicious late supper at the diner. Country fried steak suited all of us.

Buddy fidgeted and fidgeted, then finally asked the waitress when she brought dessert. "Do you know where the Meramec Caverns are? We keep seeing signs about them."

"Sure do, just down the road a piece. The caverns are just a few minutes off the road at Stanton. They are about the best thing you'll see on Route 66. The main room is so big we have dances there—coolest place around in summer. One of our kin works there for Les Dill, the owner. Tell them we sent you. They'll give you an extra special tour."

Buddy and I both turned our heads toward Larry.

He was frowning. "I see there's been a conspiracy here," he said. "Sorry kids, we have a schedule that is set. Your mother has already signed a rooming house lease and we have to be there by next Saturday at the latest. We've made especially good time so far but we can't count on good weather the whole way this late in the season. We do not have time for sidetracking."

We turned our heads toward Mother.

"That's the story," she said as she took her last bite of pie.

Buddy and I envisioned a long and boring trip.

The Missouri road was winding and narrow. I often cringed, my stomach tightening, as approaching traffic veered too close around a curve.

Through the rest of Missouri we contented ourselves with trying to guess some of the lines in the Burma Shave signs strung out along the road. I copied down my favorites. "Beneath This Stone—Lies Elmer Gush—Tickled to Death—By His Shaving Brush—Burma Shave." Another favorite was "Fire, Fire—Be Cool—Be Brave—Grab your Pants—And Burma Shave." Now and then Buddy and I counted boxcars rumbling along on the train tracks beside Route 66. I began writing down the funny names of the creeks we passed and thought up stories about how they were named. When we came to 'Turn Back Creek' it didn't take much imagination to think up a story for that one.

Larry stopped about every 70 miles at one of the many places where gas, car repairs, food and rest rooms came in one bundle. The folks that ran these tourist stops hoped to get all the traveler's business.

We wound on out of Missouri and into Kansas for a very short stretch. Mother kept a watch for trouble. She'd heard about some rough times along this stretch of the road between the lead and zinc miners and the CIO union bosses. We had no problems.

Then we crossed into Oklahoma where a sign proclaimed 'Welcome to Oklahoma, You're Headin' To The Great American West.' The first town in Oklahoma was Quapaw, named after an Indian tribe. Back at Cooke Elementary when we were rehearsing for the play 'Trails West,' Mrs. Stubel mentioned that a lot of Route 66 was laid out on Indian trails.

I began to take a deeper interest in my surroundings. The shapes and colors of the land were changing. Route 66 rolled up and down like a washboard. The people seemed different from the Easterners and Southerners I knew. Most had a weather-beaten look about them.

Wherever we stopped, people commented on our tags—asked where we were heading. One filling station owner said he'd thought about heading to California back in 1932.

"I took a look at the sorrowful folks piling up their goods and leaving kith and kin. Somehow it didn't seem right, so I plopped down here to stay."

He spit out a blackened spew of tobacco and went on talking.

"Never regretted it. Oklahoma is a mighty fine state. The whole state was parched poor back then. A fella could put on a bleached white shirt and it'd be the color of dust nigh on an hour later. Yes siree, we had us some hard years—just coming out of it a mite. The drought has eased and this here road is a blessin'."

The land did not change as abruptly in Oklahoma as I had imagined. Many towns did have Indian names. Reminders that this was Will Rogers' territory were everywhere along Route 66, especially near Claremore where he was born. Indian trading posts dotted the highway. Oil rigging crews mixed with cowboys and tourists in the diners. I began to feel as though I was in another time, a different world.

Larry had checked our tires several times by the time we began to see the signs leading into Tulsa. He was worried about the right front one.

"Tulsa. That's a funny náme," Buddy said when we spied the city limit sign.

"At the last station they said there was a nice tourist court across the river. I think we'll go on through and call it a night after we cross the Arkansas River. I've got to get that tire fixed. There's some open road ahead. We need to be in really good shape," Larry said more to himself than to the rest of us.

Soon after we crossed the river Buddy saw an interesting looking motel. The tops of the white stucco cottage fronts were oddly shaped. Some were rounded, some slanted, some saw toothed. All were trimmed in red.

"The Spanish influence with a New York name," Mother said laughing at the Park Plaza sign.

The dark haired lady behind the desk greeted us like old friends. She handed Mother a green alarm clock with a bell on top.

"I expect you'll want to get away early. Most folks do. If you want to save time ask Clara at the diner down yonder for some doughnuts for your breakfast. We've got free coffee here in the office and milk for the kids is just five cents a glass. By the way, my name is Anita and that'll be $5.50 for the night. If there's any way I can help you let me know."

Larry had no trouble finding a place to fix the tire. Station owners stayed open from early morning until late hoping to catch every car coming through.

The diner menus began to change along with the scenery. I felt adventuresome.

"Are you sure you want the chili? It might be hot," Mother cautioned.

"I'm sure."

I wasn't halfway through the bowl when I began to swallow large gulps of Coca-Cola and stuff crackers. I was determined to finish to the last spoonful. Then I ordered a piece of lemon pie piled high with cool looking meringue to pacify my mouth. It brought to mind Uncle Bill's talk about different food for different folks.

"That's a cheap meal for 35 cents," Mother commented. "No wonder so many people order it." She seemed pleased.

While I usually strived to stay on Mother's good side, I decided to end experiments and stick to the standard diner fare of hamburgers or chicken fried steak and fries.

Clara turned out to be the lady at the cash register. She also waited on the counter. When Larry asked about doughnuts, she reached under the counter and handed him a bag already packed with a dozen. She added 20 cents to our ticket.

Ever curious, Buddy took off toward the office when we returned to the tourist court.

"I gotta question to ask," he yelled back over his shoulder.

He returned a short time later. "That Miss Anita said Tulsa came from an Indian word, Talahassee or maybe Tulahassee. She wrote it down for me. It means 'old town.'"

Larry took the note. "She wrote that it is a Creek Indian word. Tallahassee is the State Capital of Florida. I wonder if there's a connection?"

My ears caught the conversation. I looked up from my book. "The 'Trail of Tears'—I remember from history. Maybe there is a connection. The Indians moved from the south on 'The Trail of Tears' in the 1830's. This must be where they went."

I asked to see the note. "If the Creeks came this way, maybe the Cherokee did too. Maybe some of our relatives came with them."

Mother looked up from the newspaper. "What makes you say a thing like that?"

"Well, you never said, but your grandmother was Cherokee."

"I never paid much attention to that tale. Who told you that?"

"Mr. Bill Nolan. We got acquainted this summer. He even asked me to call him Uncle Bill because he felt almost like family."

"He's full of tales. Always has been. You can't pay much attention to what he tells you."

There was no use arguing with Mother. When she chose to ignore something it stayed ignored.

But I knew it was true. After Uncle Bill Nolan began telling me about my ancestors, I insisted that Aunt Bea take me to Rogersville. I wanted to see the graves. My great-grandmother Sarah's grave was located in a corner of the cemetery away from all the other graves. She explained that the preacher back then didn't feel a heathen should be buried among white folks. He considered all Indians to be heathens.

"No matter how many times she went to church with your great-grandpa, she was still a heathen in the eyes of some. But out of consideration for your great-grandpa they gave her this corner."

We had stood silently for a few minutes staring at the sunken grave. Aunt Bea noticed a tear trickling down my cheek. She took my hand. Then she spoke. "There were some mighty ignorant folks back then."

Just thinking about it made me weepy again. Suddenly I felt closed in. "I think I'll get some fresh air, it's stuffy in here."

"Stay near the motel where there's light. Don' t go wandering off," Mother warned.

I stood and looked up and down Route 66. The neon signs still beckoned. Traffic still moved along the busy road. This was not what I wanted to see. I cautiously went around the last building in the motel row and peered into the night. A half moon threw shadows over the scattered houses beyond. I could only imagine the real west. I felt captured by pavement, roadside zoos, trading posts, motels, and filling stations. A strange longing came over me. I wanted to get off this road and walk where the Indians, the explorers and the settlers had walked. I felt pulled toward whatever lay beyond.

The next day we traveled farther and farther west where there was more open land. The earth rolled gently. The soil seemed a deeper red than Alabama's. Some buildings were made from rusty looking stones. I settled down with Raggedy Ann and Andy, absorbing as much as I could. I let my imagination take me off the road and off into the rugged land.

Now and then my thoughts bounced back as I noticed forlorn hitchhikers dotting the road. A woman held a small baby. Beside her, a man stood, thumbing for a ride. One small suitcase sat at his feet. Further on, I saw a large family stranded next to broken down car. One child rested on its roof. A woman stood by the road—thumb out. A man sat against a shade tree.

"How can they get a ride with all that stuff?" asked Buddy.

Larry replied. "It would take a truck to hold just the family. I expect they will abandon their goods, and—"

Mother interrupted. "They don't need all those things. They should travel light in the first place."

That remark caused me to zero in on Mother. She was a striking woman. Her dark auburn hair accentuated her pale skin and pale green eyes. She had a high forehead. A few faded freckles sometimes appeared through her powder. Mother hated the sun. She protected her skin with hats and umbrellas. I gloried in the sun. She had no use for possessions or for people who valued their possessions highly. "Some people are prouder of what they have than who they are," I heard her say often.

I wondered what could have possibly attracted her to my farm-loving father who loved his possessions, his land, his cows, his chickens—even his two-holer outhouse. He will never move again, I thought to myself. I knew she met him when they both worked for a dry goods store in Birmingham. He came up from the country to try out city life. I supposed she didn't see the signs that he would never give up country life. Plainly mismatched, their marriage must have been doomed from the start. Buddy and I had quivered through their fights until it was all over. That's when our separation from both parents began.

I studied Larry. He seemed a city fellow through and through. I wondered why Mother fought with him so much. Once she threw a plate at him. Buddy and I left the apartment quickly that day and roamed around 14th Street until we thought it safe to go home again.

Mother continually studied the map. She was not interested in the scenery or the people we met. She had a purpose. The quickest way west was all that interested her at the moment. Unlike so many we were seeing along the road, Mother and Larry had left good jobs. If there was a purpose to this moving west, I did not understand it.

I became bored with my thoughts and drawn to studying my fingertips again. When those thoughts became heavy, I decided to again read and record creek names as we passed over them. I added to my list— Polecat Creek, Catfish Creek and Soldier Creek. As we rounded a curve beyond Soldier Creek, Buddy exclaimed.

"Hey look at that!"

Beside the road stood a large perfectly round brown barn. It appeared to be two stories tall because there were windows of various sizes on two levels all around the barn. We saw a sign that let us know we were now in Arcadia, Oklahoma—home of the famous round barn built in 1898.

Oklahoma City sprawled among chunky hills blighted with oil derricks. We drove right through. That morning, Larry warned us that this would be one of our longest days. I grew more restless. Buddy and I had quiet territorial backseat fights—a kick here and a punch there. The hem of my dress became a mess of wrinkles. I longed to explore. The Chisholm Trail sign in El Reno seemed to signal me. The red earth drifted off into buff colored dust. The dust swirled in gusts.

Except for gas and a quick run for the especially clean Phillips 66 rest rooms, we did not stop to rest until we crossed the Oklahoma border into Texas. We arrived exhausted at a strange looking filling station in Shamrock. We were drawn to a tall tower with a tulip looking top.

"Well now, we don't get too many folks from the seat of the government out our way. How's things back in Washington?" asked the attendant, as Larry rolled down the window. "As a matter of fact we felt downright ignored by Washington until we got this last little piece of road paved last year. You should have seen it before that. Come a squall it was hardly passable." He glanced at Buddy and me in the back seat. "Don't get too many young'uns traveling this time of year. They look mighty hungry to me. Tell you what. Why don't you take them around the corner there back of the station? You'll find the U-Drop-Inn, all part of the business—the best eatin' in Texas. I'll just look your Pontiac over a bit and fill her up with good Fina gas. My name's Jake. I'll have it all ready to hit the road when you get back. You're bound for California I reckon."

Larry stared at the talkative man for a few seconds. Exhaustion must have really set in because he slowly handed over his keys and signaled us to get out of the car. Never had he left the car in anyone's hands before.

Buddy openly gawked at the cowboys, hats on heads, guns in holsters, sitting two tables over from us. Mesmerized, he ate his entire dinner without a peep or urging from Mother. We did not dawdle. A long afternoon still lay ahead.

"I figured you'd be heading on for a long spell. Folks don't tarry much through the panhandle. I looked your car over good. We don't want travelers breaking down, there's some dry spells between help." He nodded toward Buddy. "If you do break down, watch out for rattlers, sonny. They're mighty vicious around these parts." Jake said all this as he handed Larry the keys, took the payment and made one final swipe of the headlights with a dusty rag.

"We got rattlers back in Alabama big as any in Texas," Buddy replied. "And I go hunting them with my Uncle. I'm not scared of Texas rattlers."

"Well now. I didn't know you had some Alabama in you, boy. 'Course you know about rattlers. All the same, take care, and good luck to you."

Phew! The Rock Island Railway ran through the panhandle. All along the way there were cattle pens and mounds and mounds of manure. Handlers stuffed the cattle with feed before loading them onto cattle cars for their ride to the stockyards. That smell, mixed with the stomach-wrenching stench of oilrigs was awful. Small weary looking towns dotted with tarpaper shacks did not lure us to stop. Nor did lean-to trading posts whose signs promised rattlesnakes galore. Now and then long wandering dusty trails led off Route 66. At times we saw dust rising like smoke in the distance.

"Cowboys herding cattle," Buddy said with authority.

The sun spread a wide, waning, spectacular glow along the horizon as we got close to Amarillo. Neon signs struggled to compete with the setting sun turning Amarillo into a jumble of bright colors. Dusty pickup trucks shared parking space with saddled horses at hitching posts. Buddy and I complained of weariness. We wanted to stop for the night.

"We're stopping for gas and sodas. We'll pick up some cookies since we had our big meal in Shamrock, but we're going on down the road tonight. Remember, we change time again just over the border so we'll gain an hour. I believe we can make it to Tucumcari," Larry said.

Buddy and I groaned in unison.

While Mother and I went into a small grocery store, Larry made his routine check of the car. Buddy sidled over to a nearby hitching post to visit with the horses.

Mother questioned the storeowner about the road ahead.

"You might want to reconsider and stay here the night, ma'am. Like you supposed, the road is flat between here and Tucumcari but mighty narrow in places. One of them tired truckers comes along, there might not be room for passing comfortable. 'Sides, it's darkening up like it might come a clapper."

"We'll be all right."

"Well, good luck to you ma'am. I'll tuck this here tourist booklet that just come out into your bag. 'Least you'll know a little something about where you're heading."

Not far out of Amarillo, as if someone had suddenly drawn a shade, the night turned sooty black.

Mother gave us each a Nehi soda and opened the cookie box. The tourist pamphlet fell into her lap when she pulled the cookies out of the bag. "Let's see what it says about the towns ahead," she said. By flashlight she read to herself for a few minutes.

"There doesn't seem to be much between Amarillo and Tucumcari," she said. "You kids might like this story. It seems that Tucumcari may have gotten its name from an Indian legend."

My ears perked up.

"It says there was an Indian maiden named Kari who loved a young Indian brave named Tocum. Another Indian killed Tocum. That upset

Kari so much she stabbed her sweetheart's killer and then killed herself. Kari's father, who was Indian Chief Wauntonomauah, was so upset over Kari and Tocum's deaths that he stabbed himself in the heart. His last words were Tocum—Kari."

"Ugh," said Buddy. "Love stuff."

Mother laughed. "It also says that Tukamukara is the Comanche word for 'laying in wait for someone or something to approach'. Perhaps that is the true meaning of the town's name."

"Yeah, like robbers waiting for stage coaches or Indians waiting for wagon trains," Buddy reflected.

Mother had just mentioned that we were about halfway to Tucumcari when we came up behind a slow moving vehicle. In the headlights, we made out an old pickup truck filled with an assortment of household goods covered with old quilts and held down by two crates. As we got closer we could see that the crates were tied together and stuck out on each side of the truck. They contained chickens. Ahead, on the other side of the road, we barely made out headlights coming toward us. Larry had plenty of room to pass and veered far into the other lane in order to miss the crates. We passed safely. The approaching headlights loomed closer.

"It's a truck, going fast," Larry commented. He slowed and moved as far right as he dared. We had been warned not to get off the road. The truck whizzed past. Suddenly there was a squeal of brakes and another noise that sounded unreal.

"Damn." I had never heard Larry swear before. It startled me. I became a little frightened.

He started backing up. Buddy and I got up on our knees to look out the back window.

The pickup wasn't smashed. The big truck stopped just beyond the pickup. The driver strode back. Larry stopped our Pontiac at the pickup's front bumper just at the truck driver reached it. He carried a large flashlight.

"Of all the dad burned fool things, Mister. Don't you know no better than to be hanging stuff out of your truck all over the road? Didn't anybody tell you how narrow this road is in some places?"

A young man stood in the middle of the road. On top of the pickup cab a lone hen paced and cackled in alarm. All around us other hens fluttered and squawked then began to disappear into the night. The young man tried to grab one or two of the chickens but they were too quick. He slumped to the rusty running board of the pickup and bowed his head into his cupped hands.

"They were all we had to get us a start, me and Mary. Now there's not much use."

"Is anybody hurt?" Mother asked as she joined Larry beside the road.

The young man suddenly remembered. He stood up to look in the pickup window. "You all right, Mary?"

I leaned out the back window. I heard the faint answer. "I'm all right, Seth."

Hearing her answer, the truck driver went back to his truck, slammed the door and took off up the road.

Warily, Buddy and I got out of the car.

"Don't worry about rattlers. They'll be after the chickens," Buddy chided.

I punched him on the shoulder.

We all listened as Seth explained that he and Mary had just made a journey back to Oklahoma where their parents had shared some household goods and the chickens. The two young people had found work in Santa Rosa when they broke down the year before on their way to California. All year they worked in a filling station and restaurant saving every penny they could to put down on a small piece of land near the

Pecos River. They planned to stay in Santa Rosa and raise chickens for the local restaurants.

"Surely you can order more chickens?" asked Mother.

"Yes'um, but it takes money we don't have right now. Besides, these were some of my pa's prize layers and a beauty of a rooster. Now all I got is this one," he said as he held a struggling hen under his arm that he had rescued from the top of the pickup. All the while, Mary sat silent in the front seat looking straight ahead.

Mother returned to our car. When she came back she handed Seth two green bills. I could not tell how much she gave Seth, but I knew we didn't have much to spare. He smiled and tried to wave it off but finally accepted the money and wished us well on our journey.

We drove on in silence, each of us lost in our own thoughts. How little I really knew about hardship. I'd only begun to realize the rigors and the tragedies of the westward move. It had nothing to do with a cardboard covered wagon on the playground at Cooke Elementary—or with cowboy movies at the Tivoli.

Every set of headlights that approached caused me to cringe. In the distance, lightning sliced the sky and exposed the distant mountains. Raggedy Ann and Andy were no help. I had never thought of myself as a coward before but now I began to wonder. Stop it! I scolded myself. You're on a modern road in modern times. Think of those people who really had something to fear when they first explored the west. They had no cafes or tourist courts or welcoming neon lights. Where are those neon lights? Nothing appeared ahead except darkness broken by an occasional jagged streak in the sky. Thunder rumbled.

The car suddenly jolted "The potholes are getting bigger. I can't see too well, it's beginning to rain," Larry observed.

I grabbed Raggedy Ann, covered my head with my sweater, and sank down in the seat.

"That one, that one with the tepee sign," Buddy yelled, waking me.

It took a minute before I realized we had actually reached Tucumcari. We sat impatiently while Larry rented a room. No more than fifteen minutes passed before we all fell into an exhausted sleep.

A narrow ray of sunlight edging its way through the flimsy flowered curtains woke me the next morning. Buddy still slept soundly beside me. Mother still slept too. Larry was gone. I rolled out of the squeaky bed as quietly as I could and slipped my dress over my head. Carefully opening the door, I stepped outside.

It was as if the heavens were apologizing for the torment of the night storm. As the sun slowly rose, it turned droplets of water, still clinging to bushes and rooftops, into shimmering lights. The whole town seemed lit up like a Christmas tree. Puffy white clouds dipped down to touch Mt. Tucumcari in a morning greeting. The feeling that had gripped me now and then the day before was strong. I felt drawn to the scrubby land that lay beyond the town. It seemed as if something or someone called to me. I stood quietly for a few moments listening— wondering before I went on. I poked my head in the door of the nearest diner. Larry sat perched on a counter stool.

"Long as you're up and wide awake why don't you join me?" he asked as I came up behind him. He indicated an empty stool a couple places down the counter.

"Well now little lady, supposin' I shift a stool or two." A big barrel-chested man, who smelled like he had rolled in a manure pile, rose at Larry's right with his coffee and plate in hand.

"I thought I'd get a good breakfast this morning. We've got another long day ahead. Order what you want then we'll wake up your mother and Buddy to eat while I check out the car. We hit some mighty big pot-holes last night."

We got a late start. It was close to eight before everyone was fed and Larry satisfied that nothing was damaged on the Pontiac.

As we passed through Santa Rosa, we all wondered if Mary and Seth made it back all right. We saw the restaurant where they worked but rolled on by.

The clear blue sky seemed to stretch further and further as if in search for clouds to gather. The land stretched endlessly with no promise of anything more than the scrubby bushes and piñon pine that filled its landscape.

I daydreamed about all the cowboys I'd seen in the movies just riding and riding—going off into the distance toward the rocky peaks. By some stroke of luck they would soon come upon a ranch or a small dusty town. As the miles went by I found myself wishing I had a horse and could get out and ride off too. The west beyond the road signs kept haunting me.

We pushed on. We made a quick stop at Cline's Corner long enough to check the tires and get sodas. Buddy gawked at all the buffalo horns and steer skulls that Mr. Cline had for sale. He settled for a purple jawbreaker.

The road twisted, bumped and climbed as we made our way into Albuquerque. The town squatted down among the Sandia Mountains. Mexican flavored adobe buildings mingled among brick fronted ones. Indian crafts, Mexican pepper strings and cowboy hats mixed like an enticing stew beckoning us toward the many trading posts. We spied a diner and pulled in for dinner.

"It would be a shame not to try our famous chili while you're in Albuquerque," the waitress said as we studied our menus.

Remembering my past experience, I ordered a hamburger and a Coke. The rest of the family was equally non-adventurous. I spent dinnertime watching the people outside the diner window. I couldn't help but compare them to shoppers on F Street back in Washington. Except for a few shirt-and-tie clerks dashing here and there, the people were just too different to compare. Mexican and Indian women alike wore long colorful skirts. Many had scarves tied around dark hair and wore or carried shawls. The men's sombreros and cowboy hats seemed equal in popularity. I realized that none of my trim-waisted, flared-skirted suit drawings seemed right for Albuquerque.

As usual, we did not tarry long and soon crossed The Rio Grande. It was not really grand, but I was getting used to rivers that looked like the creek that ran through my father's farm. We began to climb more noticeably. The earth took on many colors still topped with scrub brush and crowned with cactus. Now and then a breeze sent tumbleweed scurrying across the road. And now and then high in the sky I spotted a bird, wings outstretched, riding on the wind. Oh how I wished I could soar in the sky like a bird. I wanted to see all the earth's colors and peer into those mysterious mountain crevices.

"Do you suppose those are falcons?" I asked Buddy. I had never seen a falcon, not even in the Washington Zoo. I had only read about them.

"More'n likely buzzards. They're just soaring around like that waiting for some cowboy's horse to step in a hole and have to be shot."

It occurred to me that maybe Buddy and I had spent too many Saturday matinees at the Tivioli Theater with our friends.

Mother identified the San Mateo mountains and pointed north toward the highest peak. "According to the tourist guide, that's Mt. Taylor. See, there's snow around the top."

Not too much further along I noticed black shiny rock that the road seemed to dodge. "It's lava," Mother said before any of us asked. "We're in the Badlands."

I reached for Raggedy Ann and kept a close watch on the surroundings.

The road climbed slowly making its way to Thoreau. We began to anticipate crossing the Continental Divide in just a few more miles. We gawked at the jagged mountain range.

Larry expounded. "Do you kids know what the Continental Divide is?" It didn't matter if we did or not because he was going to tell us anyway.

"This ridge we are climbing separates the rivers and streams. Those on the east side flow into the Atlantic Ocean, mostly through the Gulf of Mexico. Those on the west side one way or another flow to the Pacific."

I began to feel like I had been in a classroom all day, only it was a hundred times more exciting.

We stopped at an Indian trading post near the divide. We stood awed by the scenery. Cold stabbed at us. Again I thought of explorers and pioneers. The wind bit. We scurried inside. A beautiful Indian woman with a long braid down her back caught my attention. She sat on a stool in one corner of the trading post surrounded by all sizes of pottery. I ambled over. She began showing me all her handcrafted pottery. As Larry signaled that it was time to go, I dug thirty-five cents out of my change purse to buy a small colorfully decorated vase.

Mother doled out candy bars and Nehi that she bought at the trading post. "This will get us to Holbrook in Arizona. I don't think we want to stay in Gallup tonight. I've read that it's a pretty rough town."

Rough or not, Gallup had the most spectacular sunset I had yet seen. The whole sky was taken up by the flaming orange ball that flung its colors over the surrounding cliffs. As we entered the town the neon signs flickered everywhere, as if trying to compete with the sunset. They were no match—they would have to wait their turn. Perhaps we weren't there at a rowdy time because everything looked pretty peaceful.

Larry did stop for gas and restrooms. Buddy seemed to be out of the car before it stopped.

"Hey mister. How come this town is named Gallup? Did the cowboys and Indians used to gallop through town shooting up everything? Is that why my mother says this is a rowdy town? Do they still do that on Saturday nights? I heard that Saturday nights in cowboy towns is when everybody comes to town and anything is liable to happen."

"Whoa there, young fella." A tall white-haired man with a deeply tanned wrinkled face peered down at Buddy while going about the business of pumping gas into the car.

"I see by your tags that you are from Washington. Now let me tell you something. Everything you hear in Washington about the folks who live out west ain't always the truth. I go along with what Will Rogers used to say—ain't hardly any of it the truth."

"I didn't hear about it in Washington, I saw it in the movies."

"Is that a fact? Movie folks hang around these parts now and then. When their cameras are pointing a bunch of fake cowboys come hollerin' through town. We ain't had us a cattle drive come through here in many a year. Now, that's not to say that folks here and about don't come into town to jolly themselves come a Saturday night. That's mos' natural."

The tall man hung up the hose and shuffled to the front windshield where he began wiping. Buddy tailed right behind.

"Well then, mister, how did Gallup get such a funny name?"

Without answering Buddy, he took the $20dollar bill Larry offered and went inside the station to get change. Buddy stayed at his heels. I followed to see if there was any penny candy inside.

As the cash register clanged open, he continued. "It's on account of the railroad young man. Folks forget how important the railroad was to us folks out west. The railroad hired a heap of men to lay the line. Some stayed put here when they found a place to their likin'. Anyhow, it was back about 1880 that the railroad workers kept saying they was a goin' to Gallup's to get their pay. Now this here Gallup was just a railroad paymaster, but a most important fella' in the minds of the railroaders. It seemed as good a name as any for the town so it stuck."

"Oh." Buddy seemed highly disappointed. He had no more questions.

I dug my hand into a large jar sitting next to the cash register and got two lemon striped candy canes for Buddy and me and laid two pennies on the counter.

"Here son, take the change to your papa. Hope you all come back our way sometime. We promise not to shoot you."

After we left Gallup, the now purple-hued sunset lingered for awhile as if reluctant to give up the spotlight. I watched the shadows slowly deepen until night once again overtook us. I pulled Raggedy Ann and Andy closer to me. According to the guidebook we were entering

Navajo country. My imagination went wild as I peered into the darkness. I began twisting my dress hem.

Larry came up on a yellow bus and followed it into Holbrook. The bus pulled into the Cafe and Bus Center. Larry decided to park close by so he could go in and ask the driver about the road up ahead. All of us piled out to make a restroom stop before looking for a motel and a diner. A few people straggled in from the bus. The driver ambled over to a table at the back of the room. Larry followed.

"You say you're planning to drive through to Needles tomorrow. Well I can tell you this. Don't let it get dark on you a'fore you get onto Oatman Pass. Bad business. I'll be staying over at Kingman. It'll take me about three days to get from here to Los Angeles where you're aiming to take half that long. 'Course I have to stop a good bit."

Larry motioned us all back to the car. "We'd better get a bite and some sleep. We'll have to get up really early tomorrow and get out of here."

There was no scarcity of hotels, motels and boarding houses. Vacancy signs were abundant—the regular summer tourist season long gone. Sand whipped around our ankles as we walked from our neon-bedecked motel to the nearest diner.

Larry woke us. His spread of hot chocolate, coffee and warm cinnamon buns awaited us atop the lace covered corner bureau. Morning came draped in shades of gray. Winds of the night had brought with them an accumulation of threatening clouds and chilled air. We shivered out of bed.

After our hurried breakfast, we scrambled into sweaters and made a dash for the car. I had no idea what time it was. The sky gave no clue. We rode sleepily quiet.

I dozed, my head snapping up and down, until there was a thud and we suddenly stopped.

"What's the matter?" Mother asked in a panicky tone. "Did we lose our engine?"

The car door made a scraping sound as Larry wedged it open. He looked down. "We're buried halfway up the hub caps in sand. I didn't even see it."

Behind us a small truck pulled up to the edge of the sand. A short, fat man got out. He wore wide black suspenders to hold up his sagging dungarees.

"Don't worry. I don't see no damage," he said as he tromped around the car with Larry. The wrecker will likely be here in a few minutes. From the tracks, it appears the wrecker pulled a car out ahead of you and carried it up the road to shake out the sand."

"You're sure about that?"

"Oh yeah. Sam Thibald can smell a sand blast like a horse smells water. Makes a tolerable living with that old wrecker of his. It'll cost you five dollars to get out of here. It'll cost the same for me, even though Sam is one of my best friends. Business is business. I live up ahead in Winslow. Stayed the night in Holbrook so's I could pick up supplies early this morning and be home in time to open my store. By the way, my name's Slim," he said, laughing as he rubbed his large stomach.

As another car pulled up behind Slim's truck, the wrecker came into view. The driver maneuvered his truck into turning around on the narrow road and backed into shallow sand a short distance.

"Howdy," he said as he reeled off a cable with a large hook on the end and waded through the sand. "Third one so far this morning." He nodded toward Slim as he went about his job.

"You'd better hurry along, Sam, before the road crew hears about this one. I'm in a hurry myself. Suppose you could scurry on back here?"

"Soon as I can be sure this fella's car is all right. You know the routine."

Slim nodded and turned toward his truck.

"This is fun," Buddy exclaimed as we were pulled slowly from the sand trap.

Sam deposited us at his station, a short distance ahead in Joseph. His mechanic looked the car over, pronounced it fit and collected the five dollars due Sam.

Larry was obviously agitated. We'd lost precious time. We had been warned about the road ahead that led to our evening destination of Needles, California. We passed through Slim's town of Winslow. Signs to crater sites, Diablo Canyon and the Grand Canyon taunted Buddy and me as we passed them. Road signs also pointed out roads to towns like Two Guns and Twin Arrows. It became too much for Buddy. He slumped in his seat fretting that Larry would not veer off the road to a real cowboy town.

We began to leave the scraggily land marked by small rises topped with stone. Cactus gave way to tall pine trees. A stream of sunlight escaped the clouds and focused on the snow-capped mountains ahead. I thirstily drank in the scenery. Again the strong urge to leave the car and roam came over me.

Just as we reached Flagstaff we came upon a large campground. The campers looked comfortably settled as though they planned to spend the winter before moving on. We had passed similar, but smaller, makeshift campgrounds along the way.

As we entered the city limits I punched Buddy on the shoulder, "I know how Flagstaff got its name," I told him puffily. "Mrs. Stubel told us when we studied for 'Trails West'. The town folks cut a tall pine and put it up like a flag pole to mark the wagon trail to California."

"That's a dumb reason to name a town," he replied and hit me back.

No amount of begging and pleading swayed Larry or Mother to tarry in Flagstaff. We stopped for gas, a restroom break and a tire check.

"I think it's at Seligman that we begin to get the bad roads they talk about. We'll stop there for a good dinner and information," Mother said as we headed on westward.

Truck traffic picked up causing Larry to slow down along curves when he met them. He constantly leaned out the window for a better view of the road ahead and in order to pass slower moving traffic. My stomach tightened. I cringed down with Raggedy Ann and Andy and put my nose in a book. A loud mournful whistle announced a train's and our simultaneous arrival in Williams. People milled around the station. I glimpsed a corral of cattle down a side street. Signs proclaimed this to be the gateway to the Grand Canyon. We drove right through. By now I wanted to explore every town. Like Buddy, I began to feel sorry for myself.

"There's a sign for a Harvey House. I hoped that somewhere along the way it would be convenient for us to stop at one."

We neared Seligman. Apparently it was convenient to stop if Mother said so. She spotted the large restaurant near a motor court. The restaurant seemed a little swankier than most along the road. I smoothed my skirt and brushed my hair back. When we entered, a pretty lady with a beautiful smile and blonde hair came toward us. She wore a dark dress covered with a large white smock-like apron. As I glanced around the room, I saw other pretty ladies dressed like her. Mother said they were called 'The Harvey Girls'. The napkins were real linen. Our 'Harvey Girl' treated us like royalty. I tried to act the part.

I leaned toward Buddy and whispered when the finger bowl appeared. "Thank goodness we got some experience on the train to Alabama."

It was well past one o'clock when we left the Harvey House. Larry filled up with gas and checked the tires. The station attendant said, "You might want to rethink getting to Needles today, Mister. You've got a mighty steep and winding road ahead of you." Larry did not want to rethink anything. We continued down the road.

"Look, look," I yelled as I poked Buddy with one hand and pointed with the other.

Large mounds dotted the sagebrush-covered rangeland. Prairie dogs scurried about, dashing in and out of the entryways to their homes in the mounds. Watching for prairie dogs and laughing gleefully at their silly antics kept us occupied as we passed Peach Springs and Hackberry. We soon found ourselves deep into Indian country again. Besides prairie dogs we saw a good many wrecked and abandoned cars and trucks pushed off the highway. I wondered what had happened to all those people. In places, weeds tried to reclaim the road. Then Route 66 straightened and ran smooth into Kingman. Larry perked up. He was making good time despite all the dire warnings.

Being a movie buff, I knew that Clark Gable and Carole Lombard got married in Kingman not too long after my birthday. Never would it have occurred to me when I read about the hasty wedding that I would actually be in Kingman in the very same year. The news articles about the wedding described Kingman as an old gold mining town. As we got close, I really got excited. It turned out to be a fairly bustling town with the usual neon signs. I caught sight of the Beale Hotel and suggested we spend the night. My answer came in the form of silence. The sun nestled down into the deep red earth. Adobe and wood buildings lined the streets. Larry stopped at a station again to check the tires and gas up to the full mark. It seemed like the most prominent station in town. I surmised as I used its restroom that I might be sitting on the same seat that Carol Lombard used when she was in town. I thought the possibility so good that I could write Sue and tell her all about it.

When I came out of the restroom, I saw that Larry and Mother were both talking to the man filling the tank. He was shaking his head.

"I really think he just wanted us to stay in town for the business," Larry commented as we all returned to the car. These towns depend a great deal on tourists."

"I don't know. Several people have warned us about the road to Oatman," Mother replied.

"We made much better time than I expected so far and it's only about 30 miles to Oatman. If we have a problem we can stop there. I still think we can make it to Needles. I'd like to sleep in California tonight. There won't be much traffic this late in the season and the weather is better than we expected." Larry was determined to make it to Needles.

The sunsets got even more spectacular as we continued west. It seemed as if the sun spread out to hug the earth in reassurance that it would be back at dawn. We began a steady climb into the sunset and then turned southward. Dark mountain shadows flung themselves in our path as if in warning. A burned out shell of a car caught my eye on the road below.

A truck descending into Kingman rushed at us. Caught off guard, Larry swung the Pontiac toward the mountain's wall. Then he over compensated in trying to straighten and swerved into the now empty opposite lane. Brakes squealed. Wheels slid. Ahead of us there was a sheer drop into nothingness. A fringe of tumbleweed would not hold us back. He swerved back just as the front left tire seemed bound to go over the edge. Mother held on to the dashboard, screaming. Buddy and I held on to the front seat, also screaming. Larry finally stopped the car. All of us became stone still.

Larry finally spoke up. "It's all right. I wasn't ready for that one. Now everyone just sit back and be very, very quiet. I need to concentrate."

He didn't need to tell us twice. All of us were petrified. His stop to calm our nerves seemed only a minute. Behind us we could see head-lights in the distance. Larry recognized the danger of being run into from behind. There was nowhere to go but up into those dark hills growing blacker as each second passed. My thoughts of maneuvering this road in total darkness were fear mounting to sheer terror. My fin-gernails dug into my hands. I gripped my fists and plunged my hands between my knees while crouching up against Mother's front seat.

Beside me Buddy stiffened, then turned his face and body and bur-rowed into the back seat, hands over his ears. I opened my eyes and peeked now and then as the car swung into the opposite lane when we rounded a particularly sharp curve. Whatever angel was watching over me kept cars and trucks from coming up the mountain in the opposite lane. I hoped my angel planned to stay around for awhile. As black on black descended into coal mine darkness, I sank to the floor pulling Raggedy Ann down with me. I became convinced—the Black Mountains were about to swallow me.

"This is Sitgreaves Pass," I heard Larry say to Mother. "We'll start downhill from here."

Better or worse, I tried to decide. Worse. As Larry pumped the brakes and leaned forward in an effort to see ahead better, I died several times. I knew I would not feel it when we plunged off the mountain and rolled over and over and became a burned out shell. I'd already died of fright. Buddy suddenly kneeled beside me. A strong smell told me he had wet his pants. I felt I might soon wet my own. I did not laugh.

Larry finally stopped the car. He pulled up to the curb alongside an adobe building. I lifted my head to read the sign illuminated by a single bulb. The Oatman Hotel sat on the slope of Oatman's main street, the entrance only a narrow sidewalk away from our car door.

Stiffly, we piled out of the car in total relief. Something elusive began nagging at my memory. I couldn't bring it to mind.

We stepped into the small lobby and were greeted with a big smile by the man at the desk.

"You folks are lucky. I've got plenty of rooms left. Travel slows down a good bit this time of year. Come over the mountain in the dark did you? Bet you won't ever do that again. You're lucky too that my prices are down. I hiked them up this summer. Folks drove from all around just to sleep here because Clark Gable and Carole Lombard spent their honeymoon night here. They'd offer me twice the usual price just to stay in that room. I obliged them. It ain't available tonight. 'Sides, all the rooms look pretty much alike."

I couldn't believe my ears. But I remembered and I knew it was true. It made me feel better to know that Carole Lombard probably had been as scared as me. She may have made Clark Gable stop. She might even have wet her pants coming over the mountain.

Larry said he would take three rooms. "I think we all deserve a special treat and a good night's sleep," he explained as he handed Buddy and me our skeleton keys.

My mouth dropped open. Again I couldn't believe my ears—a room of my own! I'd never had a room of my own before—never.

The room was sparsely furnished. A large iron bed covered in a faded patchwork quilt filled most of the space. A rag rug, a straight-backed chair and a washstand completed the furnishings. I filled the washbowl and bathed all over. From my suitcase, I took out clean underwear and a fresh dress that I hung on the door hook. After slipping my nightgown on, I spun around the room dancing with my Raggedys.

I thanked my angel that night before I fell asleep. Never in a zillion years would I have dreamed the day would end this way. I tugged on the quilt and snuggled down into the old iron bed, Raggedy Ann and Andy beside me. I lay there awhile thinking. I supposed that Sue would not know the difference if I described my room and hinted that Mr. and Mrs. Clark Gable had honeymooned in it. I ran my fingertips through Ragged Ann's yarn carrot-top head. Uncle Tup's idea that someone above keeps track through fingertips jumped into my thoughts. I decided Sue would think the truth about the Oatman Hotel exciting enough.

A knock on the door jolted me awake. Mother stuck her head in. "Look who's sleeping in this morning. We're going next door to the café. Come on over when you're dressed."

Shivering, I went to the window. From the second floor I could see over the rooftops of the one-story businesses along the street. Like a stage backdrop, the morning sun slowly unveiled red hills crowned with jagged rock peaks. Sagebrush, yucca and cactus filled crevices and slopes. I raised the sash to a frigid blast. Somewhere close by I heard strange animal sounds.

"They were burros you heard little lady," the manager replied to my question as I went through the small lobby. "Most likely you'll see one or two before you leave these parts. They're left over from the mining days."

I bristled at being called 'little lady' as I made my way next door.

We all felt a hundred percent better as we took our places in the car to head on west. The sloping road down to the Colorado River had its dips, curves and potholes but they were better met in daylight. We crossed the swirling muddy Colorado on an arched steel bridge and were, at last, in California.

People along the way told us that our introduction to California would first be to its hellish side—the Mojave Desert. Still, I was unprepared for the parched towns and dried out people. Sand colored adobe homes appeared to be as much a part of the desert as the scrubby growth. To me, the tarpaper shacks that also dotted the landscape became a sign of broken spirits and dreams abandoned. Discarded cars appeared singly and in piles. My thoughts turned to wrecked lives. Would we be next? I twisted the hem of my fresh dress.

Along with the occasional trains that ran beside the highway, we wove on through the desert, seeking the distant mountains and the lushness beyond that had called so many.

Route 66 turned southward to San Bernadino. From the tourist guide we identified the strange twisted Joshua trees and the rock walled Cajun Pass through which famous explorers had passed. Then we made our descent into the land colored green.

It was mid-afternoon. "We'll stop in San Bernadino for the night and arrive fresh in Hollywood around noon tomorrow. It will give us a chance to look around a bit before we get to the rooming house," Mother said.

The first thing Buddy and I spied in San Bernadino was a drive-in hamburger stand. Of course we set up a howl.

"All right, we'll have hamburgers for supper tonight. Let's drive around and find a motel first," Larry conceded.

A pleasant looking adobe motel surrounded by palm trees and flowers was a welcome change from cactus-decorated towns. After checking in we ate our supper in the car from trays attached to the window ledge.

We spent a restless night. All of us were eager to complete the last lap of our trip into Hollywood. As I tossed and turned, I envisioned gigantic neon signs, floodlights flashing through the sky at night, movie stars strolling through the streets in magnificent furs and flashy expensive cars parked at the curbs.

*Folks in My Life*

*Fall and Winter of 1939-1940, Hollywood, California*


*Family*
       *Mother*
       *Larry, stepfather*
       *Buddy*

*Friends*
       *Jimmy, my friend*
       *Kevin, Buddy's friend*
       *Raggedy Ann and Andy*

*Roomers*
       *Maude, owner of the rooming house*
       *John Gravely*
       *Jane Shaffer (Lady Jane)*
       *Suzy Morrison*
       *The Carlsons, Marion and Jud*
       *Joe Sellers, cowboy stunt man*

# Hollywood

◆

It wasn't at all like I had envisioned. Bare brown hills served as the town's backdrop adorned by the famous Hollywoodland sign. That part looked just like the pictures I'd seen. The rest of town was actually drab. We drove north to south on Hollywood Boulevard looking for Van Ness Street, the location of the rooming house. I craned my neck trying to recognize landmarks that I knew from movie magazines. At Orchid Street I saw Grauman's Chinese Theatre. Four palm trees stood in the courtyard entrance of the pagoda-roofed building. Two lion statues stood on guard at the entrance. Bright ornate trim in reds and golds substituted for neon. I made a mental note to return to explore the concrete blocks where movie stars' prints were imbedded. The Egyptian Theater did not look any more glamorous to me than the Capitol Theater back home in Washington. Trash swirled around the entry. The most startling thing I saw was a bright pink stucco school. I wondered if that would be my school. The Brown Derby at Hollywood and Vine disappointed us. The dark brown building, which was not derby shaped, would have transported comfortably to any other city street corner.

We found Van Ness Street several blocks south of Hollywood and Vine. We turned left into our street. All the houses were similar tan stucco. We found our number. The rest of us waited while Mother made her way up the steps.

A buxom lady answered Mother's knock. She wore a bright orange caftan that came close to matching her hair. Slamming back the screen door, she swept onto the porch, acknowledged us with a theatrical wave and literally pushed Mother into the house. A full fifteen minutes later, Mother reappeared on the porch and beckoned us inside. She introduced us to Maude Freeman who acknowledged each of us with a nod. Then without so much as a spoken word she led us on a tour through the house.

The hallway could only be described as dark and gloomy. A vase of plastic flowers sat on a walnut table, the single spark of color. Continuing with her theatrical wave, Maude indicated the parlor. "Roomers welcome from six until nine at night," she said, breaking her silence. Trailing after her we got quick glimpses into the two bedrooms she said we were to occupy.

"The kitchen is yours to use. We do allow roomers to store milk and juice in the fridge. They are not supposed to cook in their rooms but we overlook a hot plate as long as they have it safely arranged. Can't have a fire hazard."

She led us upstairs, pointing at doors and explaining who lived in each room. "The Carlson's are rarely here. They are both extras—very busy. They have a little place out in the valley where they spend weekends."

We moved down the hall. "John Gravely is a character—actor that is. Eats mostly fruit, dyes his hair, much older than he looks. Harmless. Suzy Morrison works in short subjects and does bit parts. A floozy. She relies on her horoscope and swears it tells her that someday she will be discovered. At the end of the hall is Lady Jane. Quite a doll in her day. She does aristocratic old lady parts mostly. That's why she's called Lady Jane. She works enough to keep her bones fed."

Our tour completed, we followed Maude back to the kitchen. We learned that rents were fifteen dollars a week, due every Saturday morning. "We're at the high end of the rents around here because you can walk to town and we're on a quiet dead end street." Nodding toward

Mother she continued. "You pay your lease rent promptly the first of each month. The balance is your fee for running the house. You'll have a roof over your heads and enough for food until the mister finds work. The roomers keep their own rooms. You do bathrooms and the rest of the house. Brooms, mops, rags and cleaning equipment are in the hall closet." With that explanation, Maude excused herself and went to one of the downstairs bedrooms to change into street clothes.

The four of us sat at the kitchen table not sure what to do.

Maude returned, dropped keys on the table and told Mother that her address and telephone number were on the list of house rules hanging on the back of the kitchen door.

We stared after Maude.

"Well, I guess this is it," Larry said. "Might as well get our bags and settle in."

First we revisited the two bedrooms that were to be ours. Luckily, one room had one twin bed and a cot for Buddy and me—the other a double bed for Larry and Mother. There was a bureau and a chair in each room. Then we explored the parlor off the hallway. The big double window saved the room from being impossibly drab. The upholstery on the sofa and armchairs was of a color somewhere between dark blue and deep purple. The degree of sunlight seemed to determine which. Brass lamps, a radio, bookshelves laden with dusty books and assorted bric-a-brac completed the furnishings. A pretend-to-be Persian rug that clashed with everything else lay underfoot. We concluded that one of the downstairs bedrooms must have been a dining room at one time since it was located between the parlor and the kitchen. The second bedroom across the hall was in back of the stairwell.

Our first excursion was to the grocery store several blocks away. On the way out to the car we noticed that our street ended abruptly at the foothills. There were trails leading in various directions up the side of the hill. "We'll have to explore those won't we kids?" Larry said. He left

Mother out. He knew that she was not the exploring type—not if hiking was involved.

Our first supper in Hollywood consisted of a couple of cans of soup, crackers and ice cream for dessert. It tasted good after a diet of mostly hamburgers.

"Did you notice that crackers cost two cents more here? Sunshine crackers are only ten cents back home," I commented as I ate.

"But bread is ten cents, just like in Washington," Mother replied.

It was the first salvo in our duel of comparisons to the home we'd left behind.

We had just sat down in the parlor and turned on the radio when the door slammed.

A man walked past and up the stairs without even a glance in our direction.

"That must be John Gravely," I deduced. "He didn't have a wife with him and his hair looks shoe polish black."

A few minutes later the door opened and closed softly. A tiny frail white-haired woman carrying a large cloth shopping bag stepped into the parlor.

"You must be the new managers. I'm Jane Shaffer. Everyone calls me Lady Jane, as you may do also. I'm sorry I was not here to greet you. Maude did say you would be in today. This is my busiest day of the week. Saturdays I visit all my friends, go to the theater, do a bit of shopping, and treat myself to a special supper. Sundays I meditate and commune with my spirits. You will not see me until past noon. Now, tell me about yourselves."

We introduced ourselves and explained that we had just pulled up stakes and moved west.

"Now isn't that a brave thing to do. You will not regret it. This is the place to release your soul, to be who you wish to be and pretend to be whom you are not. Well now, toodle do. I'm off to my boudoir."

We looked at each other. Bats in the belfry I decided.

No other roomers appeared that night.

As usual, Larry was up first on Sunday. He sat at the kitchen table, the Los Angeles Times spread out before him.

"Great. Where did this come from?" I asked as I sat down and picked up a section.

"I found it on the porch," Larry replied. He picked up a pencil and began to make circles in the help wanted ads. "There's back issues in that basket in the parlor too."

For the next hour I chatted about everything I read.

"Looks like they don't have society ladies here. There's a whole page of movie stars all dressed up. There's Marlene Dietrich in a mink cape and Claire Trevor in a black Persian lamb coat. It looks like Robinson's Department Store is the place they shop. There's swanky evening dresses, afternoon dresses, and fur coats in their ads."

"Guess you won't be shopping there," Larry said as he circled another ad.

"From the ads, it looks like the May Company is sorta' like Hecht's in Washington. They don't have bolero suits though."

"You'll adjust."

"Victor Hugo's. I've read about that place. You and Mother should save up and go. It might be better than the dance hall back home—probably not as much fun though. It says here that Harry James will be there next Saturday, but it costs two whole dollars apiece for dinner and dancing."

"Young lady, before we start worrying about hobnobbing with the movie stars we've got to get you and Buddy back in school."

That was the first I had thought about school. The settler's children didn't go to school for months, I reasoned. Adventurers didn't go to school at all. They learned about all sorts of stuff along the way. I wasn't ready to go back to a stifling classroom.

That evening we sat in the stuffy parlor chatting with Lady Jane when Suzy Morrison clattered into the house. The click of her high heels on the hall floor, her jangling bracelets, her swishing taffeta dress announced her presence. She swirled into the room.

"Good evening Dahlings. Have you missed me? I had a 'mar-vel-ous' weekend." Her Jean Harlow white hair blended into a pasty white face accented by blood red lips. "I made the weekend acquaintance of some very influential gentlemen Dahlings. They are sure to remember Suzy when they are casting about for extraordinary talent."

I stared. I wondered if she was doing a Bette Davis imitation.

"Ladies and gentlemen, Suzy has been out practicing for a two bit part as a madam, a Chicago call girl or western bar girl. Makes no difference, she'll be ready for the role."

Suzy stamped her foot at Lady Jane's remark. It was at that moment that she noticed new faces.

"I do declare. To whom am I speaking with?"

Mother explained.

Suzy looked me over. "Do you dance, sing? Are you good at crying? What is your talent Dahling?"

I'm sure I looked puzzled as I made a quick mental tally of my talents and came up empty.

"Never mind, Suzy will see that you prepare yourself for discovery. We'd better start with your hair. Well, I must get my beauty sleep. Ta ta all." She swept up the staircase as if it were in a grand ballroom.

I ran my fingers through my greasy hair, vowing to wash it first thing in the morning.

"Wow! Is she ever a dumdora," said Buddy who had been openly gawking.

"Ignore her. It's the best way to get along. Anyway, she isn't around much. Sleeps over a lot, if you know what I mean. It will take her another hour to remove her makeup, pack herself in creams and tie up her chin." Lady Jane laughed as she too began to ascend the stairway.

We were just about to turn off the radio and go to bed when the door opened again. The Carlsons came into the parlor. They introduced themselves as Marion and Jud. They looked about the same age as Mother and Larry. Both had medium brown hair and blue eyes. They appeared to me to be the kind of people that could fold into a crowd scene and never be noticed.

Marion explained that they were returning to their room late because of the unseasonably warm weather. "We do hate to leave the garden and the fresh air. Maude told us you would be arriving. We brought you some fresh tomatoes. They are really too expensive in the store. There's an avocado too. Just leave the basket on top of the fridge. We'll take it back on Friday when—"

Jud interrupted. "Maude may have explained that we stay very busy doing bit parts. Up early. Now and then go on location. Not around much. Glad to have you on board. The last managers were a bit strange. No sense of humor at all—made a fetish of silly rules." Jud paused for a breath. "The only thing we require is cleanliness of the upstairs bathroom. Suzy tends toward messiness and can't seem to get the knack of hanging up a towel. Thank goodness she is required to keep all that powder and perfume in her room. If we can be of any assistance in getting acquainted with Hollywood, catch us on the run."

They picked up their small suitcase, another basket of fruit and tomatoes and headed upstairs. I picked up the crinkly avocado and examined it. I had never seen one before.

On Monday Mother decided it might be best if we got a little better acquainted with Hollywood before rushing off to school. The whole family spent the day walking up and down Hollywood Boulevard and in and out of stores. Except for Grauman's Chinese Theater it was no more exciting than 14th Street back home. At Grauman's we gawked at the handprints of the stars. There were old favorites of Mother's like Mary Pickford and Douglas Fairbanks. They were among the first to put their handprints in the concrete. Recently done, fresh looking blocks contained handprints of my favorites, Mickey Rooney and Judy Garland.

I felt out of place the next day as I sat in the principal's office with Mother. Thoughts of school had fallen completely out of my mind as we crossed the country. Sitting there, it dawned on me just how much I had seen and experienced in seven short days. A strong longing and sadness overcame me. Except for the road to Oatman, I wanted to be back on Route 66. Returning to a desk and pencils and paper would not be easy.

The principal's secretary gave us a tour. Buddy had been installed in the elementary school earlier that morning. Until we came to the music department it was pretty much like any other school. We entered the door and stood watching quietly.

"What are they doing?" I whispered.

"They're learning piano," the secretary whispered back.

On every desk there was a black board with white keys. Sheets of music rested on stands attached to the fake keyboards. Hands flew while the music teacher played a familiar lullaby on the baby grand piano at the front of the room.

Returning to the hall, the secretary explained. "Music and dance are regular courses here. Our drama department is very strong, as well."

I perked up. I had always wanted to play the piano and maybe I'd try dancing.

The next morning I trailed behind groups of chattering students along Hollywood Boulevard. My stomach muscles tightened—my corn flake breakfast welled up into my throat. I smoothed my best dress and wished that I had thought to polish my saddle shoes. Most of the girls wore skirts and sweaters even though it was really warm. I felt frumpish and completely alone.

It got worse. Minutes stretched as I stood waiting beside my home-room teacher's desk. No one paid the slightest attention to me. I shifted from one foot to the other while turning pages in a blank notebook—trying to appear busy.

"Hi. You must be new. Me too. Been here a couple of weeks now."

I turned to face the voice.

"My name is Jimmy. You'll probably sit in the back row with me so Mrs. Winston won't have to move everybody else. We're alphabetized you know."

Before I could reply, Mrs. Winston arrived.

"Everyone take your seats please."

Jimmy turned and walked to the back of the room.

"Let's see." Mrs. Winston picked up a sheet of paper from her desk. "We have a new student. She comes to us from Washington, D.C.—the nation's capital. Please make her welcome." I felt all eyes on me and all over me. I shriveled. "Please take the empty seat in the back. You will stay here when the bell rings. Your first class is math and I teach that class."

By the end of the week Jimmy and I had become fast friends. He lived two blocks further south of Van Ness so we walked together to and from school. He knew all about Hollywood. His family moved from downtown Los Angeles to be closer to the movie studios. His parents, older sisters and brothers worked various jobs at Paramount Pictures.

"I'll be a star one day. I'm a good dancer now. Do pretty good with the guitar too."

Jimmy struck me as a funny kid. His freckled face seemed frozen in a grin. Sun-streaked brown hair fell in a lock to one side nearly covering his left eye. He constantly wore an old baseball cap sideways on his head when outside. Jimmy automatically assumed he was everyone's friend. Classmate shuns rolled right down his arm and right off his fingertips.

By the end of the week, Mother had painted the concrete front porch of the rooming house red. The artificial flowers in the hallway were gone and in their place stood a tall Chinese vase she had found in a second hand store. "It looks Hollywood," she explained. There were several rolls of wallpaper stacked on the kitchen counter. "The hallway and kitchen need brightening." Mother seemed to be taking to Hollywood.

Buddy found a playmate up the street. Larry found a bank teller's job. The bank called him a rover. He filled in where needed around

Hollywood and Los Angeles. We settled in. But I questioned whether we fit in.

It was during my second week in Hollywood that I complained to Jimmy on the way home from school one day. "I thought movie stars would be all over the place, I haven't seen a single one since I got here."

"They're all around town. You just have to keep your eyes open. Recognizing them isn't always easy either. Sometimes they look entirely different without their makeup. A good place to hang around is the post office. Lots of them have postal boxes. We can't hang out very long though because the postmaster will give us the boot. Remind me and we'll start checking it out on the way home after school."

Two days later as we walked home, Jimmy suddenly pointed and yelled. "Hey, look. There goes one now."

I looked quickly to where he was pointing. At a red light, in the back seat of a convertible sat a heavily made up young woman with hair the color of shiny brass. She was wore a fur jacket even though the temperature had reached the low eighties. Her chin was held high, her eyes straight ahead staring at the back of the driver's capped head.

"Who's that?"

"Lucille Ball."

"I don't know her."

"Come on, sure you do—she's up and coming. I thought you were a movie buff. Let's see." Jimmy paused and closed his eyes to think. "Last year she played in that Marx Brothers' comedy, *Room Service*. It was a big hoot. Didn't you see it?"

"No I didn't. I don't happen to like the Marx Brothers. I don't go for comedians very much except Jack Benny and Rochester."

"I see all the comedies. I plan to be a comic someday. Not the usual kind—I'll mix comedy in with a little singing and dancing."

"You're pretty sure of yourself."

"Yeah, you'll see. Let's check the post office."

It was quiet in the lobby. A pretty blonde girl stood at the high writing table addressing an envelope. I turned to Jimmy and pointed over my shoulder. Jimmy shook his head. He raised his thumb and pointed back over his shoulder.

The other person in the lobby had his back turned to us. His suit was blue pin striped. Thin and very short, he stood on his tiptoes to reach the postal box.

Jimmy punched me in the side just as Joe E. Brown turned around. Another comedian. This time I recognized him. His big wide mouth gave him away.

"He actually smiled at us," I said excitedly as we followed him out.

Saturday of the same week Mother and I went shopping after the roomers paid their rents. We went in and out of each shop gasping at the price tags and rummaging through sale racks for the skirt and sweater that I sorely needed.

"Dahling, are you positive you don't have this in lavender. That's my favorite color, as you well know. If you expect my business, you simply must order my colors. I'm sure you can order this blouse in lavender. Just tell those people who it's for Dahling."

The dramatic and affected voice came from a curtained dressing room. "Seems like everyone in Hollywood imitates Bette Davis," I whispered to Mother. A moment later Miss Davis herself appeared from behind the curtain. Mother and I stood there agog and staring. I never dreamed that I would shop with the stars.

"I'm off to Sardis for lunch Madelyn. I'll stop by next week to see if you have the blouse. Do be a Dahling and try your best." In true Bette Davis fashion, she sashayed out of the shop.

That afternoon I laid my dark blue skirt and light blue sweater out on my bed to admire. Then I went into the kitchen and sat at the table while I wrote a bragging letter to Sue.

As Maude predicted we saw very little of our roomers. Lady Jane did appear in the kitchen occasionally to retrieve milk or juice from the refrigerator. Sometimes she sat at the table and talked with Mother about philosophy or gossiped about a movie star as if she were a best friend.

Buddy and Larry settled in best. Larry had his work and enjoyed getting around from bank to bank meeting new people and learning all about Los Angeles. Buddy and his new friend Kevin found a common interest in taking things apart. Neither had quite gotten the knack of putting them back together. Mother seemed restless. Cleaning Suzy's hair out of the bathroom sink and John Gravely's dye stains from the linoleum was completely against her nature. I hoped that it did not become my job.

It was a week later that Suzy disappeared. Except for a hot plate, she left nothing in her room. Her week's rent went unpaid. Mother was livid. However, a few days later, another extra heard about our vacancy from Lady Jane who was playing a bit part in a Western.

He arrived in full cowboy regalia. I peeked outside to see if there was a horse tied up to the front porch.

"Howdy," he said to Mother. "I work steady stunting for cowboy stars. Best horseman around. I heard you had a spare furnished room. I need a place in town when I'm working on the lots—spend some time on location. Would it suit you if I took a look?"

Luckily, Mother had decided to fry some garlic and onions on the hot plate left in Suzy's room. It toned down the perfume considerably.

Buddy was elated when Joe Sellers moved in. He insisted that Mother buy him a cowboy hat and did extra chores to pay for it. He became Joe's shadow anytime Joe was around.

Homesickness settled around me like a fog. I couldn't see my way out of it. Even though I usually took pride in making friends easily, it wasn't happening. I fell to studying my classmates.

One girl in particular fascinated me. She was the spitting image of Merle Oberon. She had the same dark hair and dreamy eyes with that trademark far away look. I conjured up a whole life for her as the movie star's secret child.

"She seems so sad. Why do you suppose she never smiles?" I asked Jimmy after school one day.

"The beautiful ones don't smile because smiles cause wrinkles. They don't frown either. They just look blank. Anyway, most of them are sorta' blank. That's because they depend on their looks for movie parts. Now a comic, that's different. You can't get a laugh out of people if you don't smile and laugh with them. It takes talent, not looks, to make people laugh."

"Well that settles it. I don't have the looks to be a glamour girl and I can't imagine going through life not smiling or frowning. I just plain don't have the talent to be a comic. I can't sing and I have rubber feet when it comes to dancing. They flop just any old way no matter how hard I try. I might even fail tap dancing."

"Nah, not with Miss Jason teaching you. How about the dramatic actresses? Without their makeup some of them are just plain Janes." He looked at me sideways. "Everybody can't be a lollapalooza, but I'd say you are a cut above a plain Jane. You like to study people's ways. Yeah, a few lessons and you could be on the road to an Academy Award."

I laughed. "You're kidding. I never gave one whit of thought to becoming a movie actress before I came to Hollywood. Now that I'm here, it seems to me that being part of the movie scene is like living with a Halloween mask on all the time. The real person just sort of disappears."

Mother decided weekends we'd explore. Her choices were not always to our liking.

"Let's go to Angelus Temple on Saturday. I want to hear Aimee Semple McPherson. There's a picture in one of the back issues of the paper that I dug out. She had just gotten back in town after a vacation. More than a thousand people met her at the train."

I took the paper that Mother handed me. The woman in the picture was nattily dressed in a suit and hat to match. She walked in front of a crowd that trailed behind her.

"I never heard of Aimee Semple McPherson. Who is she?" I asked.

"A famous evangelist."

"A what?"

"A preacher, in a way like a revival preacher that moves around. She still does that some. But since she built the Angelus Temple she spends more time preaching here. Many people call her 'Sister'. I've listened to her on the radio a time or two and read about her quite a bit. They claim she can heal the sick."

"Like Jesus?" I asked.

"Some say."

"I thought you didn't like preaching."

"I'm just curious."

That Saturday, Larry drove down Sunset Boulevard and found Glendale Avenue. There stood a huge circular concrete building across from a park. People milled around the park, many having a picnic supper on the grass while waiting for the evening healing service. Mother insisted on good seats so we waited patiently in line rather than sit in the park. Larry rushed forward and found seats about halfway down the ground floor on the aisle.

The auditorium was huge. Fake fleecy clouds floated across the blue domed ceiling. A huge chandelier hung over our heads. Two balconies hugged the large front platform in a semicircle. Tall stained glass windows faced us on the side of the platform.

When Buddy wondered out loud how many people the Temple held, a man sitting behind us tapped him on the shoulder.

"A little over five thousand," he said.

A coat lay open and empty in the aisle seat in front of us. Near time for the service, an usher escorted a man down the aisle to the seat. Crutches dangled under his arms as he shuffled into the seat and into the empty coat. Buddy held his nose and punched me with his elbow. The man reeked.

The organist played; a small choir sang. Then came a fanfare of music as a woman swept onto the platform fully covered shoulder to toes in white fur.

"It's only rabbit," she announced laughingly as she stepped to the microphone.

When she began to talk, a show unfolded. From the wings, props rolled onto the stage as Sister Amiee Semple McPherson preached to popular tunes of the day. *Three Little Fishes in an Itty Bitty Pool—they swam and they swam all over the dam.* Sure enough, three fish slid down a cardboard dam and off into a simulated river. 'Sister' preached about faith. She said that we all have to get over that dam, out into the stream of life without fear. She went on to say, "faith abides in us all—if only we will accept it." Dramatically, her voice rose and fell. Looking around, I saw that most of the audience was absorbed, wide-eyed and adoring. Amens rang through the auditorium. I thought of the Capitol vaudeville stage shows back home. There were a lot of similarities in the staged productions.

At the close of her sermon, she flung aside her white fur revealing a pure white dress. She stepped closer to the audience, arms uplifted. The sick, the weary, and the lame were reverently prayed for, then invited to come forward with the Lord in their hearts to be healed.

The usher reappeared. He lifted the dozing reeking man to his feet, giving him a couple of gentle shoves to start him down the aisle. As the man reached the steps of the platform he seemed to come alive and began shouting, "Hallelujah, God be praised." The crutches clattered down the steps. Worshipers jumped to their feet, shouting, arms uplifted, as others came forward. The auditorium rang in a frenzy of voices led by the woman in white. Buddy and I looked at each other in amazement and disbelief. Mother sat silent taking in everything. Larry stared straight ahead.

Each of us was lost in our thoughts as Larry drove home. Then Mother quietly said, "The power and the glory seems to have gone to her head."

I thought the make-believe of Hollywood had gotten hold of her.

Plans for the next weekend were more exciting. Skies cleared and hot breezes stirred as we headed down the coast to our destination of Tijuana, Mexico. Never in my life had I seen such beauty as unfolded on our drive. The Pacific Ocean was our constant companion. Wedged between mountains and ocean, San Diego captured me as we drove through. My heart clung there as we parked to walk through gates and into Mexico.

I was shocked. The contrast overwhelmed me. We seemed to have gone from heaven to hell within the hour.

I knew poor. Poor people lived in the dilapidated houses along the train tracks out of Washington. Poor people lived in cabins, the walls lined with newspaper and cardboard in Florida and Alabama. Poor people waved at the train from soot stained, time worn houses in North and South Carolina. Along Route 66, they lived in tarpaper shacks or camps along the road. My mind searched for a word beyond poor.

Children with stringy dark hair, dressed in filthy rags, tagged along as we explored Tijuana. While their chatter seemed almost musical, I could not understand a word. I vowed to myself to learn Spanish. Their smiles were like wildflowers growing in an otherwise barren field. Their eyes, dark and penetrating, sparkled from dust-encrusted faces. Hands stretched out in an unmistakable message, a penny, a nickel—anything. I held out my own hands, showing their emptiness. I had nothing to give. If I had, I would have given it all. I felt shamefully rich. I felt—guilty.

The main street was dirt. We wandered in and out of adobe and wooden buildings that were either bars with dirt floors or shops with colorful pottery, woven mats and sombreros. A few small restaurants were tucked here and there. Beyond the main street, one room shacks leaned on each other for support. I thought of the dominoes game that

Buddy and I often played. We'd stand dominoes on end and then touch the end domino sending them all down one after another. It looked as if a strong push or a winter wind would domino Tijuana to rubble.

We tarried long enough to have our pictures taken beside a burro. Actually, Larry straddled the burro and wore a huge sombrero on his head. Except for the picture and bottles of Coke, we bought nothing. I sighed with relief when we crossed back over the border for the return trip to Hollywood. I still steadfastly refused to call it my home.

After that, most of our exploring was done nearby. Sunday mornings Larry and I climbed the foothills, dodged the tarantulas and made a few discoveries. We found a shaft cut through one end of a hill. Tracks ran through the twenty-foot shaft. A mining car sat on the tracks. Obviously, we stood on a movie set just off the trail above our house.

One Sunday afternoon in early December Jimmy came over. It was near 80 degrees so we sat out in the small backyard, under the only shade tree, talking and watching Kevin and Buddy take apart a rusty old bicycle.

We also watched the clouds float by. "Do you ever think about heaven and death Jimmy?"

"Can't say as I do. I've hardly started living yet, least not the way I want to."

"Well, what I mean is, do you think we go somewhere after we die? I mean like one place if we're good and another if we're bad."

"Haven't thought much about that either. Mama keeps me straight or I get my ears boxed something fierce. So, I don't figure I have to worry a whole lot about it right now. Besides, I'm too busy to get in trouble what with music and acting lessons and all."

"My Uncle Tup thinks somebody somewhere is keeping track of us. Maybe up there." I pointed to a large white cloud drifting slowly across the deep blue sky. "If he's right, I think that somebody must have a lot of filing cabinets."

"What makes you say a thing like that?"

"Well, my Uncle Tup has this idea that everybody that's ever been born is marked—each and every one." I waited a minute to let that statement sink in. "He says why would anybody mark everyone in the whole world with different marks if there wasn't a reason to keep track of us."

"What do you mean, marked?"

With a dramatic flair, I slowly turned my hands, palm up, and held them toward Jimmy.

"Oh, you mean all the lines that fortune tellers use. That's horse-feathers."

"No silly, fingerprints. You know about the FBI using fingerprints to catch criminals because everybody's are different. But Uncle Tup says that certain somebody up there didn't make us all have fingerprints just for the FBI."

Jimmy studied his own hands. "You reckon that's so?"

"It does seem likely doesn't it? I've thought about it a lot. One day Mother was talking about things in the Bible. She does that often. Anyway, she said she thinks some old men in long black robes wrote the part about the meek inheriting the earth. She thinks it will be the weak who inherit the earth. She says why in the world would God want weak people who can't control themselves going on up to heaven to disturb the peace. She thinks we have to pass some tests right here on earth. That fits right in with what Uncle Tup said about somebody keeping track. It sure got me thinking."

Quizzically, still studying his hands, Jimmy looked at me.

"It'd give me the heebie-jeebies if I thought somebody was watching everything I do and keeping a record. That's downright scary."

"I've thought about that too. I expect only big things are marked down—you know, like things in the Ten Commandments. That's what Uncle Tup thinks too. Mother says there aren't many real rules from God. They all fit on one tablet, she says—just some common sense ones for getting along. She thinks the old men in long black robes made up a whole bunch of rules just to confound, confuse and separate folks. She says if all the religions didn't have so many complicated rules, most people would get along a whole lot better."

"Jeepers creepers, your mother is some kind of talker."

"Well, about some things. She's writing a book about the Bible."

We sat quiet for a long time continuing to watch the sky and listening to Buddy and Kevin discuss ways to put the bicycle back together again.

Quite suddenly Jimmy said, "Gotta' go. I'll ponder some. Let you know what I think."

Joe Sellers came out of the back door and began practicing his rope twirling tricks. Buddy and Kevin abandoned the bicycle which now lay in many parts on the grass. Buddy made a dash to our room to get his cowboy hat and a piece of rope that Joe had given him. I spent the next hour watching and laughing. I doubted that Buddy or Kevin would ever become cowboy extras—cowboy stars being out of the realm of possibility.

# Winter

◆

## Christmas Approaches

The unseasonably warm weather seemed to have a permanent hold on California. I could not imagine Christmas without a chill in the air.

I began to devour the Los Angeles Times for signs of Christmas. The paper reported the temperature as eighty-two degrees the day before. Heavy quilted bathrobes had gone on sale for $17.95. Hollywood is so expensive I thought to myself. An ad in the paper announced Aimee Semple McPherson's Christmas stage show theme—*The Bells of Bethlehem*. There were pictures of Douglas Fairbanks' funeral—pictures of movies stars, men in black hats and women in black veils. The radio weather forecaster predicted hot weather for another week.

"Is the U. S. going to war?" I asked Larry as we read the Sunday paper on December 17th.

"Some folks at the bank seem to think we probably will. Others don't. Why do you ask?"

"Well, there's this article here about a big naval battle. A German raider called the *Admiral Graf Spee* is going to battle the French and British off the coast of Uruguay. There's a picture of the British battleship *Renown* on page two of the paper."

"That's not our country's business. Besides its a long way from the U.S."

178

"But it's getting closer. Besides there's been all kinds of articles about Nazis and the French ordering more planes. Finland seems to be in a fix with Russia so the League of Nations has to do something about that. It's all right here in the *Times*."

"I wouldn't concern myself. Go back to your fashions and movies."

My frown increased as I noticed an article in the Social Activities Section about Mrs. Cecil B. DeMille and some movie starlets getting together to wrap bandages for the Red Cross. The Red Cross seemed to be preparing for war.

Then the announcement about the *Gone With the Wind* premier at the Carthay Circle Theatre caught my eye. So did the 'See Styles Section'. Barbara Stanwyck, Paulette Goddard, Mary Martin and Anita Louise dressed in classic shimmering evening dresses took up the whole page. I moved on to comics—Grin & Bear It, Tarzan and Lil' Abner.

On Monday, the 18th, huge headlines blazed across the top of the paper. "Crew blows up *Graf Spee*" off coast of Uruguay. There was an artist's sketch of the ship blowing up. The caption called it "Captain Hans Langsdorff's ship suicide." A nice Christmas tie for Larry would cost me a dollar. At Desmond's, a black crepe-sequined gown for Mother would cost $12.59, a price beyond even daydreams. There were pictures of decorated Beverly Hills homes, complete with colored lights, reindeer and fake snow. The temperature on the porch thermometer read eight-four degrees.

By Wednesday's paper war got even closer. The German merchant liner Columbus was scuttled in the Atlantic only 420 miles off New York to avoid capture by a British destroyer. The *Aracua*, a German freighter, fled from the British into port at Ft. Lauderdale, Florida. I thought about my cousins Melvin and Jamey and wondered if they were reading the war news and getting worried. Probably not, I reasoned, since they only occasionally glanced at the Alexander City Gazette. I wondered how a war might affect me. Not much I thought. Girls don't go to war.

On Thursday the 21st, Captain Hans Langsdorff of the *Graf Spee* committed suicide with a revolver in a naval arsenal in Argentina. The Carthay Circle Theatre ad suggested *Gone With the Wind* tickets for Christmas presents. They ranged from seventy-five cents to a dollar and a half.

I thought maybe if I wheedled a little, Mother might buy tickets for Christmas. When I showed Mother the Sardi's ad for Christmas dinner at a dollar-fifty, she gave me her look.

"There are perfectly respectable dinners advertised for half that young lady, we are not hobnobbing with the stars at that price."

By Friday's paper I felt completely depressed. I curled up with Raggedy Ann and Andy after school to read. A picture of the White House adorned for Christmas sent me into a blue funk. Homesickness came over me in the worst way.

The temperature dropped into the sixties by Sunday the 24th. My blues faded a bit. The Finns and the Russians still had problems. That Sunday, I saw the article that told me how the war might affect me. Heinrich Himmler, the head of the German police, urged all his black uniformed SS men to beget children, in or out of wedlock. Children were needed to replace those lost in war. A chill went down my spine as I read about it being a woman's duty to produce these children. Could a soldier just throw a woman down on a bed because it was her duty? The sneering red face of Mr. Jules jumped into my mind. Suppose the Germans did come to America. I shivered at the thought. I suddenly realized that it was not just the boys that had to worry about war and the possibility of Hitler coming to the United States with his ships and planes.

It wasn't the nosedive to forty-five degrees and the light frost that cheered me on Christmas day. It wasn't even the new brown skirt and pink sweater that I found under the small artificial tree. It was something that Mother said as we ate the fifty-five cent Christmas special in a small restaurant on Hollywood Boulevard.

"Our lease is up the first of March. We have to decide what we're going to do."

I knew my mother well enough to recognize the seeds of unrest in her voice. Maybe—just maybe, with a little luck, we'd go home to Washington. There was absolutely no guessing what Mother would do next. A worry frown creased my forehead as I crossed my fingers under the table and hoped.

After Christmas passed, the December 28th premier of *Gone With The Wind* held Hollywood in its grip. Mother decided we would be among the spectators. It seemed as if all of Los Angeles decided the same thing. We started for the Carthay Circle Theatre after a quick early supper even though the premier started at eight o'clock. Traffic backed up for blocks as we got close. Larry swung off into a side street several blocks from the theatre and luckily spotted a car pulling away from a curb. We scooted in. Spotlights swept the sky. We made our way to the source.

A hoard of Los Angeles police blocked the street in front of the theatre. It was closed to traffic. Beyond the bleachers where the lucky ones sat, a restless crowd stood ten deep. How I wished we had brought the stepladder from the cleaning closet. As the stars arrived we caught glimpses of shimmering shoulders and tops of heads. We joined in with the bursts of ooh's and ah's even though we saw little. A roar rang from the spectators as Clark Gable and Carole Lombard arrived. I had seen the King and Queen of England. Now a glimpse of the blonde tresses and shiny black hair of the King and Queen of Hollywood thrilled me down to my toes.

The next day I literally pounced on the *Times*. Full pages of pictures described Carole Lombard's long shimmery gold lamé coat, Vivian Leigh's white fur and Merle Oberon's white and silver brocade gown and ermine coat. I closed my eyes and daydreamed of having seen it all. Then I sat down to write a letter to Sue.

When I reread the paper later the pictures of the Roosevelt grand-children frolicking in the snow on the south lawn of the White House turned me back into a sad sack. I envied Sistie and Buzzie Dall. They had snow, they had Washington and they had their grandfather, President Franklin Delano Roosevelt.

Mother made her decision.

Buddy's one friend Kevin and my one friend Jimmy stood on the sidewalk and waved good-by as we pulled away from the curb that Saturday morning. The roomers were not around. We knew they would hardly notice a change so absorbed were they in their celluloid lives.

We headed east. That's all Mother and Larry agreed on. Larry wanted to go to Florida where he was from. Mother just wanted to go. They gave Buddy and me no choices other than what we chose to pack in our one suitcase and what we wanted to take for the back seat. Buddy gave Kevin the toy soldiers in exchange for a box full of nuts and bolts which he got a kick out of screwing and unscrewing. Of course, Raggedy Ann and Raggedy Andy went with me.

Mostly quiet, we rolled back along Route 66, silently picking out familiar sights. Occasionally one of us saw something new and pointed it out.

It became obvious from the start that our trip back east was to be more leisurely.

There was no one expecting us. We did not have a home. As we crossed into Arizona, Buddy and I began to whine in unison. "Can't we see the Grand Canyon? Can't we stop at the Petrified Forest? How about the Painted Desert?"

Mother gave us hope at some point into the whining. "It'll depend on the weather."

"The road's some roughed up to the south rim but it's passable. Been a mild winter," the service station attendant in Williams, Arizona replied to Larry's question. "That's the only part open this time of year. Mostly artists and photographers up there and them dumb folks that like to freeze their arse off campin' in winter."

We peeled off north toward the south rim after a hot breakfast.

"I don't see what all the fuss is about," were the first words spoken as we stood looking down into the depths of the Grand Canyon. Below, the Colorado River meandered encased in its steep rock walls.

I looked at my mother in astonishment. Then my gaze turned back to the canyon. The sight was astounding. As we stood there the late morning sunlight crept lower into the depths as if pulling back a stage curtain. I soaked in the splendor of the rocky shapes. Like tufts of cotton, icy snow clung to the stunted pines An eerie silence enveloped the whole canyon—accenting the magnificent scene. I wondered what explorers had felt when they came upon the canyon. A part of my soul was touched. I locked the scene into my memory, vowing to return some day.

Afternoon was upon us as we returned to Route 66. As we entered Flagstaff, the sun dipped low tinting the snow-capped mountains purple.

Mother sighed. "This town is like an oasis between deserts."

I looked around and wondered if she would take a notion to stay. Thoughts that we were homeless and might end up in one of the hundreds of decrepit shacks that lined Route 66 numbed me as we traveled along to nowhere in particular.

There seemed to be no hurry to leave Flagstaff. I began to worry that we were about to light here. Finally, close to ten in the morning, Larry announced that we were heading on toward the Painted Desert and the Petrified Forest.

Buddy paid much more attention than I as the guide in the Petrified Forest explained that giant trees had washed down from the mountains, were buried and turned to stone over thousands of years. Buddy insisted on stopping at a shop that sold pieces of the petrified wood. There he became most interested in the old train caboose workshop out back where the polishing took place. We bought a few nickel pieces and went on to the Painted Desert.

I stood mesmerized as the late afternoon sun played tricks. Like a magic show, the rocks and land around us turned hot chocolate brown, purple, blue and rosy red as we watched while the sun slowly sank. It was like a dance between earth and sky and I was captured in its spell. Again, as when we were in Arizona before, I felt close to something I could not see, could only sense.

Mother thought the whole day a waste of time and said so as we settled back into the car. I felt entirely different. Lost in my own thoughts, I settled down with Raggedy Ann and dozed.

That night a waitress found a crooked candle and stuck it in a piece of chocolate cake. Everyone in the diner joined in singing 'Happy Birthday'. I began my thirteenth year.

## A Moment in Time

The slam of the car door must have awakened me because on opening my eyes I found that my family had disappeared. Groggily, I raised my head from Raggedy Ann's lap. Her leg was twisted, her dress rumpled. Raggedy Andy wasn't in much better shape, having been caught under my hips. I apologized to both, straightened their clothes and lifted them to the ledge of the back window. It was then that I realized where I was.

I was in the desert. From my westward view out the back window, Route 66 resembled a long scar cutting through land already scarred beyond repair. Looking to my right, I saw a structure that looked as though it might fall in upon itself at any moment. Unpainted boards of various widths and lengths were tacked together. The tin roof sagged. Pocked with what looked like bullet holes, an old Uneeda Biscuit sign patched an opening in the side of the building. To the left of the dilapidated front door a tattered piece of canvas served as a makeshift awning for a two-seat bench. A round dusty Conoco gas pump stood no more than eight feet from the door. A trough ran along the front roof ending at a tin pipe that dropped into a wooden rain barrel. Handmade signs covered the front window—Lucky Strike cigarettes, Red Man chewing tobacco, lanterns, picks, Nehi soda and Coca-Cola promised to be waiting inside. At the bottom of the window there was a sign marked with an arrow, pointed toward the west. The single word 'Rest' was scrawled below the arrow. I figured the outhouse to be around back.

I stepped out of the car. Suddenly a peculiar feeling came over me. I felt as if I had stepped into a painting. There was total silence. Nothing was moving. My eyes roamed the landscape. I saw a few scrawny leafless bushes, low growing cactus and patches of grass, dark at the roots, dotting the barren land. To the west and north beyond the store the distant mountains appeared purple against the setting sun. Cotton ball clouds tinged in pink hung low in the sky. They seemed to cling to the mountaintops. To the east the scar of Route 66 continued and promised nothing better ahead.

There was not a car in sight. The stillness felt suffocating. Yet, mysteriously, I felt a windless wind—a breathless breath. I felt there must be something out there. I shuddered.

Just then I heard the creak of a door and voices that I recognized as my stepfather and Buddy's. Since they obviously had beaten me to the outhouse, I turned toward the store.

As I entered, the screen door banged behind me. I welcomed the noise. My mother stood at a short counter just inside the door. She was talking to a man whose face looked as if it was made of leather trimmed with a stubby white beard. His gnarled brown hands rested on the counter. He wore a baggy shirt and overalls. They looked as though they had not been washed for months.

"No ma'am. There ain't none of them tourist courts anywhere around here 'til you get over to Albuquerque."

My heart sank. In all probability we would be hunting most of the night for someplace to stay. I glanced down at the hem of my dress. It stayed just as wrinkled going east as it had going west.

Watching and waiting through unfamiliar darkness for a friendly neon sign made me nervous.

"You might try Lem Hoskins' filling station. It's about forty miles up the road. Sometimes if'n the family is away, Lem rents their rooms out. Can't tell if'n they be away or not 'til you gets there."

I looked around. An assortment of wares cluttered the small store. Lanterns hung from poles that held up the roof. Pots, pans and canteens hung from the walls. Coats in several sizes hung on pegs. Small barrels sat haphazardly around the dirt floor. Some were filled with what appeared to me to be junk. Others held bolts and nails. A few sat turned upside down, their bottoms shiny and clean. These obviously were used for seats. Behind the counter a shelf held cigarettes and chewing tobacco. Two jars on the counter held penny candy. Nothing interested me until I spied the faded red Coca-Cola cooler near the back of the store.

The storekeeper's squinty eyes followed mine. "They's ten cents apiece. I know that's a bit steep, but like I told your ma, I have to get them hauled a mighty long ways. Nothin' like a cool drink when you're out in the desert."

Mother motioned toward the cooler indicating I could have one even at twice the normal price.

"Better get one for your brother and Larry too if we've got another forty miles to drive." It was then that I noticed her Coke sitting open on the counter. I raised the cooler lid and was not surprised that there was no ice. Since there was no electricity either, the cooler merely served as a container.

Buddy and Larry came through the back door just as I popped off the third cap.

"I wouldn't go out back unless you absolutely have to," my stepfather said.

"You wouldn't like the rattler much. The tarantula was really friendly though," Buddy added as he poked into a barrel and brought out something with gears.

I looked towards the back door and then at the soda in my hand. If I planned to drink the soda, I'd have to brave the outhouse.

"Hold this, and don't drink any," I said to Buddy.

He grinned and suggested I borrow the rifle that hung by the door.

Expecting the worst, I gingerly opened the outhouse door carefully looking in every corner and all along the ceiling. It wasn't a bit worse than my dad's outhouse in Alabama. Larry, being a city fellow, had never used outhouses before this trip—that was his problem. Buddy was just plain joshing me.

Feeling better, I returned to the store and swigged down my soda while Buddy wheedled Mother into buying the thing with gears that he found in a barrel. As my family filed out, I dug into the pocket of my dress for a penny and eenie-meenie-miney-moed between the two candy jars until my finger landed on the jawbreaker jar.

"That there is a good choice, little girl," the man behind the counter said. I grimaced.

The moment I pushed open the dilapidated door and stepped outside, that feeling came over me again. Something was out there. Twice I started toward the car only a few steps away. Twice I stopped. Then I felt a strong urge to turn toward the northwest where the mountains formed their now gray background. It was then that I saw them.

Several yards into the desert stood two small children. I would have taken them for statues except that I knew they were not there before I went into the store. I glanced around. There was no car, no horse, no adults—nothing but desert and two small children. Perhaps they are

Indians, I said to myself. I started toward the car. Then, as if compelled by some force, I turned and moved toward them.

Their clothing looked like burlap. Their feet were bare. Each had hair as shiny as melted tar. Both stood perfectly still, staring at me until my eyes finally locked with the deep dark well of their eyes.

I do not know how long we stood face-to-face, eyes locked— moments, minutes perhaps. All the while we were shrouded in that mysterious penetrating silence.

Finally I blinked and the spell was broken. Somehow I knew. I knew that something had been given me, something perhaps mystical, even ancient—something of great value.

The children remained absolutely still.

I had a strong urge to give them something valuable in return. But I owned nothing of value—nothing that is, except—except Raggedy Ann and Andy. Without hesitation, I returned to the car and removed my two most precious possessions from the window ledge. No one in the car moved or said a word. I returned to stand before the children. Once again, our eyes locked. I held a doll out to each child. Each extended a hand and took a doll. In unison they nodded and turned away, as did I. It seemed perfectly natural to me that the tiny figures vanished into the vastness of the desert.

Larry did not scold me for dawdling, as he normally would have. He sat looking straight ahead, his hands in his lap as if waiting for a signal. Buddy remained uncharacteristically quiet, his eyes glued to a comic book that he had read ten times over. Mother also looked straight ahead. However, as I settled in the car she smiled the faintest of smiles the way she does when she is pleased about something.

Larry turned the key in the ignition and we set out over the scarred land to find a man named Lem Hopkins in an approaching desert night. I smoothed the hem of my skirt as the horizon turned a deeper purple and settled into coal black relieved only by a starlit sky. I faced the unknown dark of night and I was not afraid.

We found Lem Hoskins' filling station just as he was closing up. "You folks stopped just in time. No cars have stopped in for nearly an hour. That means it's shutting up time."

"Do you know of any place we can spend the night? Is there a tourist house nearby?" Larry asked as Lem filled our gas tank.

"Don't reckon there is. But it so happens the missus is away with the children visiting her ma. If you can pay a dollar a piece, I reckon I can put you up."

Lem not only put us up, the next morning he had a breakfast of ham, eggs and hot biscuits ready at sunrise. He hollered up the stairs. "Time to hit the road folks. I got to open up."

We ate heartily.

"You're sure welcome—pleased to have the company. It can get mighty lonesome around here this time of year what with the missus gone sometimes. Her ma has come down with the consumption," Lem said as we each bid him goodbye.

"That was a lucky night. Lem is a really nice man," Larry said. We all nodded in agreement.

## New Territory

When we stopped in Amarillo for the night, Larry took the maps inside the tourist court. He and Mother studied them a good part of the evening while Buddy and I listened to the radio.

The next day we left Route 66 and headed south.

"Your mother decided she wants to go to Dallas," Larry explained.

For miles and miles there were no neon lights or much of anything else.

Dallas loomed out of sagebrush and cattle ranches as if it just sprouted up for the devil of it. Mother spotted a clapboard tourist house close to town. We'd hardly settled in when she made a call on the hallway phone.

"We're going to supper at an old friend's house. I think I'll borrow an iron and spruce us up a little."

I decided this must be a very important friend if Mother intended to iron.

We pulled up in front of a large stately brick house. The shallow front porch was trimmed in white gingerbread like my grandmother's in Alabama. It looked homey.

The front door flung open. A plump but stylish looking blonde woman dressed in a lavender suit and stilt high heels came down the porch steps to greet us.

"Lord woman, I never thought I'd see the day. Let me look at you. Pretty as ever. I just can't get over it. And this must be Buddy and Sis." She grabbed us both and hugged hard. "They were little babies the last time I saw them."

I must have been a baby because I did not know this woman.

"Josie, this is my husband, Larry."

Josie! It was as if a lightning bolt struck. Josie stood before me, Uncle Bill Nolan's daughter—Mother's childhood friend.

Josie told us her husband Ned was away on a selling trip. "Hardware stuff is his specialty these days. I stayed in real estate. He sure will be sorry he missed you."

After supper Josie had to hear all about what Mother had been up to all these years. When Mother got back to the present, Josie declared, "You should have told me that you were unsettled from the start. We'll just have to get you out of that tourist house this very night. I've got loads of room here. And if you don't know where you're going, Dallas is as good a place as any. My real estate business is booming. Folks are moving in here like bees swarming on the blue bonnets. I could use some help. I've got two empty apartments right now in one of my buildings. Take your pick. I'll even give you free rent until you get on your feet. It will work out smooth as sorghum syrup as my daddy used to say."

Then and there I knew we would not be staying in Dallas.

Mother's forehead crinkled into a frown, her mouth set. "We're all settled in for a day or two Josie. Then I think we'll be moving on east. We do have some plans."

Once again Mother's independent streak won out over being practical.

Josie showed us around town and kept us fed. She and Mother reminisced. Buddy, Larry and I quietly listened to "Do you remember…" tales, hoping to learn something about Mother. Two days later we left. As we got into East Texas all of us felt relieved to be back among trees and greening up grass. My own feelings were somewhat mixed as I realized the lands of the many hues were behind us—perhaps forever, despite my vows to return.

The restaurant menus changed. Southern fried chicken, and chicken fried steak along with catfish and hush puppies became standard fare. We were definitely back in the South. We wandered northeastward through tree-lined streets of small familiar looking towns.

When we crossed the Tennessee River, I looked at the map and realized that we were no more than a hundred miles from Florence, Mother's hometown and my only real home.

"Aren't we going to go to Florence? We're so close."

Mother's lips tightened.

After glancing over at Mother, Larry said, "Your mother thinks we'd better get on up the road and light somewhere. It's time to get you kids back in school."

Tears welled up in my eyes. Feeling sorry for myself, I began to brood. Sometimes one person's independent streak could be a pain in the neck to those around them. Right now my mother was being a pain all over. I longed for Aunt Bea's comforting arms, laden table and clean sun bleached bed sheets. I felt lost. I began to relate to all the people we'd seen on Route 66 going west with a state of mind, called hope, for a destination. I sensed that we were running out of money. My chest grew tight, my stomach churned. I reached for the hem of my dress but instead of wadding it up I smoothed it out and became calmer. From somewhere deep inside, I drew on a new feeling that somehow, sometime, things would work out.

Larry's "somewhere up the road," turned out to be Knoxville, Tennessee. Mother borrowed a newspaper from beside the cash register of the first diner we came to west of Knoxville.

"This sounds pretty good. Cheap too. 'Close to University, two large rooms, kitchenette, six dollars a week.' That's about what we can afford right now," Mother said as she circled the ad with a pencil.

Cheap it was. The clapboard house had not seen a coat of paint in many years and was now a weathered gray streaked with remnants of white. Inside, the wooden floors of the front hall were worn and unpolished. Scatter rugs of various colors were haphazardly thrown about. I did not see one welcoming feature as I glanced into the curtain drawn front room.

"You came all the way from Hollywood you say. My, my—that must be an adventure if I ever heard tell of one. My name is Ellie, by the way, the widow Ellie. My husband, Joe Evans died some six years back. Wait here a minute. I'll get my keys and show you the rooms." We stood silent, not even looking at each other as we waited.

My mother saw nothing wrong with the rooms. I saw nothing right.

"I painted all these nice fruit crates myself. My, my—they are so useful. You can see for yourselves. Turned one way they make a bookcase. Turned the other way they are just right for a night table. We're close to the University. The students just love them. Can't do them a lot of harm either. You should have seen this place before I sold off all the furniture to an antique dealer. Times do change. A body does what she has to do to keep going."

Or what she wants to do, I thought as I looked at Mother.

Ellie went to the window to show Mother the view of a straggly garden. I swallowed hard. My fate now included lumpy beds, fruit crate shelves, a tiny kitchenette with a two-burner hot plate and chipped dishes that looked as if they had been retrieved from back alley trash barrels.

"It will do for now." Mother reached into her purse and gave Ellie the first week's rent.

We found the nearest grocery store and settled in as best we could.

"Ellie tells me the school is just two blocks over. She knows the principal. She will see her at church tomorrow and smooth the way for you kids," Mother said as she ladled our Campbell soup supper.

Buddy and I looked at each other and read the same thoughts in each other's eyes.

She actually gushed over us. Miss Mary Martha Gunston, principal of the school that went all the way up to eighth grade, was thrilled. "My, my. Actually from Hollywood! Why it's fate, that's what it is. Just fate."

I began to distrust everyone who began their sentences with "My, my."

Buddy and I found ourselves back in the same school building. Junior high school was another year and three more blocks up the street.

According to Miss Gunston, our fate included the annual spring 'Play and Talent Show' that involved the whole school. It ran from a Friday night straight through Saturday the second week of April. The event included catfish and hushpuppies cooked by the local Shriners, with pecan pies furnished by the room-mothers at noon on Saturday. There would be a pancake supper. No need to go home all day.

Miss Gunston declared Buddy a movie star and gave him the lead role in his class play. Never mind that Buddy had the acting talent of an Oatman burro and hated the idea. When Miss Mary Martha Gunston found out that I had taken nearly four months of tap dance lessons in Hollywood, my assignment was as a star feature attraction, a solo tap dancer.

Buddy and I were literally sick. It was one thing to have talent and be gushed over. It was quite another when the talent wasn't real. I missed Raggedy Ann and Andy something awful.

Mother found work as a temporary replacement for a lawyer's ailing secretary. Larry worked part time as a bookkeeper for a restaurant owner just opening a business. Neither was happy. Nobody was happy. Everywhere we went black factory soot settled on our clothes and hair. Our moods turned as black as the soot.

Then one day about two weeks later some mail came. I saw the letter laying on the hall table when I got home from school. It was from the Department of Agriculture in Washington. I didn't know they knew where we were.

"You mean it? Home, we're going home, to Washington, back to our old apartment?" I asked.

Buddy and I jumped all about as Mother reread the letter that gave her back her job.

"I can't say about the old apartment. Things will be tight for awhile. Larry may even go down to Florida for a few weeks to see his mother and work some there. A banker friend has some work he wants done for a couple of months. It'll help us get on our feet." Clearly, they had been making plans.

"When are we leaving? Can we leave tomorrow?" I asked excitedly.

"I think we had better finish the week out and get our pay. We'll need every cent."

Buddy and I looked at each other then found the talent to dance a jig together. I had a vision of Miss Mary Martha Gunston's face when she realized her star attractions were leaving a week before the show. I laughed until I got a stitch in my side.

*Folks in My Life*

*Spring Again, 1940 Washington, D. C.*


*Family*
  *Mother*
  *Larry, stepfather*
  *Buddy*

*Friends*
  *Richard*
  *Sue*

*Rooming House "Characters"*
  *Gloria Talbot, landlady*
  *Lester Talbot, landlady's son*
  *Eddie Baker, retired detective*

*Teachers*
  *Mrs. Morgan, homeroom*
  *Mr. Phillips, science*
  *Mr. Anderson, math*

# Spring Again—Home Again

◆

Getting home to Washington became agonizingly slow. A surprise late spring snowstorm slowed our way through North Carolina and Virginia.

Along the way Larry admired the farm country. He remarked, "I think I would like to own a farm someday."

Buddy and I silently gasped! Mother turned and gave him her look. No words were spoken. None were needed.

Finally we reached the Potomac River and made our way across the 14th Street Bridge. Larry pulled over to the curb. We stopped for a minute just to gawk at the Department of Agriculture as we came off the bridge. To me it seemed more like a life preserver than a massive white building that spawned programs like terracing and kudzu. We continued the familiar way on through the city toward Columbia Road.

Larry parked and we walked to the drugstore. The dirty slush on the sidewalks dampened our feet but not our spirits. The familiar sounds and smells were as sweet as Aunt Bea's Sunday ambrosia.

"Well now, come back for a spring dose of castor oil did you?" Mrs. Judd reached for the bottle on the back of the counter and laughingly held it up in a salute.

It was too early for lunch but we ordered grilled cheese sandwiches anyway. Buddy and I headed for the Arcade Market, hoping to see friends. Larry and Mother remained perched on the drugstore stools reading ads in *The Washington Post*. When we got back, three ads were circled.

The first we checked didn't suit at all.

At the second rooming house, a large busted, large bellied blonde woman answered the bell.

"The room I've got vacant is large like the ad says, but I'm not sure it'll be comfortable for all four of you."

Mother explained that we would be four for only a couple of days.

The landlady's hips wobbled like a bowl of Jell-O as she led us down the front hall and stopped at the first door past the parlor.

"This used to be the dining room. I reckon there were a peck of mouths to feed at a fancy banquet table. This room could more than likely seat maybe thirty people. I like to picture that. People all chatting away with a fire in the fireplace cozy as you please."

The four of us stood in the middle of the room looking in four directions. There were two chintz-covered day beds placed end-to-end under two huge windows along one side wall. They served as sofa space by day and beds by night. Near the hallway door, a double bed dominated the room. A cherry colored armchair and a comfortable looking wooden rocker sat on either side of a large walnut table against the back of the parlor wall. There was also a large chifforobe. The fireplace dominated the back wall. The dark polished mantel stood above my head. A large clock with sides that swept down like a sliding-board suddenly bonged twelve times. We stood stark still and counted every beat.

"Don't pay any never mind to 'Sassy' I call her. There is a whatcha-ma-call-it in her back. We can shut her off. When nobody's living in the room, I like to hear her bong away."

We sighed collectively.

"That there is a Tiffany lamp. She pointed to the table. I'm not all that sure myself that it's genuine but one of my women roomers who considered herself an expert offered me a pretty price for it. I'd just as leave keep it myself."

"You did say kitchen privileges in the ad?" Mother said in a questioning tone.

"The kitchen is downstairs in the basement. That's where I live. Name's Gloria, by the way. Gloria Talbot. Pleased to meet you."

Each of us shook her hand. She repeated each name as we introduced ourselves.

Gloria led us down the dark and narrow stairs. The basement was surprisingly light.

"This is what they call an English basement. I think servants used to run the place from down here. The only servant you'll see around here is yours truly—if you don't count Tessie who comes in to clean and do the laundry once a week."

The kitchen was huge. The walls were painted a pale gray that caught the light from the high narrow windows. In the center stood a massive white table. It was covered with a red checked oilcloth and surrounded by white high backed chairs. Through a half open door we had a glimpse of a bedroom.

"Bright and cheerful don't you think? Spend a lot of my time down here I do. In this corner is a hot plate set-up, six burners, plenty for everyone. I don't like anybody messing around with my stove. Out in the hall there is a little alcove with a table and four chairs. You're welcome to fix light meals and use that table."

Mother paid Gloria for a whole month. We went back to the car for our suitcases.

Buddy poked his box of nuts and bolts under one day bed. I threw my school notebooks on the other. The space against the pillow that should have belonged to Raggedy Ann and Andy looked too empty. They were long behind me. I was learning to stand on my own. It pinched sometimes.

## Challenges

I knew it wouldn't be easy but it was harder than I thought. Mr. Applebee, the principal of Powell Junior High told Mother that he would put me with my class but that he doubted that I could keep up. "From what you tell me, she's missed a great deal. It might be that she will have to repeat the year."

My heart sank just like one of Uncle Tup's fishing pole weights.

When he escorted me to my homeroom class, Mrs. Morgan remembered my name. She welcomed me and sent me to the back of the room where there was a vacant desk. Everyone turned around and stared. I had not written Sue that I was returning. Her mouth gaped open. I conjured up a smile and waved my hand.

All the questions came at lunchtime. "That wasn't very nice. Why didn't you let me know you were coming home? I felt dumb not knowing and me supposed to be a best friend and all."

Sue was right, it wasn't very nice of me after some of the bragging letters I had written to her.

The bragging had stopped in Knoxville and would not raise its head at the rooming house.

I thought I would try the truth. "Well, things didn't work out very well in Hollywood and they got worse along the way back. Now we're broke and live in a rooming house. It will take us awhile to get back to where we were."

Richard swallowed his mouthful. "Hey, but you had a great adventure. I wish my family would pick up and go somewhere. We might go up in the Shenandoah this summer and camp. That's about as adventuresome as my family gets."

I smiled a thank you. Richard always made me feel better. I wasn't ready for any boyfriends but I sure appreciated his understanding ways.

By the end of the day it began to look as if I could settle back among my friends. I wasn't so sure about keeping up with the class. The very thought of falling behind a year churned my stomach. I felt as if I were full of buttermilk clabber. My books were as heavy as the dread in my heart as I stacked them in my arms and headed to the rooming house. I refused to call it home.

For the next few weeks I struggled to complete the assignments I needed to turn in before the end of the term. History and English were a snap. To my surprise I found I was actually ahead in those subjects. It helped that California and Washington used the same history book. Mother's typewriter sat in front of the fireplace on a small table borrowed from Gloria. I pecked away doing one report after another. Because she had more time for us with Larry gone to Florida, Mother began looking over my work. Now and then she retyped a page for me.

I found one friend at the rooming house. Actually, he was more Buddy's friend. Eddie Baker, retired police detective, lived upstairs in the back room. His room overlooked the backyard and the alley. Eddie was the only roomer who spent any time in the parlor. He filled the ashtrays with Lucky Strike stubs and read detective magazines. He claimed as his the chair with sagging springs nearest the window. Short and stocky, Eddie had a nearly bald head fringed with gray hair. Near his left ear there was a scar. He had a limp and used a cane.

He promised Buddy, "Soon's I get a little ahead on my check, I'll see that you get a pair of spy glasses like mine. Lord, what a fellow can observe, even an old crippled has-been like me. Got to keep your eyes open in this world. It's a mean'un."

We began calling him Mr. Eddie. Buddy spent hours at his feet listening to stories of crimes he had solved.

When Mother went back to writing her Bible book and Buddy became plainly too restless to call out my test questions, Mr. Eddie often did the chore.

"The trick is to study lightly those you know. Then we'll go over and over the ones that snare you. Learned that in my detective work. Go over and over those clues that don't quite jell 'til all of a sudden something hits you like a busted light bulb. Always works."

Math gave me the screaming meemies. I timidly approached Mr. Anderson after school one day to ask for extra help. "How about a half hour after school for a couple of days a week? That ought to catch you up. I'll get you a pass from the office." I sighed with relief.

Mr. Anderson's offer gave me courage to ask Mr. Phillips, my science teacher, for some extra help too. He agreed to meet with me one afternoon a week to help me with back assignments. In exchange, I gave him one of the petrified rocks. He was so proud of it he showed it to all his classes.

Then Lester happened.

We were eating supper under the alcove when he appeared from the direction of the kitchen. He leaned against the wall striking a pose. He had that dark, whisker stubbled, Chicago gangster-look about him. He immediately gave me the heebie-jeebies.

"Ma said she had new roomers. You must be them. I'm Lester, Ma's one and only and the best there is." He was looking straight at me, dark eyes penetrating.

Buddy raised a hand in greeting. Mother and I nodded acknowledgment that he was there.

He stood against the wall for several minutes just staring. We were uncomfortable. Finally he said, "Nice meeting you. See you around."

He swaggered back toward the kitchen. None of us had said a word to him nor introduced ourselves. Buddy shrugged his shoulders. Mother frowned but returned to her sandwich. I shivered.

Buddy asked Mr. Eddie about Lester. "Stay clear. One of the mean'uns—bounces in and out of the pokey. Gloria still pampers him, can see no wrong to him. Mind me now, stay wary."

We settled into a pattern. For me mostly studying. I could not get back into the celluloid world of the movies on a regular basis. Even Mother got choosy. After work and on Sundays, Mother typed away at her Bible book. Buddy took things apart and with Mr. Eddie's help sometimes put them back together.

One day we invited Mr. Eddie to go to Kings' Restaurant in Alexandria. It took all three of us to help him manage his cane and his tricky leg but we did and it was a great outing.

It really pleased me that the paper man dropped *The Washington Post* into the hallway each morning. Whoever picked it up put it on the center table in the parlor for all to read. Instead of sharing with Larry on Sunday mornings, I shared with Mr. Eddie. He too grabbed the sections that I didn't want. Unlike Larry, he was into sports and kept track of all the baseball scores. While he reeled off scores that didn't interest me, I reeled back war news and other Washington tidbits that he could care less about. Then I found something of interest to him.

"Hey, listen to this. You'll love this, it's right down your alley Mr. Eddie."

"What's that?"

"A big murder. And it has my Mary Haworth involved. And *The Washington Post* too. Seems they found this Mrs. Bessie Catherine Howard with her throat cut—ear to ear. Some secretary at the *Post*, a Mrs. Fisher, told Mary Haworth about hearing loud screams and noises a couple of weeks ago when Mrs. Howard disappeared. Mrs. Fisher is a neighbor of Bessie Howard. Mary Haworth got the city editor involved, that's Mr. Frank Dennis. He got the police involved and they found her knifed up body. They think her crazy son did it."

"I do declare, a big one, huh. Wonder who'll get it? Most likely John Clemmons. He's up and coming—likes to be in the limelight. Let me read about it when you're through."

"Not much else but war news. There seems to be plenty of that these days. Mrs. James A. Farley is the society lady today. There is a new emperor penguin at the zoo. Maybe we'll walk over to see him."

"How do you know it's a him?"

"Name's Dugan."

"You don't say. I once knew a cop named Dugan."

We remained quiet for a few minutes.

"Looks like I might go to the movies this afternoon."

"I thought you weren't much interested in movies these days."

"*Broadway Melody of 1940* is on at the Tivoli. I wish I could dance like Eleanor Powell. She has the longest legs of anyone I ever saw. She keeps right in there with Fred Astaire."

The hall phone rang. I ran to answer it.

"She's asleep Larry. Do you want me to wake her? O.K. I'll tell Mother you'll call back at eleven sharp. I'll get her up soon so she'll be wide awake."

Mother was all smiles after she got off the phone. "His job is going well. They will have all the records changed over to some sort of new system by the middle of June. And the best news of all is that Mother Louise gave Larry some money for a down payment on a house. We'll start looking at those duplexes over in Arlington right away."

It dawned on me. That's why Larry was so insistent on going to Florida. Mother Louise was a pushover for her only son.

The following Saturday afternoon was dark and stormy. The rooming house was chilled and gloomier than usual. According to the *Post*, a cold front had come in and would stay around for several days. Mother and Buddy were at the barbershop. The house was unusually quiet.

I wandered into the parlor as Gloria chose to call it. The parlors I knew were front rooms kept neat at all times like Grandmother's and Aunt Bea's. This parlor looked as if an Alabama cyclone had set in to stay. The bookshelves on either side of the useless fireplace were a disaster. Movie and detective magazines lay along the bottom shelves. Gloria's collection of second hand books occupied the top two shelves as if slung there direct from the bookseller's stall and never touched again. A month old collection of newspapers lay stacked on the window seat. The springs sagged in the olive colored overstuffed sofa and in the two matching chairs. Full ashtrays sat on the two end tables. Limp lace curtains hung at the two tall windows. Gloria's pride, a Duncan Phyfe writing desk, stood along a side wall. "A real steal, got it from one of those 'everything must go' ads in the paper. A man up the street was selling out and moving to Florida."

The look of the room struck me as odd. Gloria kept the kitchen spotless. She seemed to be constantly cleaning, mopping, and polishing every surface. It was her world. She rarely left it. Tessie vacuumed the parlor a couple of times a month and flopped her dust rag around any bare spots on the tables. Gloria seemed content with that.

Restlessly, I roamed about the room emptying ashtrays and fluffing pillows. I moved to the desk. The inkpad caught my eye. The first of each month Gloria climbed the basement stairs, plopped down at the desk, collected her rents and paid her bills. She liked to give her tenants receipts stamped 'Paid'. "Very business like," she explained when she handed Mother her first receipt.

The desk cubbyholes were stuffed with envelopes and small tablets of paper. I tore a piece of paper from a tablet. Then one by one, I carefully pressed each of my fingers onto the inkpad and onto the paper. I turned on the desk lamp and stood, studying each print. This is me I thought—my own marks—on this one piece of paper. Marks like no one else's in the world. While I had studied my fingertips a lot since talking to Uncle Tup, I had not actually seen my fingerprints. There they were with all their whirlygigs. What could they possibly mean? Was it really some kind of record? Was it like a tattoo? One thing for sure, it meant something. And like Uncle Tup, I had come to think I had better worry about my own marks rather than somebody else's. Whatever the black swirls meant, to me they were becoming a big responsibility.

As I studied each print my thoughts roamed. What was it grandmother had said this past summer? I remembered. "You and Buddy will make your own mark on the world one day. Meantime, you have to be patient with folks who don't know any better than to haul you about like a piece of smoked ham."

I shook my head in silent indignation. I will not be a piece of smoked ham, I declared to myself.

The thought had barely settled in my mind when I heard a slight noise. Before I could move, someone grabbed me from behind. His hands slid down my arms; he pulled me tight against him. I felt his hardness. One of his hands began to lift the hem of my skirt. Startled out of my wits, I managed to squirm around to face Lester.

Without thinking, I stomped down hard on Lester's foot. "Get away from me! Stay away from me," I screamed.

He gasped and stepped back. My eyes met his cold dark eyes. We stood that way for moments. He stepped toward me. I stepped back against the desk. My eyes never left his. His face was flushed, his breath hot.

His hand shot up as if to grab my hair. My eyes narrowed. Slowly, his hand fell.

"I reckon you mean it. Ma thought you had a hankering for me. I reckon I did too. Figured you for coming in heat."

I said not a word but continued to meet his eyes as they narrowed. I wavered between wanting to run and wanting to stand my ground—daring Lester to touch me. I sucked in my stomach and breathed deep. I was ready to put up a fight. Without taking my eyes off Lester, I groped for the letter opener on the desk behind me.

Finally, he smirked. "Well, if you feel that strong, I'll leave you be. But you don't know what you're missing girl. I could give you some real lessons in lovin'. I got all kinds of girls wanting to crawl all over me. Who needs a baby like you? Gotta have one kiss though, friendly like. One kiss." He moved toward me again.

Suddenly, there was a loud noise. Lester whirled around. Mr. Eddie stood in the door, his cane raised.

"The next time I use this cane it won't be to bang on the floor to get your attention you good for nothing."

"Take it easy Pop. An old man like you could get hurt swinging that thing around."

"I'll tell you who'll get hurt. I made it my business to find out who your parole officer is the minute Gloria told me you were out. My advice to you is to slither down to the basement where you belong before I see to it that you land back in the slammer."

Just then lightning struck close by, heightening the electricity in the room. Not one of us flinched or moved.

Seconds passed. "Watch your threats old man. Better watch your back too."

With that he swaggered from the room laughing.

My heart pounded. I had no doubt that Lester was capable of taking what he wanted or harming anyone in his way. I saw that in his eyes.

I dropped onto the couch in relief. Mr. Eddie came over and sat beside me. He had the good sense not to touch me.

"You all right?"

I nodded.

"Lester will leave you alone now, but I'll be keep an eye on him. You can bet on that."

"He's awful. I knew it the minute I saw him."

"You're right. He's been a problem ever since he was born—in and out of jail several times in the past five or so years. I don't know why Gloria puts up with him between jail stints, except that he is her only child. She's a sucker for him."

"Thanks for being here when I needed you."

"Been wary ever since he got back. I heard you yell out—knew right away what the problem was. Lester thought I was out. I fooled him that time."

Mr. Eddie made his way back to his room. My heart still pounding, I turned to the desk and picked up my fingerprints. It took all the control I could muster to walk calmly and slowly to our room.

I bolted the door and flopped on the day bed, my heart still racing. Slowly my thoughts turned from Lester and rage to the mystical emptiness of the Arizona desert where I had left Raggedy Ann and Andy.

Lately I found my thoughts returning there often as if to a dwelling in my soul. From there I drew strength like the water from Grandmother's well.

I began to calm down and realized I was holding tightly to the finger-printed paper. Looking at my prints again, a thought came to me. I need to make some rules. Obviously, life will continue to be tough I told myself. I tore a piece of paper from my notebook, rolled over on my stomach and wrote down the number one.

I studied the number for a long time while my mind snatched at bits and pieces of conversations with Uncle Tup and Uncle Bill Nolan. I recalled Mother's Bible spats with Aunt Maime who was adamant about rules. And I thought of Aunt Bea's gentle touch with people. Those in my life with many rules, no rules and simple rules continually confounded me

Finally, I crumpled the paper tightly in my hand. No more rules. None but the simple ones God started us with. What then? From somewhere inside me a voice kept repeating, "Do your best each day. Be your best each day." I looked down at my fingertips. Did I truly believe that I was marked and my life recorded in some mysterious way beyond my understanding? What was the purpose? There had to be a purpose. I have a mark. I have ten of them. My thoughts whirled.

I can't worry about it, I decided. Let all those old men in black robes that Mother talks about do the worrying. All I can do is get up and face each day, one at a time—and be the very best person I can be. The words rang in my head as if imbedded. 'The very best I can be'. It sounded easy. I knew it wasn't. But somehow I knew that it was the only rule I needed.

To avoid Lester, I studied at the library when I wasn't with Mr. Anderson or Mr. Phillips. If I needed to go home to type a report, I made sure Mr. Eddie was in the rooming house.

The cherry blossoms long gone, the summer heat invaded Washington and settled down to stay.

Exams loomed. I became a nervous wreck. My test scores were good. Still I suffered thoughts that I might not be allowed to pass my grade. I had missed so much. After final exams, I felt all right about them. But, I couldn't be positive. My stomach churned and churned as the last day of school approached. Traditionally, report cards were handed out in our homeroom the very last thing after punch and cup cakes.

The day came. The time came. The punch turned out to be lemonade. The cup cakes were chocolate. I sat at my desk doodling my finger in the icing. To calm myself, I opened the library book I had picked up the day before—*Dr. Hudson's Secret Journal.* Lloyd C. Douglas had become my favorite writer. Mrs. Morgan began to hand out awards to the brightest students. I knew I wasn't involved. I kept on reading.

"And now we have a special award. As you know, all your teachers talk to each other about the awards that we hand out today. Some are for grades, some for citizenship, and some for attendance. This year we have decided to have a special award for the best effort made by a student."

Her words droned and she began to hand out awards while I decided it was taking too long to learn what Dr. Hudson's secret was about.

"This student not only completed all her daily work, she completed back assignments for which she did not expect a grade. The assignments were graded. So today, I am pleased to give her a certificate of excellence along with her report card promoting her to the next grade with high marks."

I looked up from my book. Every head turned to the back of the room as Mrs. Morgan laid the report card and certificate on my desk.

My lips quivered. My eyes began to tear. Led by Sue, my classmates applauded.

I had changed over the year from spring to spring. I learned more than I could have imagined—grown up some might say. And my life began to take yet another turn.

On Saturday, the day after school let out, Mother, Buddy and I boarded the bus at the post office and rode along Route 1 to South Arlington. We got off at 23rd Street. It seemed like a nice neighborhood. There was a small library on one corner. On the same block there was a drugstore, a grocery store, hardware and a fire station, all near the bus stop. We walked four blocks over to 26th Road. There we found two blocks of duplex houses. Several were for sale.

Mother talked to a salesman. Buddy and I walked around the neighborhood and returned to the sales office just as Mother came out with Mr. Goode, the salesman.

"I'm glad you're back," Mother said when we returned to the office. We're going to look at one of the houses in the middle of the next block."

The duplex had a living room, dining room and a small kitchen downstairs. Steps from the kitchen led to a basement. Upstairs were two bedrooms and a bath. In the back, a terraced yard backed up to woods. The front yard boasted a tree, one of the few on the block.

"I can give you a check in a few days for the full deposit. I can leave a partial one today to hold the house. About when may we move in?" Mother asked Mr. Goode.

"That sounds like a deal to me. You say your husband has a job when he gets back?"

"He starts to work on the first of July for Riggs Bank. I can get that verified for you."

"Then I'd say you probably could move in around that time. We can rush the paperwork through. Let's go back to the office. I need more information and there are some papers to sign."

Buddy and I sat down to wait on the steps at the end of the sidewalk in front of our new home.

"Listen," Buddy said.

"What?"

"The train. I can hear the trains across Route 1. I love trains. I bet if we follow that path at the end of the street we can even see the trains across the road."

"Well, I guess that's one plus."

"S'matter."

"Nothin' I guess. I just hope this works out. It will be wonderful to have a real home—almost too good to be true after what we've been through."

"Yeah. Mother said we might stay here all summer if we move."

"She did. Not go to Alabama?"

"I heard her talking to Larry on the phone. She said you were old enough to look out for us."

I couldn't remember a summer without long train trips or shifting about.

"I saw something about a playground program at Nellie Custis School on the bulletin board in the sales office. It said up to high school age. I wonder what all they do."

"Probably baseball and stuff like that. I don't know if they let girls play," Buddy replied.

A family across the street laughed as they got into a car with a picnic basket.

"The boy looked about your age Buddy. You'll find some friends."

"I guess."

"I saw three girls coming out of the library where we got off the bus—a blonde, a redhead and a dirty-blonde like me. They seemed nice. Maybe I'll get to know them—but I'll miss Sue."

"What will we do for furniture?"

"Mother will look in the ads. She can get cheap stuff that way."

"I hope it's not orange crates."

"Me too."

Just then a boy on a bicycle came to a screeching halt in front of us. He had a bag slung over his shoulder. He seemed a little older than me, good looking with a nice smile. A lock of dark hair fell across his forehead.

"You moving in?"

"I think so," I answered.

"You're going to need a paper. Here, take a sample of *The Evening Star.*"

"I'm partial to *The Washington Post.*"

"O.K. then I'll deliver the *Post.* Makes no difference to me, I deliver them all. Tell you what, I'll keep an eye on the place and when you move in I'll come back and sign you up. Meantime, here's a copy of the *Post.*"

"I think that will be all right. There aren't any drugstores really close by to buy the paper. I'll ask my mother."

He went pedaling on his way, throwing papers as he went.

"Look at that. All we'll have to do is pick up our own paper from the porch. It'll be nice to have our own things and a house just for our family—no creeps to worry about."

"Whose a creep?"

"Lester."

"Oh. Yeah, he is."

"Do you suppose he'll have to go to war?"

"Who, Lester?"

"No, the paper boy," I said as I watched him wheel around the corner and out of sight.

"How would I know?"

"Mr. Eddie says before long all the men are going to war. He's ready to sign up."

"He's too old and crippled."

"He thinks he would make a good spy."

Buddy looked back at the front door of the duplex.

"Mother said she would make me a room in the basement and I can have my stuff down there. Maybe I can make a workbench. I bet I can find some leftover lumber somewhere."

"I don't guess you are ever going to have a pony Buddy."

"Don't reckon."

We sat for a few minutes each lost in our own thoughts.

I was thinking I would like to have one of those kidney shaped dressing tables with a flowered skirt like my cousin Ellie's.

Buddy spied a boy at the end of the street. "I think I'll go ask him some questions."

I unfolded the paper and turned to Mary Haworth's column and then the comics.

I stood up to take another look at the house. I wondered who lived next door. Then I looked up and down the street. It seemed peaceful. It seemed right. I remained standing as I saw Buddy coming back down the street.

"He says there's a hobo camp just up the hill behind those houses." Buddy pointed up the street across from where we sat.

"He says we can sneak up there and watch them sitting around the campfire. He says sometimes they get into arguments but they don't bother folks that live here."

"That's comforting."

"He says sometimes they knock on the door and ask for food. He says they know just who the suckers are."

I laughed. "Do you suppose hobos will like Mother's tomato recipe?"

We sat quiet another minute or two.

"Are hobos all he knows about?"

"Well, he did say Nellie Custis School is just a few blocks away up on 23rd Street close to where we got off the bus. You have to take the bus to go to the movies near Alexandria and kids play all the time in the clay pits way over on the other side of 23rd Street."

"Seems like you've found a friend already."

"He'll do. But he's a year younger than me."

I sat down again. Anxious. Mother appeared at the sales office door. She waved a paper as she started down the street toward us.

Buddy held his little finger up to mine. We clasped them together. At last, we were going to have a place of our own.

Buddy walked up the street to meet Mother.

I refolded *The Washington Post* and rubbed my thumb several times across the front page. I rose and walked to the front door of the duplex and pressed my thumbprint into the brick beside the door. The smudge of ink blended into the cracks and crevices. My home. My mark!

# *Epilogue*

———————— ◆ ————————

Luck was back.

*Mother did not get the wanderlust again until my senior year in high school. She waited impatiently until I graduated before she, Larry and Buddy moved to Florida. I remained in Washington and went to work at the Department of Agriculture. Mother would eventually divorce Larry and move back and forth between Florida and Washington as the mood struck.*

*That first summer in our new home, I ran the mile race in the summer sports program. I high jumped also. I broke the records for both events and my picture was published in the 'Community News'. I felt less a failure.*

*We stopped going to Alabama in summers. The third summer I got a Thursday night and Saturday job at Lerner's Shop on F Street. Later I switched to L. Franks Ladies' Shop.*

*It was a wonderful neighborhood. Mother didn't seem to mind when I joined a church. It really didn't matter which church I joined or even if I joined. All of us kids roamed from one church to another depending on what was going on. The preachers seemed to think we had some chance of going to heaven despite our Halloween antics each year. We all attended midnight mass and each other's hayrides and picnics. Nobody called us sinners.*

*Once in awhile, we got on a bus and went to the Reed Theater in Alexandria. We weren't all that interested in movies.*

*I became friends with the redhead, the blonde and the dirty-blonde like me whom I saw that first day. We're still good friends.*

*Cousins Melvin and Jamey did go off to war. They came home safely.*

*Buddy became a mechanical engineer and has continued tinkering all of his life.*

*In early June of 1946, The Washington Post interviewed June brides who were busy planning their own weddings while waiting for the last of the South Pacific servicemen to return home from the war. They interviewed me. At last, my picture was smack in the middle of the "Style Weekly" section.*

*I married the paperboy that June. For the past fifty-four years he has seen to it that I always have my favorite newspapers.*

*Along came daughters Tere and Bonnie and sons, Mike and Bob. Then came granddaughters Corey, Jessa, Kate and Lauren. Also, grandsons, Bryan, Scott and Jaret. Yet another generation is making an appearance. And so life goes on—one generation replacing another.*

*I used only one "real" family name in my story. My great-grandfather's name really was Solomon.*

*When "Uncle Tup" died, Florence pretty much shut down for the funeral. People kept coming up to "Aunt Alice" to say how much they were 'beholding' to him. He didn't seem to want them to talk about it while he was living they said.*

*With one or two exceptions, the aunts and uncles who nurtured and influenced my life are gone now. But not forgotten.*

*Before she died, my stepmother, "Ilene", wrote me a letter of apology for the way she had treated Buddy and me. By then she had two children of her own who were treated quite differently.*

*As I sat beside my mother's deathbed, now and then she roused and murmured a few words. She told me that I was the only one who had ever understood her. I felt sad about that because I never really had. I just knew that she was a very intelligent woman, born out of place and in the wrong time. Once in those final days she asked, "Do you remember those two Indian children out in the desert?"*

*That was the first time they had ever been mentioned.*

*"Of course I do Mother."*

*She smiled the faintest of smiles like she always did when she was pleased. Then she drifted away.*

As when reading a good mystery, I continue to work my way through the clues to the 'secret of life'. They are there—as are all the cures for our ills if only we can find them. I do not necessarily think that the clues are in any bound volume.

Like "Uncle Tup", I do backslide when a church seeks to stifle my inclination to accept that God marked all humankind as his—not just some of us. I will not be chained to rituals that separate.

This I know. We live on a very small ball precariously placed in a vast unknown universe. To my way of thinking, we would be very wise to hold each other's hands.